# PERFECT WIVES

# BOOKS BY LAUREN NORTH

*My Word Against His*
*She Says She's My Daughter*
*The Teacher's Secret*
*I'm Her Mother*
*For Better, For Worse*

*All the Wicked Games*
*Safe at Home*
*One Step Behind*
*The Perfect Betrayal*

# PERFECT WIVES

## LAUREN NORTH

bookouture

Published by Bookouture in 2025

An imprint of Storyfire Ltd.
Carmelite House
50 Victoria Embankment
London EC4Y 0DZ

www.bookouture.com

The authorised representative in the EEA is Hachette Ireland
8 Castlecourt Centre
Dublin 15 D15 XTP3
Ireland
(email: info@hbgi.ie)



ISBN: 978-1-80550-170-1
eBook ISBN: 978-1-80550-169-5

*For Matt Hazel*

# PROLOGUE
## SATURDAY, 18 OCTOBER

Text message thread between DC Amanda McLachlan and DS
Sara Sató

10.45 a.m.
Amanda
*Sorry, boss, I know it's your day off, but we've had a
development with the Jonny Wilson murder. One of the
residents of Magnolia Close has just confessed.*

Sara
*Who?*

Amanda
*Georgie Bell at No. 6*

Sara
*I thought she had a rock-solid alibi.
I'm at a trampoline park with my nieces. I'll get there as
soon as I can.*

11.03 a.m.
Amanda
*Something weird has happened. Another resident has confessed. Tasha Carter from No. 12.*

Sara
*They killed him together?*

Amanda
*She says she did it alone. I've put her in interview room 2.*

11.21 a.m.
Amanda
*A third woman has just confessed!*

Sara
*Let me guess – Beth Smith from No. 3.*

*Keep them separated. I'm walking in now.*

PRESENT DAY

# ONE

## GEORGIE

There are a lot of things I regret about the last three weeks, but killing Jonny Wilson isn't one of them – which makes my intended destination this morning, weaving through shoppers and market stalls, completely insane.

'You can do this, Georgie!' I say quietly to myself, like I'm talking to my eight-year-old son Oscar, telling myself what I tell him when I'm cheering him on at sports day.

I say the words like I'm not alone right now – more alone than I've ever felt in my life, and that's saying something.

'There's no can't. Only won't,' I whisper, but my mantra is swallowed up by the bustle and noise of the shoppers around me. Straight ahead, a teenager strums a One Direction song on his guitar. He sings without nerves or hesitation, like he's singing to more than the army of pushchairs and pensioners that roam this sleepy market town of north Essex.

I keep my stride determined, ignoring how scared I feel. Ignoring the fact that my pulse is hammering in my veins like one of Oscar's wooden spoons hitting a saucepan when he was a toddler.

*Don't think about Oscar.*

Too late.

My perfect boy, with the shaggy blond hair from Nate and the boundless energy that's all me. 'My two pocket rockets,' Nate calls us with that sideways smile and the wink that makes Oscar giggle and scrunch his eyes shut, trying to copy the gesture.

My family. My life. My everything.

'What the hell are you doing, Georgie?' I mutter under my breath, not caring if I seem crazy to anyone looking my way.

My feet stop dead as I search for an answer. A man with a bag of Halloween decorations swinging from his wrist and three sourdough loaves stacked in his arms bumps my shoulder, mumbling an apology but tutting at the same time.

Doubt creeps in. Should I turn back? I picture myself spinning on the heels of the cute suede ankle boots I was so excited about before all of this started, imagining myself wearing them to the school firework display and nights in the pub with Tasha and Beth. Even to the estate agent's where I work part-time.

Maybe I should be wondering how I ever felt excited about footwear, but even now I feel a tingle of joy when I look at them. Just knowing I didn't have to think about how much they cost when I bought them. I could just have them. When you've grown up with nothing, being able to buy whatever you want never stops meaning everything.

I blink, forcing my thoughts back to the moment. It's not too late to go home. I could do it. I could walk the half mile home to Magnolia Close, slip through the wrought-iron gates, down our private road to the circular close containing the twelve pristine, bespoke homes. I imagine Nate in our huge, open-plan kitchen with the decadent light fixings and the white marble counter-tops. I see his six-foot-two frame bent over the expensive espresso machine with the bean grinder I bought him for his birthday last year – because God forbid he use the Nespresso pods like a normal person. He'll be clean-shaven, showing off his strong jaw and classic good looks. Those piercing blue eyes that watch me.

I see Oscar too, kneeling on the rug in the playroom, scraping through the boxes of Lego, searching for the perfect piece to complete the rocket he's building. Oscar is tall for his age. Smart too, just like Nate. But, unlike his father, Oscar takes the world as it comes. He doesn't search for hidden truths or question every motive. Oscar is happy-go-lucky like me. He's perfect.

The ache for my son is suddenly fierce. I long to scoop him into my arms, tell him I love him, tell him I'm doing this for him.

I grit my teeth. 'You're no coward, Georgie Bell,' I murmur.

No. No, I'm not. I could turn back, but I won't. Not after the message this morning. Not after everything I've already done. I force my boots forward on the cobbled street. Big girl pants on. Isn't that what I say to Oscar when I throw on my workout clothes, even when all I want is to curl up on the sofa and watch *Bluey* with a bowl of Coco Pops?

I pass the last market stall. The rich scent of frying batter makes my stomach growl. If only I was like Beth – tall and slender with long auburn hair – who loses her appetite at the whisper of a crisis. Or Tasha with her Sri Lankan parents who has no idea how beautiful she is. A part of me wants to stop at the food stall, buy Oscar a brownie and Nate a fruit scone. Maybe a donut for me. I shove the thought aside before it can take root. Today is a low day. I do not eat carbs on low days. Even if my world is falling apart.

My hand smooths over my flat stomach, reminding myself that every sacrifice is worth it. I'm the same size and weight at thirty-nine as I was at twenty-one, and that takes work. The strict calorie intake, the punishing workouts, the 6 a.m. Peloton rides are all worth it for the appreciative glances Nate gives me. *Used* to give me, but I won't think about that right now.

The bike used to face out to our garden – bushy trees and

neat borders. But I moved it to the spare room at the front to watch the comings and goings of Magnolia Close, waving at Beth's husband, Alistair, as he leaves number three for the commute to London in his tweed jacket and carrying his old leather briefcase. In his forties, but with his hair already completely grey, he looks every bit the distracted university professor he is. Knowing as he leaves the gates that later, at the school drop-off, Beth will tell us a story of what Alistair forgot that morning. His wallet sometimes, his tie another day. I'll laugh and pat Beth's hand, and Tasha will hoist little Lanie higher on her hip and suggest a quick coffee that I'll offer to host.

Everything was so easy. Did I ever pause to take it in? How Nate could make me laugh with just the quirk of his brows. How every day was a breeze. Until it wasn't.

In a blink, the market stalls are behind me and the tower of the cathedral pokes up above the last of the shops. Ten more steps and I'll be at the end of the road, standing on the corner, staring at the police station.

I take a deep breath, drawing the air slowly into my lungs. It does nothing to calm the fear.

One, two, three steps.

Everything was so perfect until Jonny Wilson moved into number two Magnolia Close eighteen months ago, and slowly – so slowly I didn't even see it coming – my dazzling, extraordinary life began to unravel.

'I hate you, Jonny Wilson,' I murmur. 'I'm glad you're dead.'

Actions have consequences. And Jonny? Well, he reaped what he sowed.

Eight, nine, ten steps.

There's the corner. There's the police station. An imposing, five-storey modern building, all glass and chrome.

I look for a gap in the traffic. A bright-green bus whizzes past, pushing a gust of wind through my sleek, honey-highlighted blonde bob that costs more at the salon than I earn in a month. Thank God for Nate's salary.

Then a white Tesla rounds the bend and, for a heart-stopping second, I think it's ours. That Nate has dug and dug in that way he does, putting it all together, and come to stop me. He's going to kill me when he finds out what I've done.

Panic constricts my airway. I scrunch my eyes shut, blocking out the watery autumn sun and the road and the police station. Will Nate see I'm doing this for Oscar? Will he understand one day? Or will he hate me? Will Oscar?

I open my eyes to find a gap in the traffic. Taking it as a sign I'm doing the right thing, I dart across the road, ignoring the angry yell of a cyclist. I'm up the steps and pushing through the glass doors before I can change my mind. The heels of my boots tap against the polished floor, a countdown to something I can't take back.

The waiting area is busy. A mother bounces a crying toddler on her lap while filling out a form. A white-haired man dozes in the corner, his mouth slack. At the front desk, a bored-looking officer with a buzz cut lectures a trio of teenage girls in baggy jeans and cropped vests. They could be thirteen or eighteen – who can tell anymore?

By the time I'm across the waiting area, the girls are turning to leave and the officer is looking at me with an expectant glance. Anxiety coils tight in my chest, but I close the gap.

'Can I help you?' he asks.

I nod, forcing myself to look straight at him.

*Own your power!*

'I'd like to talk to Detective Sató please.'

He raises a single eyebrow. 'May I ask what it's regarding?'

I swallow down the lump lodged in my throat. Shoulders back. Gaze straight. For Oscar. For Nate. For Beth and Tasha and my big, beautiful life in Magnolia Close. I may not have been entirely honest with the people I love, but that doesn't make my need to protect my life – protect them – any less. I will fix this for all of us.

I offer my most determined, take-no-shit smile. There's no going back. Whatever happens next, it's done.

'I'd like to confess to the murder of Jonny Wilson.'

18 DAYS EARLIER

Magnolia Close WhatsApp Group

Ryan (No. 9)
*Has anyone seen Mr Pickles? He's gone walkabout
again.*

Jean (No. 5)
*Bill says he saw him sunbathing on top of Steve's car
earlier.*

Steve (No. 4)
*Fur everywhere. He's lucky he's cute!*

Andrea (No. 7)
*A gentle reminder to bring bins in promptly please. The
close looks so untidy when they're left out.*

Andrea (No. 7)
*The gate was propped open again today. ALL – please*

*make sure it's shut. We don't want any unexpected visitors!*

Dan (No. 9)
*Anyone else having trouble with their key fobs not working? Or is it just me and Ryan?*

Jean (No. 5)
*Mine is working fine. Bill's good with electronics. Want him to pop over later and take a look?*

Dan (No. 9)
*Lifesaver! Thank you.*

Susie (No. 11)
*Does anyone have any self-raising flour? Florence is baking cupcakes and we've just run out.*

Beth (No. 3)
*I've got some, Susie. Will pop it over now. I've got a parcel for you to drop over anyway.*

Susie (No. 11)
*Love this close! Thank you xx*

PTA WhatsApp Group

Georgie
*A reminder we're meeting in The Anchor Inn at 7 p.m. to finalise details of the PTA quiz next week.*

# TWO

## TASHA

I sip from the huge wine glass in my hand, savouring the hints of cherry and dark chocolate. Georgie, Beth and I have claimed our usual table in the corner of the pub, near enough to the fire for the warmth but not so close our hair will smell smoky tomorrow. I love The Anchor Inn. Love that it's five minutes from Magnolia Close and the school – the perfect location for tonight's PTA meeting about next week's quiz night. I love the exposed beams, the soft amber lighting, the rich scent of roasting meat and rosemary from the restaurant side of the bar. I love the wine they serve too.

It's my second glass, and it's a fight not to gulp it down as fast as the first as I try to stop my mind racing right back to the never-ending to-do list in my head. Of course it goes there anyway.

Across the table, Georgie and Beth are finalising one of the quiz rounds. Like always, Beth is quiet. She's happy for Georgie to take the lead as she nods along, absently twirling a lock of her long red hair. I can't seem to hold on to the conversation.

Have I paid for Matilda's ballet classes? Did I order a new

swimsuit for Sofia? My phone is resting on the table, and I'm itching to pick it up and do it now. When else will I get time?

Georgie says something I don't catch, but the cackle – that raucous Georgie laugh – makes me smile. She's what Marc calls a 'go-getter'. He doesn't mean it as a dig, but it always stings. I tried to explain it once, how it felt like a comparison. Like what he was really saying was he wished I was more like Georgie. But my husband just pushed a hand through his short dark hair and rolled his eyes before he stuck my comment in the box of 'I guess we're just different'.

Georgie's notebook snaps shut. 'Done,' she declares, and I realise I've barely listened to a single word she's been saying. I'll add 'terrible friend' to my growing list of failures.

Another gulp of wine. If I can't stop the list, then maybe I can drown it.

A wide grin spreads over Georgie's face as she reaches for the bottle and tops up our glasses.

'So,' Georgie says with a light double clap of her hands – the kind of gesture that would be annoying from anyone else, 'I'll collect the wine and snacks on Monday, and you've got the tablecloths to iron, haven't you, Tasha?'

I nod, adding 'find the tablecloths' to tomorrow's list.

'A bad turnout tonight,' Beth says with an arch of her brows.

Georgie waves a hand like it doesn't matter. 'The other mums always say they'll come and then send their excuses.'

'Like we don't have kids to put to bed too,' Beth says.

I nod. All that and more. Tonight's meeting is the last thing I need. Especially with Marc leaving for the airport in three hours. A two-day business trip to Brussels – something about helping a client streamline a new human resource filing system. He's the only one in his company who speaks French, Dutch and Italian, so it's always him who's sent. He's a project manager. His job is to make chaos look easy. The gliding swan, serene above the waterline while the frantic paddling happens out of sight. He's brilliant at it. Efficient. Organised. Cool under pressure.

I just wish he'd bring even a fraction of that energy home. Because when it comes to our life – to our girls, our house, our marriage – I'm the one juggling the chaos. I'm the one staring down the barrel of two nights and three days of solo parenting while he eats dinner in a hotel restaurant and sleeps in crisp white sheets, returning home with a suitcase of clothes that need washing, telling me how exhausted he is. How hard *his* life is.

And it's Wednesday tomorrow. It isn't one of Lanie's nursery days, which means I'll have to take her to the super-market then across town to my parents. Then back for Matilda's assembly, school pick-up, the drop to Beavers, tidying, cooking, the ever-growing pile of washing, and reading with Sofia and Matilda.

Opposite me, Georgie straightens the neckline of her navy cashmere jumper and snaps a selfie with her wine. Three taps on her screen and it's on her Instagram story. I look down at my yellow silk top and feel dowdy. It's my only nice top. The one I grab without thinking and always wear.

There's a lot I didn't know about life before meeting Georgie. Before moving to Magnolia Close when Matilda was four months old. I remember following the removal van down the narrow private road and through those big black gates, squeezing Marc's hand, barely believing we were moving from a two-bed flat in town to a detached house in a private gated community, thanks to his promotion and an inheritance from his granny.

Georgie was the first one out of her door to greet us – wide smile and two bottles of wine. *'I didn't know if you preferred red or white, but thought you'd need both after moving day is over.'*

Over the years, I've learned a lot from Georgie. Like the

importance of a good sports bra when tackling a busy day. Like always keeping frozen pizzas in the freezer for when a doorstep chat turns into a playdate and tea for the kids. Like sending voice notes to myself on WhatsApp with reminders to do something, grab something, be somewhere.

But if there's one thing I don't buy into about Georgie, it's her mantras.

*'You get out what you put in.'*

I'm sorry, but that one is utter crap. If I got out of life what I put in, then my life would be all glitter and sunshine. All I do, every minute of every day, is give and stretch and juggle. All I do is put in!

I shut the thought down, clenching my teeth together until the hollow scream whipping around my vocal cords settles into a throbbing in my temples.

'I know the other PTA mums are flaky,' Georgie says. 'But we get a lot more done just the three of us. And now we can talk about us instead of making awkward small talk with the other school mums. But first we need more wine.' And with that, Georgie is out of her chair and striding to the bar.

More wine is the last thing I need. I push my wine glass further away on the dark oak table. I just won't drink any more. Two glasses is plenty. Two means my head won't be foggy when ten-month-old Lanie shouts for breakfast at 5 a.m. with her wide, gummy smile and those bright brown eyes that melt my heart even when the exhaustion feels like I'm wading through sludge. Not to mention the lecture I'll get from four-year-old Sofia, who, as the middle child, is as precocious and opinionated as my mother-in-law. I can already imagine Sofia's sing-song voice on the walk to school tomorrow morning. *'Wine is very bad, Mummy. You are very bad.'*

I had no idea wines like this existed before meeting Georgie seven years ago. Even Marc's become an expert since we moved to Magnolia Close, and we've shared countless bottles of wine with our neighbours. He says his expertise is in his blood. His mother is Italian, his dad English. It's one of the reasons we were so drawn to each other when we met in college. With my Sri Lankan parents and his dark Italian looks, both of us felt like we didn't quite belong.

Marc even jokes about running away to the countryside and building his own vineyard one day when the girls are grown up. *'I'll use my full name of Marco, and you'll be my Tesoro,'* he'd say in an Italian accent, calling me his treasure. Sometimes when I lock myself in the bathroom, press my hands to my eyes and hold back the tears – grabbing a minute of peace – I imagine that other life. What it would feel like to run away from it all and start again.

But that's all it is – a dream. We have a life here. Responsibilities. Bills to pay. The Magnolia Close community. The girls are happy and settled, and there's my parents, of course. I can't leave them.

My thoughts draw back to tomorrow, and the taste of the dark cherry Pinot Noir turns sour in my mouth as tomorrow's tasks stack up. Like always, the stress feels like I'm being buried alive, weighed down, running out of air.

My eyes drag back to my phone, sitting face down on the table. I'm really not sure I did pay for the ballet classes. I can't forget again. There was something else I need to remember. Something about the garden...

For a moment, it feels like the guilt will consume me – a monster from one of Matilda's nightmares swallowing me whole. That constant feeling of disappointing everyone. Marc. The girls. My parents. Especially my parents.

I hate this feeling.

It's just... since the summer, everything has felt harder, bigger. Impossible. The smallest things – a forgotten PE kit, a lost shoe – send me spiralling. Before the summer, I had hope.

There was a light at the end of the tunnel – a way forward. Now, there's no escape.

And it's all Jonny's fault. He is the reason – the sole reason – my life is as hard as it is. All my stress, every burden I carry, is heavier because of what he did.

I wish Jonny Wilson was dead.

# THREE

## TASHA

Outside, the night presses against the windows. A reminder that the October half term is only weeks away. Then Halloween. Then Christmas. I should start making a list of presents I need to buy...

Georgie returns with another bottle of red and tops up our glasses. I can feel her energy humming around me. What I wouldn't give to be my friend for just one day.

'How are your parents, Tasha?' Georgie asks with so much concern, I feel the prick of tears at the back of my eyes. Georgie might be a go-getter. She might spend money without thinking and cajole us into nights out and helping at the events she organises, but she's also kind and thoughtful and really cares about me. About all of us.

I reach for my wine and take a sip, determined not to cry.

'Dad had another fall last night,' I tell them. 'He was on his way to the toilet and his legs gave out.'

'Oh God, Tasha,' Georgie says. 'What happened?'

'Nothing,' I reply, swallowing down the hurt threatening to close my throat. 'That's how I found him this morning. Mum couldn't get him up. They didn't call me. They said they didn't want to be a bother. Mum covered him with a blanket and waited for me to arrive after the school run.' My voice cracks despite my resolve.

I blink hard, trying to block out the image – the sag of my dad's thin frame beneath the throw, his pyjamas damp with urine, the sour smell clinging to the room, to me. The way his rough hand had gripped mine, apologising for causing a fuss and asking why I'd taken so long to get there. Always swinging like that. Gratitude and frustration in the same breath.

Across the table, Beth's own eyes swim with tears. 'That's awful, Tash,' she says, reaching to squeeze my hand. Her fingers are cool, but the gesture is full of warmth, and I'm grateful for my friends and the moments they make me feel seen.

I met Beth soon after Georgie. She knocked on the door the day after we'd moved in, little Henry – eight months then – in a baby carrier on her chest. *'I made cookies. They're gluten- and nut-free. I wasn't sure if you had any allergies.'*

I couldn't believe it – not one, but two other women on Magnolia Close had babies a similar age to Matilda. And then there was Lily at number two, with little Joshua already a toddler. We became a foursome. Play groups and rhyme time at the library. Coffees that turned into lunches, park trips that lasted until dusk. We forged a friendship in the trenches of motherhood – through every sleepless night, every milestone, every meltdown and row with our husbands. It was hard when it all fell apart with Lily and she and Kevin moved away, selling their house to Jonny. It was a difficult time for all of Magnolia Close, but I still have Georgie and Beth. Some days, it feels like these two women sitting with me now are the only two people who truly see me.

'And they still won't accept a carer?' Georgie asks, dragging my thoughts back to the table. Typical Georgie, always so practical. It's not her fault, but she doesn't understand. Neither of them do. Care is for family. Not strangers. And I'm the only family my parents have here. I am their everything.

They always planned to return to Galle at the southern tip of Sri Lanka to live with my cousin and the extended family when they retired. But then Mum needed her hip replacement and Dad was diagnosed with stage two prostate cancer. They still talk about going home, but deep down, they know they're too frail.

I shake my head. 'If only...' I trail off, biting down on the inside of my lip, stopping the words from coming. It's not like I haven't said them before, a hundred times over since the summer when it all went from bad to worse.

Beth's face hardens. 'Jonny.'

I nod, taking another gulp of wine. Sod tomorrow!

'I really hate that man,' Georgie says, her voice sharp.

My gaze glances to the bar, scanning the faces for any other Magnolia Close residents. I don't want to be overheard talking about our neighbour. However angry I feel, I'll keep the peace for the sake of the Magnolia Close community.

'I'm sorry, I know I've said this before,' I say, unable to stop myself, 'but I just can't get over it. Why would he object to our planning permission for the extension, when he can't even see our house from his?'

'None of us would've seen the extension,' Beth says. 'Jonny just did it out of spite.'

I heave in a breath, swallowing down the anger threatening to consume me. The extension we'd planned was small. A single-storey with a bedroom, a kitchen-living room, and a bathroom. Somewhere my parents could've lived independently but still had me on hand when needed. It was the perfect solution. Saving me the hours driving across town and back every day to take care of them. All that time eaten up and it still doesn't feel like I'm giving them enough. They need more.

'Just be grateful you don't live next door to him,' Beth says, venom carrying in her voice. 'Last night, Henry kicked his football over the fence. Jonny threw it back five minutes later, all the air gone and a massive slash through the leather. That was a brand-new ball Henry bought with his eighth birthday money. He was so upset.'

A frown pinches Georgie's brows. 'Why does he even live on Magnolia Close? He won't even join the WhatsApp group. A single man in his forties living among all couples and families. All those women he has coming and going.'

'I passed one coming through the gates once,' Beth says, 'and she was wearing a wedding ring. Strolled right up to Jonny's door and was kissing him before she was even inside. It's disgusting.'

'And you never see the same one twice. It gives me the creeps.' Georgie shivers.

'It makes me miss the Gallaghers,' I say, mentioning Lily and Kevin.

Georgie shakes her head. 'No way,' she says. 'They're still dead to me after what Lily did. What we need is Jonny gone and a new family in the close.'

We fall silent for a minute, and it feels like I'm not the only one fighting back my anger towards this man.

We all hate Jonny.

Georgie picks up her wine glass, swirling the liquid before her gaze lands on me. 'Sometimes I think about doing something.'

'Like what?' Beth asks before shooting me a look. *Typical Georgie*, the look says, and the three of us burst out laughing. And just for a second, I forget my to-do lists and my guilt and I'm just me – just a woman enjoying a glass of wine with her friends.

Beth sweeps her long dark-red hair over one shoulder, still laughing. 'Are you going to write him an angry letter like the one you sent to the council when the bin collections kept skipping our road?'

'Hey.' Georgie grins. 'That worked, didn't it? And no, I don't mean a letter.'

There's a mischief to her expression that makes me laugh again. 'I'm sorry, Georgie,' I say, 'but you couldn't even dispose of Oscar's goldfish when it started swimming upside down. You made me come over and get rid of it.'

Beth laughs too, then she stands. She brushes a hand over her emerald-green corduroy skirt, looking effortlessly elegant and so serene. Nothing seems to rattle Beth. It's like she's been to hell and back these last six years and now nothing can touch her.

She nods in the direction of the toilets before she steps away. On the other side of the bar, a waiter clears a table, stacking plates and sweeping away crumbs. I should leave soon. I told Marc I'd be home by ten.

'We really should do something about Jonny, Tasha,' Georgie says again when it's just the two of us.

'I wish we could,' I reply. Wish more than anything there was a way out of the frazzled, never-a-second-to-spare, too-many-things-to-do, everything-piling-up feeling I live with. A life Jonny trapped me in this summer when he objected to our extension.

But wishing and dreaming won't get me anywhere.

I'm about to lighten the mood, make a joke about Georgie needing a new notebook if we're planning... what? I'm not actually sure what Georgie means by 'do something'. But there's movement from the corner of my eye, and I turn to see a woman approaching the table. She's younger than us – early thirties, I guess – with edgy, short black hair, a low-cut black top revealing creamy white skin, and a look on her face like she just overheard our conversation.

As a slow smile spreads across her red lips, I remember something my mum used to say when I was little. Her voice echoes in my thoughts and a shiver races down my spine.

'*Wish for the devil and he shall appear.*'

## FOUR

### BETH

*You should've told them.*

The know-it-all voice sings in my head as I dab cool water on my cheeks. God, I hate that voice. Does it always have to sound so smug? I ignore it and stare at my reflection in the tarnished mirror of the pub toilets. There's an ugly sheen of sweat on my face that refuses to be absorbed by the organic, cruelty-free foundation I dabbed on earlier in between serving Henry his lentil Bolognese with his favourite bow-shaped pasta. Also homemade, of course. There's little I can do about the onslaught of processed food Henry is exposed to out in the world, but at home, I keep things natural.

*You've left it too late.*

That voice again, dragging me back to my reflection in the mirror. I've been in the toilets too long as it is, but I'm so tired. I don't think I've ever felt this exhausted. Not even when Henry was a newborn, waking every few hours.

The face staring back at me burns with the news I need to share. I take a deep breath, smooth down my cardigan and tug at the green skirt I made last week. I didn't realise the fabric bunches a little around the waist. Sloppy. I'll unpick it tomorrow and do it right.

*Chicken.*

I grit my teeth. I'm telling them now.

But as I step out of the ladies' room, my feet falter. There's another woman at our table. A stranger. Any resolve to share my secret with Georgie and Tasha disappears.

'Beth!' Georgie waves me over like I was planning to beeline for the door. Which had crossed my mind. 'This is Keira.'

'Hi.' Keira raises a hand as I give her a polite smile. She looks a little awkward. And a lot out of place. Thick eyeliner rims her eyes, adding an intensity to her face. I'm not one to judge, but she looks like she'd be happier in one of the trendy bars under the railway arches in the centre of town.

'I hope you don't mind me joining you,' Keira says, her Irish accent strong.

'Of course we don't,' Georgie cuts in as I take a seat beside Tasha, noticing the new bottle of red that's appeared since I left. And the inch added to my glass. I don't even like red wine. But Georgie pushed ahead, ordering the bottle before I could ask for a water. Then the glass was in my hand, and it would've been rude to refuse.

'Keira will be a new mum at Magnolia Primary,' Georgie announces. 'She's joining the PTA, and she's just bought a ticket for the quiz night. I'm going to put her on one of the parents' tables.'

'Except I'm hideously late for the meeting. I'm so sorry,' Keira says.

Georgie waves the apology away. 'Her daughter, Rowan—'

'Is joining year three,' Keira finishes with a smile. 'She was hard to settle tonight. I think it's all the changes. We only moved back to my mum's at the weekend. We're on Dove Street. Anyway, I didn't mean to intrude.'

I know Dove Street. A narrow road of terraced houses, crammed in like biscuits in a packet. It's the cut-through people use on the walk to and from town, and there's always litter in the gutters.

'No one who buys wine is intruding.' Georgie grins, clinking her glass to Keira's.

I share a brief look with Tasha. It's not the first time Georgie has adopted someone on a night out. Although usually they disappear pretty quickly when we start talking about our husbands and our lives and they realise we're not as interesting as Georgie has made us out to be.

Georgie and Tasha are my best friends. Honestly, they're my only friends. The only ones who've stuck by me for the last six years. Would they have done the same if we didn't live on Magnolia Close? Maybe not, but that's why our community is so perfect. We look out for each other. No one outside of Magnolia Close understands how special that is. It's why people rarely move away. Why would you want to leave that?

'I was just filling Keira in on Jonny,' Georgie says. 'I was telling her about Henry's football.'

My anger rises to the surface. How dare Jonny do that!

'And his objection to my planning permission,' Tasha says, her voice a little too loud. A sure sign she's going to regret the wine tomorrow. 'He even called the planning officer at the council. Can you believe it?'

'And the way he looks at all of us.' Georgie shudders. 'Like he's undressing us with his eyes. All those little comments about how we look. It's sexual harassment dressed up as compliments and friendly jokes so we look like we're over-reacting if we say anything.'

'Yes, that's exactly what it is,' Tasha says. 'He's repulsive, and I hate him.'

I nod, feeling the raw, jagged edges of my own anger. 'And the worst part is, the men can't see it,' I say.

Georgie rolls her eyes. 'Exactly. You know Nate actually thinks he's cool.'

'He turns on the charm for them,' Tasha snaps. 'They see his flash car, his white teeth, his Rolex, not to mention the women that come and go, and they think he's the ultimate bachelor.'

Tasha's right. I think of Alistair and how he only sees what a great guy Jonny is. But Jonny is all charm and back slaps with the men in the close, and then something else entirely with the women. I hate the way I catch him looking at me from an upstairs window when I'm in the garden, tending to my vegetable patch.

We always try to be good neighbours in Magnolia Close. I love where we live. I love how it's shut away from the rest of the world, like it's our own little sanctuary. But I don't know how much longer I can stand living next to a man like him. When he's home, a low-level hum of unease thrums through my body. An anxiety I can't shift. Some days, I want to scream with the unfairness of it. Alistair needs to be close to London. Our life is here. Our life is in Magnolia Close. We love our home and our community – our friends. We'll never leave.

'He said the football caught on his rose bush,' Alistair said last night, completely ignoring the gaping knife wound in the ball.

'Did you at least tell him to keep his music down in the evenings?' I asked. 'I can hear it in Henry's room when I go in to check on him in the night.'

'It's not that bad,' Alistair replied, a calming hand taking mine. 'And he's a music producer, Beth. He has to listen to it loud.'

At the table, I check my wrist for a hairband, find none and scoop my hair behind my ears instead. I know the long red waves are my best feature. It makes me seem more interesting than I really am. How many times have I heard the expression 'a fiery redhead' when I'm nothing like that? Too many. My hair is really just a distraction from the sharpness of my face. And skin so pale that Alistair can trace the veins with his finger. But right now, I'd give anything to tie it back. Just as I'd give anything to be home in the dog-print pyjamas I made myself for my birthday, curled into Alistair's side, watching the latest detective series on Netflix.

Poor Alistair never gets the plot. He always has half a mind on whatever research project he's undertaking or his students and the courses he teaches as a professor at the London School of Economics. I'm forever having to pause the show and explain the twists while he makes us both herbal tea.

If I was home, I could distract myself with TV or Alistair or knitting. Anything so I didn't have to think about Jonny. I hate that he saw me that day seven months ago. It was March. I remember the daffodils swaying in the cool breeze as I made my way to the train station. I'd told Tasha and Georgie a white lie about a great-aunt's funeral so they'd look after Henry for me after school for an hour. I thought I could get to my appointment and back without anyone knowing. The last person I expected to bump into that day was Jonny.

When I escape to the toilets again, just for a moment of peace and the cool water I dab on my cheeks, I return to find my wine glass is full to the top, the dark liquid nearly spilling over the rim. My friends haven't noticed I'm not drinking it.

Keira's jaw is tight, eyes narrowed as I take my seat again. 'This Jonny sounds just like my ex, Richard. He's making my life hell. I'm coming out of the divorce with next to nothing. He's trying to take half my business. I have an online activewear shop that's doing pretty well, so of course he wants a piece of that. And he's even fighting me for joint custody of Rowan. That man has barely spent five minutes with his daughter in her whole life. He's just doing it to hurt me. If only he'd die before we get to court, it would make my life so much easier.' Keira's accent is stronger in her anger, the rhotic R more pronounced. 'But there's nothing we can do about it,' she continues. 'We're stuck living in a world where men like this are fucking up our lives.'

I flinch at the expletive, feeling like a prude as Keira catches the movement and quirks her eyebrow in a way that's almost challenging.

*She thinks you're a fool.*

I don't care that Keira swore. I'm just so used to watching my words around Henry.

But before I can explain, Georgie jumps in. 'We should do something. Really do something.' The wine has left a dark stain on her inner lip. This time we don't laugh.

Keira leans forward, elbows propped on the table. 'You should kill him.'

# FIVE

## GEORGIE

*Disrupt. Evolve. Own it.* The mantra from my Instagram story this morning flashes through my mind as Keira's words hit the table. Her lips are quirked up, like she's fighting a smirk at the bomb she's just detonated on our boring Tuesday night drinks in this sleepy local pub.

Of course she's joking. She doesn't really mean we should kill Jonny. Beth and Tasha's faces – gaping mouths, wide eyes – though... the laughter bursts out of me, head thrown back, that full-belly, wild cackle – what Nate calls my witch's laugh. The thought makes me laugh even more. And now they're all giggling too, caught in it, like we've tipped over into a giddy hysteria we can't control.

It consumes us. I can't speak, can barely draw a breath. Beth is doubled over, head practically in her lap. I've never seen her like this before, and it only makes me laugh harder. Tears fall down Tasha's beautiful face, her long black hair slipping out of her ponytail as she gasps for air. She waves her hands in front of her eyes, trying to stop the tears. But they're happy tears, and it's been so long since I've seen anything but strain and sadness in my friend.

Finally, the moment begins to ebb, and Tasha wipes her eyes. Beth straightens up, her cheeks almost the same colour as her hair. 'We must sound like a pack of hyenas,' she whispers, shooting a look across the bar.

'Let them stare,' Keira says at the exact moment I'm thinking the same. She picks up her glass and winks at me.

I flash her a grin, deciding in that moment that Keira and I are going to become good friends. I love Tasha and Beth. Tasha is always the first to offer to help. Beth might be quieter, but she's steady and reliable. I wouldn't be me without them. But they can be heavy sometimes. Their emotions and their worries and their endless talk of their problems. I hate myself for thinking it, but sometimes – only sometimes – it feels like they suck the air right out of the room. I don't blame them. Life hasn't been fair. Not with what Tasha has to deal with every day with her parents, or for Beth and her fertility struggles. It's changed her. The bright woman I met when Nate and I first moved to Magnolia Close ten years ago no longer exists.

There are days when I shut the door after another coffee or playdate and exhale like I've been underwater. But Keira looks like she's all fun. She's whip-smart but doesn't strike me as someone who wants to play by the rules, and I love that. So what if she lives outside of the close? Maybe there are things we can learn from her.

Beside me, Keira refills my glass, and I feel her watching, like she's trying to get the measure of me. I pull my shoulders back and run a hand through my sleek bob. I don't know what test I'm taking here, but no way am I failing it.

Keira's charcoaled eyes move to each of us in turn, and when she speaks again, her voice is low like a secret. 'But would you do it?' she asks. 'I mean, if you could get away with it. If there was a way you could never be caught... would you kill your neighbour?'

My reply rushes out without hesitation or thought. 'I would.'

Keira gives me an approving nod, and even though I'm thirty-nine years old, happily married, confident in who I am, I can't help but feel myself glow under her praise. 'Go on then, Georgie,' she says. 'How would you kill this Jonny fella?'

I think for a moment, tilting my head to one side, biting my bottom lip. 'I'd stab him,' I reply. 'Right in the gut. Three times. One for each of us,' I add, shooting a look to Tasha and Beth.

There is no shock at my words. No laughter. My friends know I mean it. Those lecherous looks he gives us all. The winks. The comments, especially to me.

*'That husband of yours is one hell of a lucky man, Georgie.'*
*'That workout kit should be illegal.'*
*'You'll give a man a heart attack wearing that.'*
*'Looking gorgeous today, Georgie.'*

Tasha and Beth know I hate Jonny as much as they do. Even if they don't know all the reasons why.

Keira looks to Tasha next. 'What about you, Tasha? Would you kill your neighbour?'

Tasha swirls her wine, staring at the legs around the inside of the glass before replying. 'Yes. But stabbing is too risky,' she says. 'What if he overpowered you?' she asks me.

'I'd sneak up on him,' I reply. 'Bill and Jean have a key to Jonny's house from when the Gallaghers used to live there. I've got a key to Bill and Jean's. I'd pop into theirs when they were out, get the key, then sneak into Jonny's and bam!'

'Poison would be easier,' Beth says in a soft voice. 'Something in his coffee machine or his milk.'

It's my turn to shake my head. This is fun. This is real friendship – laying our fantasies bare.

'Too much risk of collateral damage,' I say, ticking off the issues on my fingers. 'What if the cleaner eats some, or a guest?

Or some poor delivery guy who accepts a coffee? I couldn't live with myself.'

Keira looks thoughtful, and for a moment it's like we're actually planning this. The thought sends a giddy thrill shooting through my veins along with the wine.

'You're right,' Keira says. 'No poison. It's not just the collateral damage. There's too much risk he'd survive. But Tasha is right. Men are stronger than us. It's a fact, and there's no point pretending otherwise. Stabbing is too risky.'

Tasha nods. 'I would use sleeping pills,' she says, rifling through her bag and pulling out a box. 'These are my dad's prescription tablets. They'd knock Jonny out so he couldn't overpower me. And then—' She makes a vague stabbing motion that has me grinning.

'What about you, Beth?' Keira asks. 'If poison's off the table?'

I'm surprised Beth is joining in, rather than shaking her head and staying quiet like always, but she's as caught up in this as the rest of us. 'Stabbing is messy,' she says. 'Suffocation would be better. A pillow over his face while he's knocked out from the pills,' she says, nodding to Tasha's bag.

That's Beth. Always wanting things neat and tidy.

Keira claps her hands, her grin wider than ever. 'Yes. That's perfect,' she says, leaning forward and placing her palms flat on the table. 'So you'll slip him some food laced with sleeping tablets. Wait a bit. Then go in and kill him. Either stabbing,' she says, gesturing to me and Tasha. 'Or suffocation. Or both.' She laughs. 'And it gives you a window.'

'What window?' Tasha asks, a hiccupped giggle slipping free.

'A window of time when the murder happens. That's when you need to make sure you all have an alibi,' she replies.

A bubble of laughter threatens to spill. 'But if we have an alibi... how do we actually kill him?' I ask.

Keira's voice is still low as she flicks a glance to the near-empty pub before looking back to us. 'You'd be each other's alibis,' she explains. 'You lie to the police. You lie to everyone except each other.'

There's a pause. A breath where it feels like the air shifts.

'You could murder Jonny next week, during the PTA quiz night,' Keira continues. 'It's perfect! Those things are always wine-fuelled chaos. One of you could slip out and kill Jonny. Then all three of you swear you were with each other all night.'

Tasha's wine glass hovers halfway to her lips. The air is sparking with something dangerous. It's just a game – a bit of fun. And yet the mention of the quiz night makes it feel suddenly real, and I'm no longer sure if I should laugh.

My heart pounds like I'm about to sprint into something unknown, something dangerous, and, secretly, I love it. My life is bright and wonderful. I have my gorgeous Oscar and my husband, Nate, and Magnolia Close and my part-time job, and Tasha and Beth. I keep busy and I keep fit, and one day soon my Instagram Mum Mindfulness account will go viral and I'll be a proper influencer. I already have over ten thousand followers. Just one perfect post and everyone will see that I'm someone. But the waiting and trying can drag me down sometimes, pull me too close to the mundane. Nights like this, shaking things up – having fun – feel like fuel. Like pure energy.

Tasha exhales in a breathless laugh. 'You make it sound so easy.'

'That's because it is,' Keira replies with a shrug. 'You've got a plan for how you'd do it. You make sure he consumes the sleeping pills before you get there. Then you've got a window during the PTA quiz where there'd be lots of witnesses who won't notice one of you slip away for half an hour. You've got each other to be alibis too. There's just one really important thing to remember.'

'What?' Beth asks, her tone light as she rolls her eyes, like she's waiting for Keira to deliver the punchline. To burst into another fit of giggles and tell us she's joking.

But there's no humour in the way Keira lifts her glass and takes a long sip of wine, allowing a dramatic pause. I swear we're all holding our breaths, waiting for her reply.

'Whatever you do' – her voice is stone-cold, her eyes fixing on each of us in turn – 'you have to lie to the police. Your alibi has to be watertight. You stick to your story. You were together all night, running the quiz. As long as you say nothing to the police, you'll get away with it. No one will ever know.'

Beth lets out a nervous laugh. 'Obviously you're not serious?'

Keira tilts her head, no longer smiling. 'What if I am?' she asks.

That's when the mood shifts.

Tasha sets her glass on the table and pushes it away. Beth's laughter dies in her throat. The words *no one will ever know* seem to vibrate in the air. The wine is suddenly thick in my head, the room spinning in the edges of my vision, but it's not enough to muffle the unease I feel when I glance at Keira. She's watching me again, dark eyes steady.

Then she laughs. A loud, brittle laugh void of humour. I glance at Tasha then Beth. They look rattled and uneasy. For the first time tonight, I feel out of my depth. Like we've swum too far from the shore and don't know how to get back to safety.

Keira has made our talk of Jonny's murder feel all too real.

This was just for fun... right?

# PRESENT DAY

# SIX

## BETH

*You shouldn't be here.*

I shut the voice down and clutch at the plastic bag on my lap. The fear is unbearable. The bare walls of the police interview room feel like they're inching closer with each passing minute. How long since the officer ushered me in here and asked me to wait? Twenty minutes? Thirty? Are they watching me through the two-way mirror? I squeeze my eyes shut then regret it instantly when the floor tilts. My stomach lurches. Bile burns the back of my throat. I snap my eyes open, holding myself statue-still.

The chair beneath me is broken. A screw is loose, making the plastic shift against the metal legs with every tiny movement, scratching at the frayed edges of my nerves, making my stomach twist again. I stare at the fluorescent lights, counting the tiny dead bugs trapped inside the plastic cover. The faint smell of coffee and sweat press in on me. I wonder if the chair I'm sitting on has been thrown against the wall or against another person. If that's why it's broken. If someone else sat here, waiting. I wonder what would happen if I just walked out right now.

*You swore you wouldn't speak to the police.*

It's too late to second-guess everything we've done to get here. The only way out of this mess is to confess to a murder. To lie to Detective Sató.

*It's you that smells of sweat, you know?*

The voice again. Always so smug. My mother's voice maybe. She always was a know-it-all. Lived for 'I told you so'. Like when I was sixteen and dated the popular boy at school.

*'He'll break your heart.'*

Or when I finished law school and began my training.

*'It'll be a waste of time when you give it all up for children.'*

I did give my career up. But not for the longed-for children. Just one. One perfect boy. Henry. Who turned eight last month and loves trains and books about space. Who is sweet and thoughtful, always thinking to include four-year-old Sofia in the games with Matilda and Oscar. He loves football, but not playing in matches when the other dads shout from the side-lines, and the other boys call him 'ginger' and 'carrot top', like his beautiful hair makes him less than everyone else.

My mother died the year Henry was born; she never got to see him or tell me all the things I was doing wrong. And still, she lingers in that voice. She would've revelled in my sadness and my heartbreak of the past six years.

A noise shatters the silence. My gaze snaps to the door as it opens and the tall, slender frame of Detective Sató steps into the room. The fear threatens to take over again. My hands shake, rustling the plastic bag resting in my lap.

This is it.

Sató's hair is pinned into its usual bun at the nape of her neck, and she's wearing a fitted blazer with jeans and a jumper. She looks more casual than the previous times I've seen her during the investigation into Jonny's death. But then it is a

Saturday. Alistair will be wondering where I am by now. I told him I was going for a walk with Tasha and Georgie this morning. He'll assume we've got caught up talking. He'll be putting the dirty laundry into the wash. Running the hoover around. Always thinking of me and Henry. I know he'll understand what I've done.

'Good morning, Beth.' Sató sits down in the chair opposite me.

My mouth fills with saliva, and my hands worry at the edges of the plastic bag on my lap.

'How are you today?' she asks.

The question is an opener. Chit-chat. A technique to build a connection between us. I ignore it. 'I'd like to confess please.'

'Yes, DC McLachlan told me. What exactly are you confessing to?' Sató asks.

I swallow again, but it's no good. The chair shifts beneath me. The walls and the floor too. I've been fighting this feeling all morning, but the floral scent of Sató's perfume, the reality of sitting in this small, windowless room and why I'm here – it's too much. I dip my head and heave into the plastic bin liner. The sound of spattering liquid fills the room, the smell of my vomit making me heave again until my throat is raw and tears are stinging at my eyes.

It took a year to fall pregnant with Henry, and so when he was six months old, we started trying again. Months stretched into a year. Then eighteen months. The doctors were sure it would happen. But it didn't. Tests. Hormone drugs. More disappointment. Tasha fell pregnant with Sofia, and I tried to be happy for her as we paid for round after round of IVF. Eating into our savings, leaving us counting every penny. It's the real reason I make my own clothes. Buying new things isn't an option right now. A year ago, I had no idea how to make clothes. But I worked the problem. Researched. Learned. Found the solution. Practised until it was perfect.

Years of nothing. Years of heartbreak. Then watching Tasha fall pregnant for a third time, the swell of her belly growing round. It wasn't fair. I'd done everything right. Followed every piece of advice. Alistair and I both stopped drinking alcohol and caffeine, then we cut out refined sugar and processed foods. I took up yoga to calm my mind and keep my body fit. I even changed our washing powders and soaps and moisturisers, keeping anything with chemicals away from our skin. I took so many vitamins I swear I rattled most days. I stayed positive for as long as I could. I even took Georgie's advice and visualised that positive line on the pregnancy test.

Six years of failure.

We did everything right. So why wasn't it happening for us?

It was that question that drove me to go to London that day in March when Georgie and Tasha looked after Henry. The day I bumped into Jonny on the street as I was coming out of the clinic.

To see the one person I detested most in the world when I was at my most vulnerable was truly awful. And now finally I'm healing and Jonny is dead and I am here. Even in death, he's a selfish bastard.

When I'm done retching, I lift my head. Sató is no longer in her seat but standing by the door, one hand already on the handle, poised to get help. 'Are you OK?' she asks.

'I'm pregnant,' I tell her with a weak smile I don't try to fight. Because even with my world imploding, Alistair and I are finally having the second baby we have both longed for. A brother or sister for Henry. Our perfect family complete at long last.

'Would you like a glass of water and a moment to yourself?'

'No,' I reply quickly. I can't stand to wait anymore. I tie the handles of the bag tightly together and place it by my feet. 'Thank you, but I have some water here.' I reach into my handbag, past the Tupperware of ginger biscuits I made yesterday, ignoring the weight of the other object sitting beside it, and pluck out my water bottle. I fight the urge to gulp it back and take a small sip, before pulling out another bin liner just in case.

'I'm happy to continue,' I add. Terrified, more like. The same terror I've lived with for weeks. More even. The second I found out I was pregnant and my entire world became about protecting this wonderful, perfect baby growing inside me.

But there's no going back now, even if I wanted to. And I don't. I'm glad Jonny is dead. Whatever comes next, that fact will never change.

Sató retakes her seat without a word. We go through the mechanics of the interview. She asks me if she can record it, and I agree. I give her my name and address and finally she says, 'What do you want to confess to, Beth?'

*Don't do it!*

I ignore the voice. I take a breath and meet Sató's gaze. Her eyes are dark and disbelieving. 'The murder of Jonny Wilson. I killed him. I acted completely alone.'

Sató sighs like I've just made her day a lot harder. You'd think she'd be happy to have a confession.

'Do you know how many people confess to crimes before they're charged, Beth?' she asks me.

'No, I don't.'

'Neither do I,' she admits. 'But it's not like TV shows and Hollywood films would have us believe. Confessions don't come after gruelling interviews, or even out of the blue,' she adds, gesturing a hand at me. 'They come after the Crown Prosecution Service has accepted the case. After the lawyers have advised their clients on their best chances. That's when we see confessions. So you'll forgive me if I'm a little surprised by your confession today.' She pulls out a notebook from the inside pocket of her blazer and reads something before looking back at me. It's an act. She's allowing her words to settle, to unnerve me before moving on.

'Why should I believe you?' she asks.

'Why wouldn't you?' I reply.

'Because I have your two friends, Georgie and Tasha, also in this police station. Also confessing to the same murder. I'll tell you this now, Beth, Tasha isn't doing well. She's very upset.'

I bite down hard on the inside of my lip. My pulse is drumming in my ears. Poor Tasha. This isn't fair on any of us but especially on her. She's already gone through so much with her parents and what Jonny did to ruin her chance of making a home for them on Magnolia Close. If there was a way to stop this from happening, I'd do it. But we're all sitting in the same out-of-control car and there's no way to stop what's coming.

*It's just a tactic. She's trying to rile you.*

For once, I listen to that voice. Grab hold of the words and force myself to stay calm. 'They're lying,' I say. 'They're trying to protect me because of the baby.' I place a hand on the small bump of my stomach.

Sató considers this for a moment. 'That's some friendship. Giving up their lives and their families, going to prison for murder so you can walk free.'

I don't reply. There's no point trying to explain the closeness we share – how Magnolia Close has made us more than friends. We're family. I remember my training as a solicitor. Sometimes it feels like another lifetime. Another person. Other times it feels like yesterday. I won't be drawn into talking – giving more than I intend in the silences Sató is leaving me. I stay quiet, like always. People mistake this as shyness, but it's not. I just prefer to sit back and watch and listen.

The detective shakes her head. 'It still doesn't answer why I should believe you over your friends. Right now, I'm inclined to think all three of you are lying, so I'll remind you that wasting police time is a criminal offence. I could charge all three of you.'

*I told you she wouldn't buy this. She's too smart for you.*

I hold back my plea for Sató to listen. Hold back the fear

threatening to eat me alive. I'm not scared of this room or this detective. I'm terrified of the reason we're all here. And that's something Sató, with her sharp eyes and her neat handwriting, will never understand.

The nausea returns. A roiling wave that starts at the top of my head before moving its way down my body, all the way to my stomach. My fingers fumble with the new bin liner, opening it up, getting ready. I force my gaze up to Sató again. 'You should believe me. Because I killed Jonny. And I can prove it. I can tell you exactly how I did it – how he died – which I believe hasn't been made public yet.'

'It hasn't.' There's a spark in her eyes now. I've caught her attention. 'How did you kill Jonny Wilson, Beth?'

'I stabbed him three times in the stomach with a kitchen knife and then suffocated him with his pillow.'

The words hang in the air, just like Keira's did that night in the pub when she'd first suggested killing him.

Sató doesn't move. Doesn't blink.

I close my eyes, just for a second, just long enough to see Keira's smirk at the table and hear Georgie's wild laughter in my head followed by Tasha's hiccupped giggles. We thought it was a game that night. What fools.

The nausea surges. I clutch the bin liner, hunching forward as my stomach twists inside out.

I feel Sató's eyes on me as I dry-heave into the bag, my stomach already empty. When I'm done, I wipe my mouth with a tissue and force myself to sit up straight. 'Do you believe me now?'

I don't breathe as I wait for Sató's reply.

Magnolia Mums WhatsApp Group

Tasha
*I think I'm dying! Why did we drink so much red wine last night???*

Georgie
*I don't feel great either. But it was a fun night.*

Beth
*It was weird!!!*

Tasha
*Was it?*

*Why?*

*OMG I just remembered!*

Beth
*We need to talk after drop-off.*

# SEVEN

## GEORGIE

'Muuuummmmeeee!'

Even from upstairs, Oscar's shout is piercing – a jackhammer to my lingering headache. I wince, pressing my fingertips to my temples before plastering on a smile.

'I'm in the kitchen!' I call back, my voice light, like I'm not feeling every drop of wine from last night thudding against my skull. I take a deep breath, willing my heart rate to settle after my sixty-minute Peloton session.

'I will never regret the path I take,' I murmur to myself, pushing aside the desire to rake over the decision to drink so much or to inhale two slices of toast when I got home at midnight. Regrets root me in the past. 'And you, Georgie Bell, are about living in the present and looking to the future.'

I take a photo of my spinach smoothie – or sludge according to Nate and Oscar – and add a quote before posting. Last night's wine glass shot has reached eight thousand views. Not enough, but Rome wasn't built in a day. I'll add a reel after the school run. Something in my kitchen. My followers love this space as much as I do.

I take a long sip of my smoothie. It's actually super tasty.

Spinach, strawberries and blueberries and banana, Chai seeds, turmeric and plenty of ice. The cure-all of smoothies.

Oscar skids into the room, already dressed in the school uniform I laid out for him last night – charcoal-grey trousers, a white polo shirt and a red jumper with the Magnolia Road Primary School logo on the left breast. It's clean on, but somehow in the journey downstairs he looks like he's been dragged through a bush. My heart swells with love as I crouch down and he rushes towards me. I scoop him into my arms, inhaling the scent of fabric softener and shampoo.

'Good morning, baby,' I murmur into his mop of sandy, untamed hair. 'Do you want some of Mummy's smoothie?'

'Yuck!' He wrinkles his nose, already wriggling free before making a running leap towards the cereal cupboard.

'Coco Pops it is.' I laugh, reaching for a bowl, my gaze pulling to the floor-to-ceiling bifold doors overlooking the garden. I catch sight of a familiar black-and-white cat balancing perfectly on the fence that separates our garden from Andrea Jenkins' at number seven. I smile, grabbing my phone and adding a message to the Magnolia Close WhatsApp group:

*Just spotted Mr Pickles in my garden. Hopefully he's on his way home.*

The cat is always going AWOL. I think he's got a second home outside the close, one that feeds him Dreamies and Whiskas instead of the organic dried food Ryan and Dan have delivered once a month.

I turn in time to stop Oscar before he pours the entire contents of the cereal box into his bowl.

'Mummy,' he admonishes me as I take the box from his hands. 'I can do it.'

'I know you can, buddy.' I reply. 'I'm just helping.'

'I don't need help,' he says, tipping the milk too fast so it spills out of the bowl and onto the dark quartz worktops. He definitely needs help, but I let him do it. I can clean up later.

He carries the bowl to the table and flicks on the TV to an episode of *Paw Patrol*. I stay in the kitchen area, drinking my smoothie and taking a moment to be grateful. Even with a headache pulsing behind my eyes, I never want to forget how far I've come from the girl at sixteen who left school with little more than a sharp tongue and a handful of bad grades. I never want to take this for granted.

I tap out a WhatsApp note to myself – a reminder of the content I can use for my reel.

*There's nothing that can't be fixed.*

Nate grew up with this kind of comfort, but I didn't. He has no idea what it's like for your parents to have to choose between heating or food, but I do. I remember the nights I went hungry and the ones I wore my winter coat to bed. It's why I'm grateful every day for this life, and for Nate and Oscar.

The kitchen is my favourite part of the house. Dark-blue walls, soft-grey cabinets, brushed-brass fixtures, a statement island that looks straight out of an interiors magazine. It's open-plan with the units one side and a spacious dining area the other. The room stretches the entire width of the back of the house, opening out onto a patio and the rattan corner sofa that gets the sun all day in the summer.

'Georgie Bell, you need coffee,' I say to myself, looking up and catching Nate grinning from the doorway.

'You know talking to yourself is a sign of insanity, right?' He strides into the kitchen in his usual working-from-home outfit of grey jeans and a navy cashmere jumper, looking both casual and put-together. And good too. His dark-blond hair is still thick despite the years, damp from the shower and styled away from his face. His strong jawline has only grown sharper with age too. The lines at the corners of his eyes make him look distinguished rather than tired. He barely works out, save for a few weights in the spare room once a week and the occasional round of golf, and yet he still has the body of the thirty-year-old man I married. Some might say it's unfair considering the effort I put into keeping myself looking this good, but I prefer to think of myself as lucky to have a husband who is still so hot.

Nate moves to Oscar first, ruffling his hair and kissing the top of his head. I watch them – father and son – and send another thank you into the universe for my family.

'What does insanity mean?' Oscar asks as my Nespresso machine hums.

Nate huffs a laugh before he replies. 'It means it must have been a fun night if Mummy is drinking coffee before nine a.m.'

He crosses the room to me, looking for a moment like he might loop an arm around my waist and kiss my neck like he used to in the mornings. When did it stop? I see him start to swerve away from me and quickly shake my head, pretending I thought he was coming towards me. 'I need a shower,' I say with a smile.

'That, Mrs Bell, is definitely true.' Nate smirks, reaching for my coffee and taking a sip before pulling a face. 'God, Georgie, how do you drink this black?'

I roll my eyes, taking back my mug. 'Because I'm a superior human.' And because milk has extra calories. I keep that last thought to myself. Nate doesn't need to know all the small things I do that add up to me looking this way.

His eyes crinkle with amusement. It's a smile that still makes my stomach flip and makes me wish he had touched me a moment ago. 'Debatable,' he says, reaching for a bowl and heaping in a helping of granola. 'What on earth do you still have to talk about with Beth and Tasha? You see them every day.'

There's something about the comment that makes me hesitate. I search Nate's face. He's not accusing or irritated. Just... something.

I shake it off, force a smile and sip my coffee. Nate is just being curious, that's all. He likes to know what everyone is doing. 'It's the PTA quiz night next week,' I reply lightly. 'Lots to organise.'

He makes a pained face. 'And I'm going to that?'

I pretend I don't see through his question to the one he's really asking – do I have to go? – and give a breezy, 'Yes. Rosie is babysitting,' I add, grateful for the teens who live on Magnolia Close. Bill and Jean next door have two daughters. Rosie is sixteen now and always happy to babysit for some extra money. Not that Nate and I go out as much as I'd like.

There's a whoop of joy from Oscar. 'I love Rosie. She reads the best bedtime stories.'

I smile, pretending his comment doesn't sting a little. Story-telling skills aside, I know I'm his world.

I turn back to Nate. 'You're on the Magnolia Close table with Alistair, Marc, Dan and Ryan, Bill and Jean, and Susie.'

The table plan makes me think of Keira, and my thoughts drag back to last night and the strange sense that our jokey fantasy about Jonny was something more. I shiver before pushing the thought aside and focusing on Nate. 'They need your encyclopaedic knowledge of capital cities and cocktail ingredients.'

'Can't wait,' he says, drawing in a long breath like he's steeling himself for it.

'It'll be fun,' I say. 'My events always are.'

I glance at the clock on the cooker. There are still thirty minutes before we need to leave for school. 'Have I got time for a quick shower before you log on?'

Nate flashes me another pained face before nodding. 'If you're quick. I've got a meeting in fifteen minutes.'

'Great,' I reply, grabbing my phone. 'Quick selfie for my

socials.' I scoot in beside Nate and snap a photo of us both smiling, knowing my followers love to see me and Nate together, even if Nate's smile drops the moment the photo is taken.

I'm halfway to the door when Nate calls my name, and I turn back.

'I'm out tonight,' he says. 'Did I tell you?' His eyes are on his coffee machine as it grinds the beans.

The whir of the grinder fills the kitchen, and I wait for it to stop before I speak. 'I don't think so.' He didn't and we both know it, but I play along.

He pulls another face. 'Sorry,' he says. 'It's a company social event at the London office. I wasn't sure I was going to go, but I feel like I should. You're not working today, are you? You can collect Oscar.'

There's a pause. It's just long enough for the niggling doubts to creep in – the thoughts about Nate and my marriage I'm trying so hard to ignore. Thoughts that make me feel like Nate is holding something back.

'Better get cracking if you want that shower,' he says with a smile that doesn't reach his eyes.

I nod and turn away, but the worry is still twisting in my gut. There was a time when we couldn't leave a room without a kiss, a touch on the arm, a whispered joke. Now it feels like I'm always holding my breath, hoping he'll look at me the way he used to, hoping he doesn't say something that we can't come back from.

I climb the stairs, telling myself whatever that moment was with Nate just now, I'll fix it later. But even as I do, I'm already wondering how many more 'laters' we've got left before they catch up with us.

# EIGHT

## GEORGIE

Twenty-nine minutes later, I'm in a clean burgundy activewear set and my hangover is lingering in the very back of my mind in the same way my interaction with Nate is. He's been going out in the evenings more recently. Once or twice a week. Old friends and work socials. I wouldn't mind if it didn't feel like he was avoiding me.

We used to go out together all the time. Even when Oscar was a baby, we'd still have regular date nights. Live music bars were our favourite. Sharing a bottle of wine before pulling each other onto the dance floor. Nate's hands roaming my body as we swayed to the music. Then once a week became once a month.

I jog down the stairs and call to Oscar. 'Time for school. Shoes on please.'

Oscar straps on his shoes before standing up, hands on hips, chest out, throwing himself into the superhero pose we do every morning. I copy the movements with a smile, trying to feel the energy of the pose.

'Got everything?' I ask.

'Got everything,' he repeats with a firm nod.

'You sure?' I grin and hold up his bright-red book bag.

He smacks his hand to his forehead, making me laugh as I open the front door and we step onto Magnolia Close.

The twelve houses are set like the numbers on a clock, built in grand red brick with white sash windows. But that's where the similarity ends. Each house is bespoke. Each offering something different from its neighbours. Ours – number six – sits at the top of the close opposite the gates, and it's the grandest of them all – three storeys and my huge open-plan kitchen, perfect for hosting. But the garden is small – a strip of lawn with two borders of shrubs and rose bushes.

Beth and Alistair are three doors down at number three. And Tasha and Marc's house – number twelve – is at the bottom of the close, nearest to the gates. It's smaller than the others, but it has the largest garden plot, which would've been perfect for the extension she so desperately wanted. And on the other side of the gates to Tasha, tucked slightly back, next door to Beth and Alistair, is number two – Jonny's house. The only house without hanging baskets or a flower bed at the front. The only house that hasn't put their bin away from the collection yesterday.

Just looking at Jonny's black front door causes a familiar pulsing anger to stir in my body. I cast around for a mantra, something positive and bright, but when it comes to Jonny, all I have is this hate.

Oscar pulls me along to where Beth and Henry are already waiting like always. I spot Tasha across the close, struggling with Lanie's pushchair at her front door while hurrying Matilda and Sofia along.

We meet by the gates, and the children move together like a pack of wolf cubs, Oscar leading with Matilda at his side, heads bent close. Henry trails behind, his red hair neatly combed, his uniform straight in a way Oscar's never seems to look. He's holding out a conker in his hand, showing it to little Sofia. Her eyes widen in delight, and she nearly trips on her book bag in her excitement.

I fall into step beside Beth and Tasha and slide my sunglasses on before assessing my friends. Tasha, even with her flawless skin and model-like beauty, looks washed out. In her pushchair, ten-month-old Lanie is grizzling, shoving a rice cake into her mouth with sticky fingers. Beth is faring better. The grey pallor beneath her skin is the only giveaway that she's feeling last night's excesses. Her long auburn hair is neatly braided. The black skirt she made herself is paired with a pea-green jumper she knitted last month. She reminds me of Nicole Kidman in an autumn *Vogue* spread.

I'm desperate to dissect last night in the pub and Keira. Unease sweeps through my body when I think of the way she slipped so confidently into the chair beside mine. How quickly the conversation turned to murder. But the children are only a few steps ahead and at that age where they hear and repeat everything, so we make small talk instead.

'Alistair nearly missed his train again this morning,' Beth says, rolling her eyes. 'He had to run back to the house for his phone. He barely made it.'

I feel a pang of something in my gut I don't like. It's not jealousy exactly. It's just... Alistair is in London every day. So is Marc, Tasha's husband. Or he's constantly off on business trips. Nate used to commute too, but his job shifted to remote working, and now he spends all day in his study on the third floor. There's never a moment to miss him. Never a moment to be alone in my home. No stories to trade at the end of each day. He's just... always there. At least he's out tonight. I think about popping into town for a new underwear set. Maybe some candles too. Waiting for him when he comes home late.

It's only a five-minute walk to Magnolia Road Primary School. It sits on the edge of the town and has a village-school feel to it – welcoming and friendly. Its low buildings stretch out in a neat cluster, connected by glass walkways and edged with flower beds and vegetable patches the children care for in gardening club. It's ranked as one of the best schools in Essex, and only those in the small catchment area get a space. I see the desperation in the parents who pop in on a weekly basis to the estate agent's on Park Street where I work part-time. I swear some of them look ready to kill to get their hands on a property inside the catchment.

The metal school gate clangs, causing Tasha to wince as we make our way to our usual corner of the playground. Oscar charges into the melee of playing children without a backward glance, and I scan the groups of waiting parents. It's mostly mums with a few dads and grandparents thrown in. It takes me a moment to realise who I'm looking for – Keira. But there's no sign of the sleek black bob or those sharp charcoaled eyes anywhere.

'Strange,' I murmur to myself. I'm sure she said her daughter Rowan was starting today.

The bell rings, and there's a scramble to grab bags and coats and say goodbyes, and then the children disappear. Beth and I wait for Tasha by the gate as she deals with Matilda's daily wobble – the tears and the clinging to her mum's legs. I swear I catch her little sister, Sofia, rolling her eyes as she walks, perfectly composed, into the reception class. God, with Sri Lankan and Italian blood, she could be a supermodel when she grows up. All three girls are the perfect mix of both parents and jaw-droppingly beautiful.

And then it's just the three of us, with Lanie asleep in the pushchair, and finally, we can talk about last night.

I flash a mischievous smile, trying to lift the mood, but it's Tasha who speaks first.

'I'm sorry,' she says, rubbing her forehead. 'But what the hell was that last night?' She sighs, scrunching her eyes shut for a moment. 'I feel awful,' she says. 'Marc was waiting by the front door when I got home. He had to leave to catch his flight for his business trip, and I told him I'd be back by ten. He was fuming. He almost missed his flight.'

I feel a familiar pang of sadness for Tasha. She's juggling so much. I drop my hand around her shoulder and give her a hug.

'We lost track of time, and I lost track of my belongings,' Beth adds with a sigh. 'I left my scarf at the pub last night. So annoying. I only finished knitting it last week. I'll pop in later and see if it's still there.'

'Can you check if they've got one of my gloves too?' I ask, showing her the lone suede glove from the pocket of my jacket.

Beth nods before flicking a glance at the passing parents. 'Did anyone see Keira this morning?' she asks, her voice low.

I shake my head. 'I swear she said Rowan was starting today, but maybe it's next week. There was something...' I trail off, not sure how to explain the prickling thorns in the pit of my stomach this morning when I think of Keira.

'Odd about her?' Tasha finishes for me. 'Yeah. What kind of person joins a table of women and then starts talking about murder?'

'Definitely unhinged,' Beth mutters in reply. 'Let's have the next PTA meeting at your house, Georgie. I don't want to repeat last night.'

'So we had a strange encounter with someone and let our hair down a bit,' I say, trying to make light of last night, even though it feels like more to me too. 'It's not a crime.'

'Come on, Georgie,' Beth says. 'It was more than that. Planning someone's murder *is* a crime,' she adds so quietly I almost don't catch it.

'We hardly planned it,' I scoff.

Beth raises her brows at me. 'We talked about how we would kill someone and when we would do it.'

'We didn't mean it,' Tasha protests.

'I know,' Beth replies. 'But I don't know if the law would see it that way. Conspiracy to commit murder constitutes a crime under the Criminal Law Act 1977. Ten years to life in prison.'

I always forget Beth was a lawyer before having Henry. We were friends back then too, of course. Grabbing an occasional coffee or glass of wine. Sitting together at the Magnolia Close social events. Nate and I moved to Magnolia Close as soon as we were married. When our gated community had only just been built. We'd both been renting in London – him in a high-rise in Canary Wharf, and me in a studio flat in Islington. Before Nate's family moved away, he'd grown up around here and liked the idea of commuting to the office, having something grand to come home to.

We bought number six before the close had finished being built, moving in within a few days of everyone else. I think that's why the community is so strong – because so many of us started together.

Back then, I'd wave at Beth as she left for the office each morning, hair swept back, suit sharp – a different person to the Beth standing before us now. It was only when she started her maternity leave that we grew closer. Two pregnant bellies waddling into town. Then six months after Oscar was born, David and Mags at number twelve left us to move to Spain, Tasha and Marc bought their house and we became a trio. Then a foursome on the times Lily from Jonny's old house joined us with her boy Joshua. Before her betrayal anyway.

The weight of Beth's words settles over us as we turn down the private stretch of road that leads down to the gates of Magnolia Close.

'Look,' I say as we reach the gates and I tap my key fob against the control panel. I hold the gate for Tasha as she steers the pushchair through, and we walk slowly into the close, not ready to say goodbye. 'We had too much wine and we let off steam. Let's just forget about it.'

But before Beth or Tasha can reply, there's a movement

from outside number two, and my blood starts to boil before I fully register who I'm seeing.

Jonny.

Tall and broad-shouldered. His short dark hair is gelled at the front just enough to catch the light. He isn't good-looking the way Nate is, but there's something about him – an easy confidence, the kind that makes people lean in when he speaks, laugh a little louder when he makes a joke.

I hate this man. I hate how self-assured he is.

Of course, we all would've preferred another family moving in after the Gallaghers left, rather than a single man, but that didn't stop us throwing a late-spring street party to welcome him to Magnolia Close.

Even on that first meeting, he was obnoxious and pushy. Not caring that I was happily married, a mother to little Oscar. He liked what he saw and had the gall to follow me into my kitchen when I'd left the party to refill the ice bucket. Eighteen months on and I still remember the hot grasp of his hand on my arm. That tongue jerking into my mouth before I could stop him.

Who does that? Who accosts a married woman who lives on their street and tries to kiss them while their husband and child are mere feet away?

I should've told Nate then and there. Told everyone what Jonny was like. But I didn't want to cause bad feelings and animosity among the residents. So, stupidly – foolishly – I chose to believe Jonny when he said he didn't want to cause trouble.

By the end of the street party, Jonny had charmed his way into a round of golf with Nate and Marc that's turned into a regular event. I swear if I told Nate now what Jonny did that day, he wouldn't believe me.

I swallow the bitterness crawling through me. At least Beth and Tasha are with me. Jonny is always trying to get me on my own. Always finding a reason to step into my space, touch my arm, remind me of that street party. Remind me what he whispered in my ear.

We keep walking into the close, and even though I tell myself not to look his way again, I do.

Jonny leans against the gleaming black paintwork of his BMW 5 series, arms folded, watching us. His lips curl into a smile like he knows what we talked about in the pub last night with Keira. Like he's daring us to even try. And with the anger pounding in my chest, I find myself wishing last night was more than a bit of fun.

# NINE

## TASHA

A dull throb pulses at the base of my skull, in perfect rhythm with my racing heart.

I can't even—

That man.

My grip tightens around the pushchair handle. This hate is like nothing I've felt before. It spreads through my veins like a dark poison – a living thing making my fingers itch, my teeth clench. Of course, Jonny just stands there, looking smug. Looking like he doesn't give a shit about belonging. He's not one of us.

Does he even realise the damage he's done? How thanks to him, there's no way out of the day after day of me putting in and getting nothing back. I would give anything – do anything – for a little more air.

Hot tears sting my eyes. I wish I'd remembered my sunglasses. The morning sun is too bright, slicing through the trees, leaving me feeling exposed. My stomach churns – whether from last night's wine in the pub or the weight of today, I don't know. If I'm quick, I can straighten up the house before Lanie wakes, then bundle her into the car to visit my parents.

*I mustn't forget to take the prescriptions with me that I collected yesterday.*

I hope my parents are having a good day. And Lanie too. No tantrums – those bunched fists and her face so hot, that screaming fury when I have to coax her out for another errand instead of to a toddler group. Maybe we could visit the swings before school pick-up.

Like always, I wonder how much easier it would be if I had a sibling. Someone to share this burden with. Sometimes I think I had Matilda, Sofia and Lanie to fill a house with the big, noisy family I never knew growing up.

Jonny's mouth quirks into a smile, dragging my thoughts back. He's good-looking, and he knows it. Tall, with that square-jawed, old-school kind of handsomeness that makes people stop and glance again. And even though I hate myself for it, I wish I'd looked in the mirror this morning before leaving the house, or brushed my thick black hair into something other than a scraped-back ponytail. But it's all surface with Jonny. A polished shell. Because Jonny is rotten on the inside.

I will myself to move, but my feet remain rooted. It feels like talking about Jonny last night has summoned him. He isn't usually moving around this early on a weekday morning.

'Hello, ladies,' Jonny calls with a wave. Even his greeting makes anger flare. I know I'm not imagining it either because I'm sure Beth flinches beside me.

'Ignore him,' Georgie mutters, turning her back, always so much stronger than me.

And usually I would. Usually, I'd grit my teeth and shove the hate down and picture my happy place – that wide-open space, rolling fields, the sun on my face, fresh air.

But not today. Maybe it's the hangover. Maybe it's the weight of everything I'm carrying, pressing down on me. Or maybe it's last night. Our whispered plans. I don't know what makes me do it, but suddenly I'm moving, my steps quick, my breath fast.

I grip the pushchair, wheeling it forward around the curved pavement.

The words when I throw them at Jonny are sharp. 'Do you have any idea what you've done?'

Slowly, like I haven't spoken at all, Jonny raises an amused eyebrow.

'My parents are elderly,' I hiss, too angry, too tired, too hungover – too everything – to back down now. 'They're alone and struggling. All I wanted was a small single-storey extension in my garden so they could live with us, and you had to object. What does it matter to you? Why do you care?'

I hadn't realised how much I've wanted to know the answers to these questions until they're out and I'm heaving in a breath. I've asked them to myself, to Georgie and Beth, to Marc countless times. For months, the not-knowing has eaten away at me. Ever since that letter from the council rejecting our planning application.

I called the planning officer, trying to understand, begging for the application to be reconsidered. In the end, the exasperated officer let slip: 'I'm as confused as you are, Mrs Carter, but between you and me, one of your neighbours is a golfing buddy of my boss. He put in the objection personally. There's no way on earth you'll get approval for so much as a shed now. I'm sorry.'

Beth and Georgie were as outraged as I was, but Marc hadn't wanted to talk about it. Hadn't wanted to ask Jonny what the hell he was objecting for. 'What's done is done,' Marc said. 'Let's just leave it now.'

Jonny looks momentarily surprised by my outburst then shrugs. 'You've got five bedrooms, Tasha, same as the rest of us. Give your parents one of them.' He cocks his head, gaze flicking to Lanie, asleep in the pushchair, then back to me. 'It's not my fault you decided to have so many kids.'

Bastard! Does he think I haven't thought about doing that? The nights I've lain awake. All the hours I've spent churning it over. Matilda and Sofia would adjust to sharing a room. My parents could have the room with the second en suite, and Lanie would have the small room next to ours. Marc would still have his study next to the living room downstairs for when he has to work, although I swear he mostly just uses it as a place to escape.

Yes, we have five bedrooms. I'd give one to my parents in a heartbeat, but my mum struggles so much with the stairs. She needs to be in a single-storey home. And our downstairs is small. A kitchen-dining room, a living room. Marc's study. No play-room. Just our huge garden – all that wasted space. Even if we could convert Marc's downstairs study into a bedroom, we'd be living on top of each other. And Marc already complains about the noise and the mess of toys and shoes and discarded clothes. Like I don't try to keep it tidy. Most days, it's sweeping leaves in a hurricane.

He even says the house and Magnolia Close make him feel claustrophobic sometimes. What happened with Lily and Kevin didn't help. It left a bitter taste in everyone's mouths the way they acted at the end – the rudeness. The theft. But Marc didn't like how the Magnolia Close community turned on them either. How none of us said goodbye.

I wonder how Lily and Kevin are doing now. Despite everything that happened, I miss Lily being part of our friendship group. Her son, Joshua, was two years older than Matilda, Oscar and Henry, but she was there for every coffee and play-date. Always with a guiding hand as we navigated weaning and potty training, then tantrums and the first day at school. Then she and Kevin announced one Christmas they were leaving, and it all turned so very ugly.

Marc says it's as though the gates of our community are keeping him in rather than others out. Cabin fever. He was the same on the cruise around the Greek islands a few years ago. Sofia got sick, and Marc was stir-crazy. We ended up flying home from a different port a week early.

I couldn't expect my parents to cope with the chaos of our family when Marc and I barely feel as though we survive it most days. The extension was the perfect solution for everyone.

'You wouldn't have even seen the extension from your house,' I reply, voice cracking with the rage pounding through my blood. 'You didn't have to object. You didn't have to go as far as calling the planning office.'

Jonny sighs like he's already bored. 'Look, Tasha. Don't get emotional on me. If you want, send Marco over,' he says. He's the only one in Magnolia Close to ever call my husband by his full name. 'He didn't seem too cut up about the plans not going ahead when we spoke the other day, but I'm happy to explain things to him man to man.' His smile widens, and there's a delight dancing in his eyes. 'Oh, but he's not here, is he? Where is he again?'

'Brussels,' I say through gritted teeth. 'He's visiting a client.'

'Of course he is,' Jonny replies. It's exactly the kind of comment I tell Marc about, the kind he never understands.

I can already see Marc's face, his slight frown, his bemused expression. *'What's the big deal, Tash? Jonny was agreeing with you.'* Then he'd roll his eyes playfully, and we'd shove it into Marc's box of *'I guess we're just different'*.

I really hate that box. I was so sure it would shrink over time. But twenty-five years together, it feels sometimes like it's only getting bigger.

But there's something else just beneath the surface of Jonny's comment. Could he know something about my husband I don't? Fear shoots through me so fast, I don't draw my next breath. It's the same fear that keeps me awake at night, niggling at my thoughts whenever Marc gets home later than he promised. Or when he goes straight upstairs for a shower instead of kissing the girls goodnight or greeting me. It's the fear he's had enough of nappies and bath times and cold dinners I didn't have time to reheat. A fear he's had enough of me.

Tears swim in my vision. Suddenly, it feels like a fight to keep upright. I'm already at breaking point. Marc and our marriage – it's too much to think about on top of everything else.

A hand touches my arm. I jump, jerking away before realising it's Georgie. Beth appears at my other side – my two friends urging me away. But I'm not done. Jonny has to see. He has to know what this is doing to me. I can't keep spreading myself this thin.

I open my mouth, ready to say something more, but Jonny jumps in, gaze shifting to Beth.

'I hear congratulations are in order,' he says. 'Alistair told me the good news last night. Another little carrot top to join our wonderful community.' His grin widens, and his next words sound mocking and insincere. 'I'll try to keep my music down when the baby arrives.'

Georgie gasps beside me. 'You're pregnant?' she asks Beth with an expression halfway between happy and confused.

Beth's face pales, but she gives a slow nod. 'Yes. I was going to tell you last night, but then Keira...' She trails off.

'That's wonderful,' I say, feeling a rush of joy for my friend. Beth is pregnant. After all this time, her dreams have come true.

'Oops.' Jonny chuckles. 'Did I spoil the surprise? So sorry, Beth,' he says, like he's anything but.

And then he's gone, jumping into his ridiculous car and starting the engine with a loud rev. He pulls out, and a second later, his window buzzes down. 'Looking good today, Georgie. I'll see you later, yeah?' He winks.

He gives a sharp beep of his horn before speeding towards the gates. A split second later, Lanie wails, and I scoop her out of the pushchair, rubbing slow circles on her back as she buries her face in my neck. Her little body is hot and unsettled. *Please don't be coming down with something.* I make a note to check if we've got Calpol.

Georgie claps her hands – one, two, three. The moment with Jonny is over for her. She grins at Beth. 'I can't believe you're pregnant! This is wonderful news!' She throws her arms around our friend. 'How far along are you?'

Beth hesitates then lets out a breath. 'Twelve weeks. The first scan was on Monday. Everything's fine. After all that IVF, we fell pregnant naturally in the end. I still can't believe it.'

Jealousy nips at the edges of my joy for my friend. Beth gave up her job as a solicitor when Henry was born. Now he's at school, she spends her days cooking meals from scratch, making her own clothes, doing as she pleases. What I wouldn't give!

All she's wanted since I've known her is a sibling for Henry. Completing her family. Everything has finally worked out for her. I push the jealousy away. It isn't fair to feel this way, like Beth and Georgie's lives are perfect and mine is not. Beth's fertility struggles are written in the lines of her face.

I reach out, hugging Beth too, and the tears pricking my eyes now are only happy tears. She deserves this.

Georgie is the first to pull back, looking Beth up and down with a playful smile. 'No judgement here, but last night, the wine—'

Beth shakes her head. 'I wasn't drinking it. You just didn't notice my glass was getting fuller.'

'God.' Georgie laughs. 'No wonder I feel awful. Tasha and I must have polished off the best part of two bottles before Keira arrived with the third.'

Beth sighs, and the shine of her joy dulls. 'I'm sorry you had to hear it from Jonny,' she says. 'After everything we've been through to get here, I was looking for the perfect time to tell you.' Her voice wobbles, and she takes a breath. 'I guess Alistair assumed I'd have told you last night and thought it fine to tell Jonny.'

The smile drops from Beth's face before she speaks again. 'The way he said he'll try and keep his music down and how he was leering at you, Georgie... God, I hate him so much.'

I think of the knowing in his voice when he spoke about Marc. And suddenly there is no space for my joy for Beth and her longed-for second baby. All I feel is razor-sharp hate. The kind that has taken root in my body and won't ever let go.

PRESENT DAY

# TEN

## TASHA



'So you killed your neighbour because he objected to your planning permission?' There is no emotion in Detective Satô's voice. No disbelief or accusation. It's just a question, the same way she's asked every question in the weeks since Jonny's death – calm and methodical, giving nothing away.

My throat closes – an invisible fist squeezing my airway. The sob comes from nowhere, guttural and shuddering. We swore we wouldn't talk to the police. Not one word except to give our alibi. And yet here I am. 'Yes,' I whisper.

How will this end?

I feel like I'm navigating a cliff edge at night with a blindfold, one wrong step from plummeting. Any step now and hands will reach out and shove me over.

Hot tears streak down my face. My nose runs. The tissue in my hands is soaked through, disintegrating in my damp fingers. I reach for another from the box Satô nudges towards me across the table. The interview room is cold and windowless, lit by a strip light that hums above me like a warning. The walls are painted a shade of pale grey that is somehow both clinical and grubby. One wall is dominated by a two-way mirror. I try not to think about who is watching. The table is scratched laminate, its edges dented. The chairs hard plastic. I wonder if Georgie's and Beth's rooms are nicer.

'What's the time please?' I ask, pretending like it's not the second time that question has slipped from my lips since Sató took the seat opposite me in the tiny interview room and I stumbled through my confession.

The detective glances at her watch, and it strikes me how composed she is. How self-assured, not a hair out of place. Another woman who has her shit together, as Georgie would say.

Like Georgie and Beth. They trust their judgement, stand by their decisions. They don't question every thought that races through their mind. They don't shut themselves in the bathroom, sink to the floor and cry five times a day. I bet they don't throw themselves at their husbands the moment they step through the door, desperate for a break, terrified they can't make it through another hour.

'It's eleven thirty,' Sató replies.

Only eleven thirty. Panic claws through me, like a thousand flesh-eating insects crawling over my body. It feels like I've been here for hours and hours. Is Lanie awake from her nap now? Is she grumpy, wanting her milk? Are Matilda and Sofia wondering why I'm not with them? Is Matilda crying? The weight squeezing my chest is crushing.

I can't cope.

Can't breathe.

It's too much.

I close my eyes, scrambling for my happy place. Those green rolling hills. But all I see in my mind is this room.

'Tasha, look at me.'

The command in Sató's voice has my gaze snapping to her face.

I give a gulping apology and wipe my eyes.

'I need you to calm down,' she says. 'Tell me what's going through your mind. Tell me why you're so upset.'

I try. I take deep breaths, but how do I explain this? This buried-alive feeling I've lived with for so long? No air. No escape. 'Because I killed someone,' I reply, trying to give her the words she wants to hear.

'Why don't you tell me about the night of the quiz?' Sató suggests, her voice still even. If she's annoyed, she's not showing it. 'I have a list of over fifty people who have stated you were with them for the entire evening.'

I press my hands in my lap, gripping them together to stop the tremor that's taking over my body. The PTA. I don't know why I ever agreed to it. I don't even have time to keep my own life in order, let alone bake for cake sales or organise fundraising events. But no one says no to Georgie. Not even Marc.

Take a day off to run the barbecue at sports day? Sure. Collect the fireworks from the wholesaler on the one evening that week he's home early enough to tuck the girls in? No problem! He never hesitates. Never sighs or complains.

I try not to notice the way his smile comes easier for her. The way his posture softens when they talk, always a little flirty, but then isn't that just Georgie's way with everyone? Nate is the same. They really are the perfect couple. The way he comes on the school run just to spend those extra minutes with Georgie and Oscar. The way Georgie looks at him. How are they still shiny and new, and Marc and I are... tired? Worn out, it feels like most days.

'Tasha?' Sató's voice is a jab in the ribs.

'I snuck away,' I blurt out. 'Beth was in the toilet because of her morning sickness, and Georgie was being Georgie. Doing everything ten times faster and better than anyone else.' I try to keep the bitter edge from my voice, but it's there anyway. 'I was delivering the food platters to start with, but then everyone was settled and the quiz was underway, and I was on kitchen and clear-up duty.' I stop myself saying more. 'Sorry, what did you say the time was please?' The question slips out before I can stop it. I can't keep hold of what Sató is telling me.

The detective's eyes narrow a fraction. 'It seems the time is important to you, Tasha. Why is that?'

Fresh tears brim in my eyes before falling easily down my face. I can't put it off any longer. I draw out the clear plastic sandwich bag with the yellow silk top inside. The fabric is stiff in places and creased all over from being stuffed behind the washing machine. I place the bag on the table, and despite the fact I'm giving Sató all the evidence she needs to charge me for murder, I'm glad to be rid of it.

'This is what I was wearing,' I whisper. 'This is what I wore when I killed Jonny.'

Sató stares at the yellow top, the colour of spring sunshine. The colour Marc always says he loves on me. '*La mia bella*,' he said when I wore my yellow top the evening I left for the quiz night. The blood patches have dried to a muddy red.

I see the detective's mask of calm slip for a moment. See the tension lurking beneath it.

'For the recording,' Sató says, 'Mrs Carter has placed an item of yellow clothing on the table, which appears to have bloodstains on it.' Her gaze flicks back to me. 'Whose blood is that, Tasha?'

'Jonny's,' I reply.

'I'm going to pause the interview now so we can take this item of clothing into evidence. Then you're going to walk me through every minute of the night of Jonny's murder again.'

I scrunch my eyes shut, bite my lip and nod.

'It's eleven forty-five by the way,' she says as she stands, opening the door and motioning for an officer to help.

I close my eyes again. Am I losing my grip on reality? It feels like another hour has passed. How is time moving so slowly in here when the hours slip away like sand through my fingers when the girls are at school and Lanie at nursery? They'll be hungry now. They like an early lunch. Jam on toast for Matilda. Ham-and-cheese crackers for Sofia. Lanie in the high chair chewing on the toast crusts. The longing for them is visceral.

When will I see them again? Will I ever—?

I drop my head in my hands and stop trying to fight the sobs. Sató wants to rake over every minute of the quiz night.

She doesn't know that Jonny's death was just the start.

Magnolia Mums WhatsApp Group

Tuesday, 7 October, 6.00 p.m.

Tasha
*Voice note: So sorry, I'm running late. Just leaving now. Matilda started crying and that set Lanie off. God, I hope they're OK when Marc leaves in a bit. I'm just walking up the close now. Be there in— Damn, I forgot the table-cloths. Sorry. Sorry. I'm going to be ten minutes.*

Georgie
*Don't worry! I've only just got here, and Beth is running a few minutes behind too. There's still an hour before people will arrive.*

Beth
*Do you think Keira will come?*

Georgie
*She did buy a ticket.*

Tasha
*But we haven't seen her since. So weird!*

## 10 DAYS EARLIER

Magnolia Mums WhatsApp Group

Wednesday, 8 October, 7.34 a.m.

Georgie
*Well done last night, ladies! I haven't got the final numbers yet, but I think it's our most successful quiz yet. We totally pulled that off.*

Beth
*Sorry I spent so long in the toilets with my morning sickness. Did Keira show?*

Georgie
*No!*

Tasha
*I know this is an awful thing to say, but I'm glad she didn't come. I still feel like there was something really odd about that woman.*

Beth
*How did she even get Rowan a space in the year 3 class?*
*It's full.*

# ELEVEN

## BETH

The evening the police arrive in the close is like any other. The sound of Alistair's singing fills the house – a silly, made-up version of 'Row, Row, Row Your Boat' that has Henry in hysterics in the bath. I always love this time of day. When Alistair rushes home from work, kicks off his shoes, scoops Henry straight into his arms and declares it, 'Daddy bath time.' And I'm banished downstairs to relax while he spends a precious hour with Henry before reading him a story and tucking him into bed.

There's a break in the verse, and Alistair's singing becomes a shout. 'Beth – are you putting the dinner on?'

I glance down at the oven gloves in my hands and then the vegetable pot pie I made earlier. I should've known he'd want to do it after putting Henry to bed.

'I might be,' I call back.

There's a silence that makes me smile. I imagine Alistair whispering something to Henry. Sure enough, my little boy's voice carries down the stairs. 'Naughty Mummy. Daddy says you're supposed to be sitting on the sofa and he's cooking dinner.'

Alistair's voice follows after his son's. 'That's right. Mummy is growing a little brother for you and she should be resting.'

I laugh. 'Or sister,' I call back, quickly placing the pie in the oven before doing as I'm told and moving to the living room at the front of the house to sit down. I place a hand on the small bump hiding beneath my leggings. It still doesn't feel real. But I already love this tiny human more than I can put into words. The truth is I don't care if it's a boy or girl. Alistair doesn't either. We just want our family to be complete, and soon it will be.

*Unless something goes wrong. Unless Alistair finds out.*

I shut the voice down before it can take root. Nothing will go wrong. I won't let it. Six years of failing. Of my life shrinking inward, losing friends who didn't understand.

*'You have Henry. Just be grateful.'*

Of course I was grateful. Of course I love him. But I wasn't like Georgie with her 'one and done' outlook. Knowing my family wasn't complete was a sickening hurt I couldn't put into words.

The guilt of what I'm keeping from Alistair feels like a stone lodged in my oesophagus. Unmoving and uncomfortable. It's there when I draw in a deep breath. There when I swallow or eat or throw up. It's guilt for what I was doing in London when Jonny saw me. I lied, of course. Gave him a story about being lost and popping into the building to ask for directions, like anyone does that anymore. He nodded, said nothing, but I could tell he saw through the lie. It would break Alistair if he ever found out. He is the perfect husband. The perfect man. I never want to hurt him, even if I did this for him. For us.

The living room, like the rest of the house, is a patchwork of colour and textures. Carved dark-wood artwork hangs on mint-green walls. There are two velvet sofas – one blue and one orange – both have two cushions on each seat, made from fabrics that catch my eye. Chunky blankets I've knitted hang over the arms, perfect for the nights Alistair and I curl up together to watch TV. The coffee table – an upcycled trunk I found at a car boot sale – bears the faint scent of lavender from the candle I lit earlier. Homemade, of course.

After my fertility issues, it's become a little obsession to keep everything natural. All food. Soap. Shampoo bars. Even my own candles. It takes hours every day, but it's worth it to know I'm keeping toxins out of my body and away from my baby.

I can't fathom how people don't seem to care about how much plastic and chemicals they pump into their bodies or how much damage it does.

I drop onto the sofa, my foot nudging one of half a dozen woven baskets I keep filled with books, half-finished knitting projects and Henry's wooden toys tucked into the corners. I move the basket next to the others where it belongs, annoyed with myself that I left it out after using it earlier.

Boho chic, Georgie calls my house, always with a warm smile and a glow of admiration when she picks up one of the cushion covers I've made. 'You really should start a business, Beth.'

That's the difference between Georgie and me. She thinks we should always be trying to better ourselves. My life is about Alistair and Henry and Magnolia Close. I don't need to fill it with anything else.

I sink against the squishy cushions and sigh. The quiz night last night was exhausting. Rushing around. Juggling the nausea with everything I had to do between throwing up in the toilets.

Tasha looked frazzled and on the brink of tears all night, spending most of the evening in the kitchen. She probably had a fight with Marc. He's hardly the supportive type, the kind of man who sees childcare as her job.

Georgie was in her element, of course. The star of the evening in a red, sequinned cocktail dress.

*She looked like a magician's assistant, if you ask me.*

But why shouldn't she shine? I argue back, picturing my mother's tsking eyeroll and wondering what it would've been like to have a beautiful, fun mother like Georgie when I was at school. My mother had me late in life. I've always suspected I was an answer to loneliness and a lifetime of failed relationships rather than any maternal need. I still remember the whispers in the playground.

*'That's her mum? She looks like my grandma.'*

I didn't do the normal things the other children in my class did. Trips to the park and ice creams. Weekends and holidays were spent visiting the wool shop, then sitting side by side with my mother as she kept an eye on my knitting. Telling me the gossip from the office where she worked as a secretary. Names and people I didn't know or care about.

It was only as an adult looking back that I realised how odd it was that she didn't have any friends. She took on no involvement in school life – the assemblies or the PTA. To her, school and work were things to endure until we could be together again. I know she was disappointed when I left her to study law at university. She did everything she could to talk me out of it.

The sound of gurgling water fills the house, quickly followed by a squeal of delight and the thud of little feet. I smile and close my eyes, meaning to rest them for a moment. Except there's something I can't quite put my finger on – a niggling worry like I've forgotten something. It's just the exhaustion though. I don't forget things. I don't make mistakes. It's not who I am.

My mind turns to Keira. She seemed so friendly that night in the pub. But when I look back, all I can think about is the way her sharp eyes watched each of us. It's been more than a week now, and Keira hasn't appeared at the school gates, and she didn't come to the quiz night either. No texts. No follow-ups. It's like she's disappeared into thin air. Like she never existed at all.

I must doze off because the next thing I know Alistair is placing a kiss on my cheek and pulling me into his arms.

'Hey,' he whispers as I open my eyes. His face is close to mine, the scent of Henry's bubble bath lingering on his skin.

I reach a hand up, touching the soft grey beard Alistair has grown this year. His hair turned grey overnight the year Henry was born. We joke that it was the stress of the birth. I call him a silver fox. His reply is always to laugh and pat his stomach. *'More like a silver sloth.'*

I know he feels the odd one out with Nate and Marc. Nate is tall and broad – effortless charm too. Then there's Marc – Marco – with his olive skin and dark eyes. Quieter than Nate but just as handsome. Both of them play golf with Jonny a few times a month. They always invite Alistair to join them, but he doesn't play.

'Why would I want to spend my weekends hitting a ball around a field for hours and missing out on spending time with you,' he always says when I ask him if he minds. 'Besides, you know me – I'll forget which direction I hit the ball in before it's even landed.'

Maybe Alistair isn't conventionally handsome. His chin is a little weak, his stomach a little soft, but he has the kindest hazel eyes. He might be a bit forgetful sometimes, but he's warm and solid, rushing home every night from his work at the university to be with us. And best of all, he treats Henry and me like we're his entire world. I wouldn't trade that for anything.

Emotion sweeps through me, tears brimming in my eyes. 'I love you,' I say, swallowing down the rising guilt. I did this for him, I remind myself.

His smile widens into a boyish grin that reminds me so much of our beautiful boy. 'I love you too. Sorry. I didn't want to wake you, but dinner is ready.'

'I'm glad you did or I won't sleep tonight.' I yawn, drawing in the scent of the pastry and herbs. 'How was work today?'

He lights up in the way he always does when he talks about his students. 'Actually, quite good. One of my second-years, Freddie – the one who always wears those really baggy jeans – he finally cracked the problem set on marginal cost theory. He even challenged me on one of the models, and he was right.' Alistair brushes a bit of flour from his sleeve then pauses, almost sheepish. 'By the way, I saw Jonny on Monday. He asked if I could be a witness to a form he needs to sign. I suggested he come for dinner on Saturday. Is that OK? I think he was after a home-cooked meal. I could do my famous aubergine parmigiana.'

My stomach clenches, and heat flashes through me like a slap. Jonny. Signing a form will take less than a minute, but he wants to spend the evening with us. I can't help but think this is just another way he wants to leer over me. Rile me. But I nod, masking my anger with a smile because even if my hate for Jonny burns like fire, Alistair sees only the good in everyone. 'Sounds good.'

It's just as I'm pulling myself to my feet that the first flash of blue light fills the close, followed by the slam of car doors. One then another. Later, I'll remember this moment – the scent of lavender and pastry, the weight of Alistair's arms around me – as the last time everything was normal.

Magnolia Close WhatsApp Group

Wednesday, 8 October, 7.44 p.m.

Andrea (No. 7)
*Does anyone know what's happening?*

Bill (No. 5)
*I expect it's a break-in. I've still got mates on the force,
and one of them said there have been a few in the area.*

Ryan (No. 9)
*3 police cars for a burglary?*

Jean (No. 5)
*I hope everyone is OK! Keep us posted x*

Susie (No. 11)
*Hug your loved ones extra tight tonight!*

# TWELVE

## GEORGIE

I'm on the sofa with Nate, scrolling through a positive mindset account, looking for content ideas, when the Magnolia Close WhatsApp messages start landing. My eyes snap to Nate. He's lost in his phone too, neither of us paying attention to the documentary about a '90s pop band streaming on the TV. I imagine seeing us from the outside – a stranger peering through the window. Two people together but so far apart we're almost lost. Nothing like the Instagram story I posted of us cosying up together an hour ago.

Last week's attempt at romance ended with Nate returning late from his company social, tired and grumpy, asking me why I was still awake before disappearing into the bathroom. He didn't even notice the candles or the new lilac underwear set I was wearing.

Have we even spoken today? Other than perfunctory comments about dinner and our evening plans? At least he's not out tonight. *Be the one to make a change.* I say the words in my head and promise myself I'll find a way to connect with Nate. There's nothing fundamentally wrong. We're just... no longer close.

In the back of my mind, fear pricks like a dark thorn, and I wonder just for a moment if he's somehow found out about my past. I shove the thought deep, deep down. Even thinking about it feels like it could spark something, and I want that part of my life to stay buried.

Nate has swapped his day clothes for a dark-green hoodie and grey joggers. His hair is ruffled, stubble shadowing his jaw. As the second message lands, he looks up, checking if I've seen.

Then, without a word, we're on our feet, moving to the window, my phone still gripped in my hands as I wait for more messages to arrive.

'Turn off the light,' Nate says, and before I can question why, he adds, 'So we can see better.' We may not be in a good place in our marriage right now, but if there's one thing I can rely on, it's Nate's curiosity. He always has to know what's going on.

I flick off the lamp, plunging the room into darkness. The only light is the dim glow from the ornate black streetlights and the strobing flash of blue from the silent police cars. My thoughts turn instantly to Oscar. He'd love to see the police cars, but he's already asleep, and it feels wrong to wake him.

Nate and I stand at the window, shoulder to shoulder, watching the officers move up the pathway to number two – Jonny's house. Ryan's message echoes in my head like a siren. Three police cars. Six officers. All heading for Jonny's door.

This isn't a noise complaint.

This isn't a wellness check.

This isn't nothing.

A chill climbs the length of my spine and wraps itself around my ribs.

'What the hell?' Nate mutters, pulling out his phone. 'I'm messaging Jonny.' I watch his fingers fly across the screen before he taps send, and I read his message.

*Everything all right, mate?*

We wait for the blue tick or the notification that Jonny is typing, but neither come.

My gaze moves back to Magnolia Close. The usual tranquillity and peace looks ugly in the flashing blue of the silent sirens.

A minute passes. Nothing happens. No movement inside Jonny's house. No blue tick on Nate's screen.

'Do you think—?' I start to say, falling silent again as two officers step from the front door, their expressions grave. They're followed by a woman in leggings and a loose T-shirt. Hair pulled into a high ponytail. Her hand keeps moving to her neck, rubbing it as though she's in pain.

'Do you know who that woman is?' I ask Nate as one of the officers kills the blue strobe of the silent sirens, one after the other.

'It's his cleaner,' Nate replies without missing a beat.

Of course Nate knows. He misses nothing when it comes to Magnolia Close. Who's coming and going. He's not a gossip. He just... observes. Details. Movements. Patterns. It's why he's so good at his job in compliance – running the whistle-blower programme at the investment bank in the city, investigating internal misconduct, piecing together scraps of information until he's built a case strong enough to take someone down. He would've made a brilliant detective – patient, methodical, asking gentle questions that make people tell him things. But there's far more money in corporate investigations, and Nate has always been pragmatic like that.

It's how we met. Eleven years ago, I was working at the same investment bank. I'd climbed my way up from the post room then reception, answering calls, fetching coffee, and eventually landed a job as personal assistant to three high-level fund managers. One of them was Reggie Chamberlain.

One morning, just as I was stepping into the office, Nate

introduced himself. He was running an internal investigation into Reggie, looking at irregular trades and offshore accounts. Nate was calm and polite. He wanted to know everything. What time Reggie usually arrived? Who did he meet with? What he did between meetings? Where he went for lunch? Did I know anything about his nights out? Nate made it seem like I held the key to something big. And, in the end, I did. Two months later, Reggie and his junior were fired. Nate emailed to thank me. Then he asked me to dinner.

Nate made me laugh, and I made him soften, stripping back that hard shell and one-track mind. We clicked, and it was easy in a way that things rarely are. He grew up never having to think about how much things cost, thinking everyone had a ski holiday in winter and two weeks in a nice hotel by the beach in the summer.

When I told him what Christmas was like for us – second-hand board games and books from the charity shop, the cheapest frozen turkey, Mum and Dad not buying each other gifts, Nate couldn't believe it.

A week later, in the middle of July, he threw me a surprise Christmas Day. Decorations and a mountain of presents piled beneath a tree. A full turkey dinner with all the trimmings. Christmas music on repeat. It was ridiculous and perfect and the most thoughtful thing anyone had ever done for me.

We fell madly in love. The dream couple. At least, that's how it started. As soon as we were married, we bought our home in Magnolia Close. The first thing Nate did was choose his study. The room on the top floor at the front with a clear view of all the other houses. The perfect view to watch the comings and goings of our neighbours.

Nate checks his phone again. Still no reply from Jonny. 'The cleaner must've found something and called the police,' he says.

'What do you think it was?' I ask.

Before Nate can answer, another car pulls in – a grey unmarked Ford that parks beside the first police car. A navy van follows closely behind. No writing on the side.

'Whatever it is, it's not good,' Nate replies.

We watch in silence for a while, then Nate suggests a glass of wine, and I smile and hurry to the kitchen. 'Bill thinks it could be a break-in,' I say when I return with two glasses and hand one to Nate.

He nods. 'Jonny has a lot of recording equipment, although there's no way someone got it out of there without any of us seeing. More likely they've found something. Maybe Jonny was a secret drug mule?'

'Not the drug boss then?' I smile, and even though we're standing in our living room, in the dark, pondering the terrible fate of our neighbour, I take a moment to step out of myself and think how nice it is to be sharing something with Nate. I rest my hand on his arm and close the gap between us.

There's movement outside Jonny's house, and Nate shifts away from me. I tell myself it's to get a better look at the woman in a dark suit as she gathers the officers, gesturing at the other houses. A moment later, they're spreading out, walking quickly. The first officer to move makes their way to Beth and Alistair's house. Somehow, I can't imagine them standing at the window like we are.

More officers fan out, and although I track the movement of an officer beelining straight for us, I still jump when three hard knocks rattle the door. We set our wine glasses down, and I step into the hall and open the door, Nate a second behind me.

The officer is younger than I first thought, with an angry shaving rash on his neck. His uniform is stiff, his expression neutral – but there's a flicker of energy in his eyes.

'Good evening,' he says. 'My name is PC Henshaw. I'm with Essex Police. Do you mind if I ask your names please?'

'I'm Georgie Bell,' I say. 'This is my husband, Nate. Is something wrong?'

He nods, pulling a small notebook from the pocket on his vest. 'Does anyone else live at the property?'

'We have a son,' I say, frowning. 'Oscar. He's eight. Why? What's going on?'

Nate's already stepping forward. 'Is this about Jonny?' he asks.

PC Henshaw's expression shifts – something tightens in his jaw. He looks directly at Nate, steady and grave. 'I'm very sorry to inform you... your neighbour, Jonathan Wilson, was found dead earlier this evening.'

Jonny is dead.

The words tumble through my head, bouncing off the edges, trying to find a place to settle.

Dead.

There should be something – shock, horror, sadness. Anything. But my body won't move. My mind just... stills.

And then it hits me. *Relief.*

It surges through me like a wave breaking free. My legs wobble slightly with the sudden lifting of something I didn't even realise had been so heavy.

Since Jonny moved to Magnolia Close, he made his intentions crystal clear. He wanted me, and he didn't give a damn that I was married. Didn't care I hated his guts either. And underneath that leering was the knowledge that with one conversation, he could've exposed the past I've worked so hard to keep hidden. Because Jonny didn't just walk into my life eighteen months ago when he bought the house at number two. He'd already been in it a long time before...

# THIRTEEN

## GEORGIE

'He's dead?' I ask. It's not that I don't believe it – more that I want to be sure.

PC Henshaw gives a grave nod. 'I'm very sorry if this is upsetting for you, but we're now going door to door to establish a timeline for his death. Were you close to the deceased?'

I shake my head at the same time as Nate nods. 'We were friends,' my husband says. 'We played golf regularly and hung out at social events.'

There's a need rising in me to correct Nate. To backtrack and brush over. To tell PC Henshaw that it was only golf once or twice a month, and the social events four times a year. Hardly besties. Hardly worth noting down our names or any connection we had to Jonny. But I keep the words pinned inside. I have a habit of rambling when I'm nervous, but Nate hates it when I speak over him or correct him. It's one of the few things we've argued about during our marriage.

'And when did you both last see Mr Wilson?' the officer asks.

I swallow, trying to grab hold of my thoughts. *Breathe, Georgie.*

'I saw him arrive home yesterday,' I say as heat prickles my skin, burning me from the inside out. 'I was on my way out to the school. We were hosting a PTA quiz night, and I was setting up for that.' I grit my teeth, force myself not to say more.

PC Henshaw scribbles something in his notebook. 'Time?'

'Around six.'

Beside me, Nate clears his throat. 'I had a text exchange with him after that. He wished me a good night at the quiz. That was around seven. I asked him if he wanted to play golf at the weekend, but he didn't reply.'

'And this quiz,' PC Henshaw asks. 'It was yesterday evening? You were both there?' he asks.

I nod. 'Most of Magnolia Close were there too. It was a fundraising event for the local school.'

'I came back with a couple of the neighbours around nine thirty – Alistair Smith from number three and Marc Carter from number twelve. Georgie stayed to tidy up.'

'I got back about eleven with Beth Smith and Tasha Carter,' I confirm.

The officer makes another note.

'How did he die?' Nate asks.

'I'm afraid I'm not at liberty to divulge that information. However, we are treating Mr Wilson's death as suspicious. I will need to take your contact information, and you can expect a visit from the senior investigating officer in the coming days.'

My pulse pounds in my ears. This wasn't an accident. This was murder.

Who would do this? I try to think. Maybe it was a break-in and something went wrong. Maybe one of the husbands of the women Jonny slept with found out what he was up to. Or maybe someone hated Jonny as much as I did.

For an awful moment, I think I say the words aloud, but Nate is reeling off our phone numbers for the officer and neither is staring at me.

I think of my walk to the school yesterday evening. Me in my red sequinned dress and heels, carrying a box of quiz sheets and props and wishing I'd driven the short distance to the school. Seeing Jonny's car turn in as I'd reached the end of the private road. Gritting my teeth as he pulled over and climbed out.

'Wow, Georgie, you look stunning,' he said, leaning close, his breath stinking of whisky despite the fact he was driving.

The slow wink, the shiver of fear that raced down my spine. And how much I wanted to kill him in that moment.

I fight the urge to slam the door shut. To race through the house and out into the garden and the cold night air. Last night I'd wished him dead. And now he is.

# FOURTEEN

## TASHA

My heart hammers against my ribs as the detective steps away, and I shove the door closed, twisting the lock with fingers that barely feel like my own. It takes me two tries before the lock turns into place.

Why did she come to our house? Detective Sara Sató with her neat hair and her suit and her polite apology for disturbing our evening. Why did all the uniformed officers go to the other ten houses and we got the detective? I didn't like the way her eyes kept flicking back to me even when Marc was answering questions.

The horror of it all is squeezing me tight.

I turn to Marc, needing his solid strength – his support – but the hall is empty. He was just here. Sitting by my side on the sofa among the mess of puzzle pieces and Barbie dolls as we answered questions about Jonny.

Have we seen anything suspicious? No.

Do we know of any trouble Jonny was having? No.

Do we know of anyone who might want to harm him? *No*, we said in unison. But I couldn't stop thinking of Keira and how that answer to Detective Sató felt like a lie.

'Marc?' I call his name softly, desperately hoping Lanie doesn't wake. Where four-year-old Sofia finds every excuse not to go to bed and eight-year-old Matilda cries if the light isn't left on, ten-month-old Lanie is the easiest to fall asleep. But she's the easiest to wake too, and I can't be a mother right now.

There's no reply from Marc, and so I go in search of him. The hall is cluttered with little shoes, kicked off and forgotten beside the empty shoe rack. The living room is an explosion of pink plastic toys and teddies and dolls. I should've tidied it away by now. My eyes snag on a sticky stain on the coffee table. Jam? Chocolate from the biscuits they had after school? Another thing to clean. I'll add it to the list alongside filling in Matilda's permission slip for the school trip to the zoo next week and finding the box of my dad's sleeping pills I collected from the pharmacy. I swear they were in my bag the other night and now I can't find them.

All the endless jobs nagging and prodding and pushing at me, all still in my head. And yet something has shifted. I might not watch TV police dramas like Beth, but even I know what suspicious circumstances means. It means Jonny was murdered. Someone came into our perfect community and killed him. The obvious questions will be running through everyone's heads.

Why?

How?

Who?

They knot and tangle inside me too, leaving me nauseous. I need Marc.

I find him outside, pacing the length of the patio in slow, hesitant steps. When we first moved into this house, I had dreams of sitting in this garden at the end of the day, savouring a herbal tea, enjoying the view. A lawn that stretches out towards a small copse of trees. Flower beds at the edges, now completely overgrown. Ivy strangles the fence posts, and the hydrangeas I once planted with such hope have long since sprawled beyond their borders, drooping under their own weight.

I can't remember ever sitting out here. The day never seems to end.

The light from the house spills onto the patio, illuminating Marc's face. For a moment, I see the gangly, out-of-place teen with the sharp hip bones I fell in love with when I was seventeen. He's filled out. Aged well. That dark Italian hair and broad shoulders, an easy smile. Then it's like I see him properly for the first time in months and the man before me is a faded version of my husband. He's lost weight, and there are dark circles around his eyes.

I step outside to join him, the October night air pushing through the thin fabric of my jumper.

Marc is holding an unlit cigarette in one hand and a cheap plastic lighter in the other. I'm about to call his name, but the cigarette makes me pause. Marc hasn't smoked since college. And where did he get that cigarette from? What if one of the girls had found it? The questions disappear when I see the anguish in his expression. He looks... shaken.

'Are you OK?' I ask, my own need for support pushed to one side.

Marc shakes his head – a jerking movement – before continuing his pacing. His thumb scrapes over the metal of the lighter, flicking the orange flame on then off.

'Marco,' I plead. 'Talk to me. What's going on?'

'I've just been told my neighbour – my friend – has died. What do you think is going on?'

'I wouldn't call him a friend. He blocked our planning permission, remember?'

It's the wrong thing to say. I know it the second Marc's dark eyes blaze.

A muscle ticks in his jaw as he speaks. 'Is that all you think about? Our neighbour has been murdered in his home and all you can think about is an extension?'

The venom in his voice stings, and instantly my throat is aching with emotion. Tears threaten behind my eyes. 'I just…'

I don't know how to finish the sentence. Jonny was an awful person. Do I care that he's dead? No. Do I care that a week ago, Beth, Georgie and I talked about how we'd kill him, and in some twisted nightmare reality, he's now dead? Yes. It's rattled me. If anyone finds out what we said that night, will they think we had something to do with it?

I watch the grief and worry war in my husband's eyes and pray he never finds out what I said.

'Don't turn on the tears, Tasha.' He sighs, and the bitter edge to his voice reminds me of his mother and how she talks to me like I'm less than she is. Less deserving of respect or kindness.

I was so excited to meet Marc's parents that first time, three months into our relationship when he brought me home for dinner. Marc's mum, like my parents, grew up in another part of the world. I thought my understanding would connect us, but I was wrong. Marc's dad was welcoming enough, but his mum spoke over me at the table, using Italian so I wouldn't understand. But I caught the gist. I wasn't the nice Italian girl she wanted for her son. I'm still not. Eighteen years of marriage. Three beautiful grandchildren. And my Italian mother-in-law still treats me like I'm temporary.

I bite the inside of my lip, fighting back the tears and the hurt and the sudden rush of anger towards Marc that I don't want to feel. Anger for all the times he didn't stick up for me to his mum, saying he wouldn't take sides between the two women he loved but allowing his mum to be openly rude to me. Anger for all the times he's not here. In the office all week then disappearing on Saturdays to play golf. Anger for all the times it feels like he doesn't see me.

'You never liked that Jonny and I were friends,' he continues, voice rising.

I try not to think of Lanie's bedroom window above us.

'Because he was an asshole to every woman on this close,' I reply. 'If you knew—'

Marc shakes his head. 'You just didn't get his sense of humour.'

I grit my teeth. Marc is wrong, but fighting is the last thing I want to do. I draw in a long breath, releasing it slowly. 'Please, Marco. I don't want to argue. I'm sorry you're upset, but so am I, and I need you.'

Something hardens in his expression at my plea. 'And what about what I need? Have you ever stopped to think about that? It's always about you, Tash.' He throws a hand in the direction of the house. 'I come through that front door every day knowing I'm about to have all of your day's troubles heaped on me along with a crying wife?'

'I don't cry every night,' I say quietly.

He rubs at his temples, squashing the cigarette in his hand. 'You do, and I hate it. I wish I could make you happy. I wish I could make everything right, and I'm trying. But right now, I've just been told my friend is dead. Yes, my friend. I don't talk about Jonny to you because I know you hate him, but we hung out, we messaged. He was someone I trusted and liked. Someone I confided in.' Marc's voice cracks. 'But instead of offering me support, once again you twist this to being about you.'

His words sting.

'I'm sorry,' I whisper. 'I didn't know you were so close.'

'Yeah, well, there's a lot you don't know—' He stops then, pinning his lips together as though physically stopping himself from saying more.

Marc rakes a hand over his face before sighing. 'I'm going to bed. I'm sleeping on the sofa in my study. I need some space.'

He turns to me, and I see a hollowness in his eyes. He opens his mouth. Stops. Starts again. 'You have no idea how much I'm trying to fix everything. No idea what I've done for you.'

He strides into the house without a backward glance, leaving me open-mouthed, hurt cleaving at my chest as I replay our fight. Marc rarely raises his voice. He doesn't lash out. I don't recognise this version of my husband. He and Jonny were friends. Good friends. How did I not know? Or did I simply choose not to see it?

The conversation from last week with Jonny replays in my mind.

'*He's visiting a client,*' I'd said.

'*Of course he is.*'

Jonny had said it so casually, but his tone... it was like he knew something about Marc's business trip that I didn't.

The thought leaves me with an awful sick feeling that I've been focused on all the wrong problems. Like I am a sinking ship, trying to scoop the water out with my hands, keep myself afloat a little while longer, instead of trying to find the source of the leak.

No. Marc and I are solid. He was upset about Jonny, that's all. We'll talk tomorrow, and it will all be OK. But I'm not sure I believe it. Something I don't understand has shifted in my marriage tonight.

Outside, alone in the dark of the garden, I bury my head in my hands, wishing I could just disappear. Be somewhere else – someone else – just for a little while.

I need help.

I need to talk. Not about Marc. But Jonny.

My hands shake as I pull out my phone and send a message to Georgie and Beth.

*I'm freaking out. Can we meet quickly? Outside*
*mine? xx*

The replies come fast, and five minutes later, we're huddled in the shadows beside my house.

'I haven't got long,' Beth says first. 'I told Alistair I was dropping a casserole dish back to Jean.' She pulls her cream shawl tight around her shoulders, long hair braided down her back, and glances over her shoulder. Two of the police cars and Detective Satō's car have gone, leaving only one car and the blue van behind. Light streams from Jonny's windows.

'Me neither. Nate was in the shower. He doesn't know I've popped out,' Georgie adds. 'I can't believe Jonny is dead. Who would do this?'

'Some man who found out he was sleeping with his wife is my guess,' Beth whispers.

Georgie nods. 'That's what I thought too. Or a break-in gone wrong.'

'I can't believe it either,' I say, emotion cracking in my voice.

Georgie's gaze lands on me. 'I know it's awful that it happened, but I'm not going to pretend I care Jonny's dead, and you'd better not either, Tasha. This is good news for you. You can reapply for planning permission.'

Her words land with a jolt. I've been so fixated on Jonny's death, I haven't stopped to think about what it means. A whole new future opens in front of me. One I thought was as dead as Jonny is now. My parents living with us. The perfect solution to all my problems.

I swallow, focusing on Georgie's question. 'I'm not upset he's dead.' My voice dips lower. 'I hated him as much as you did. But he's dead after we joked about killing him. More than joked after that weird woman – who, by the way, still hasn't been seen since – pushed us to go into insane levels of detail.'

Beth hugs her arms around her chest. 'You know no one saw him today, right? He went into his house last night and never came out again. What if he was murdered during the quiz night like Keira suggested?'

'Then it's like Keira said – we've all got alibis,' Georgie says. In the darkness, her mouth forms a tight line. 'And no one knows what we talked about in the pub last week.'

'Keira knows,' Beth says, her voice barely a whisper.

My legs feel suddenly like they might buckle. My mind starts to race. If Keira talks to the police...

If they find out that we joked about killing Jonny on the same night he was murdered, what happens?

We'll be arrested. Questioned. The whole of Magnolia Close will turn against us. It'll be like the Gallaghers all over again. But worse. At least I'll still have Beth and Georgie's friendship. And the girls will have their friends. I couldn't bear it otherwise.

Georgie places her hand on my arm. 'It's OK,' she says, seeing the fear written on my face. 'Where is Keira anyway? Like you said, she didn't show up to the quiz night. Her daughter hasn't started at the school. We've got nothing to worry about.'

'But don't you think that's even weirder?' I ask. 'It's like she's disappeared into thin air. It makes no sense. Why would she say she was a new parent if she wasn't?'

'She didn't look like a parent, did she?' Beth says. 'Maybe she gets a kick out of joining strangers on nights out and pretending? Who knows. The important thing is, we didn't kill Jonny. We say nothing to the police. Only that we were together all of yesterday evening.'

She shoots another glance over her shoulder, and I follow her gaze to Jonny's house.

Two men in dark overalls push a gurney out the front door, its wheels bumping. My eyes are drawn to the black body bag lying strapped to the top. Jonny's body. But now it's not him I'm thinking about. It's the night in the pub with Keira, and the exact moment she joined our table. Not walking through the door from the street but moving towards us from somewhere else in the pub. As though she was lingering just out of sight. Listening to our conversation about Jonny before deciding to join us.

She's the only person who knows what we talked about that night. I squeeze my eyes shut and pray I never see her again.

# PRESENT DAY

# FIFTEEN

## GEORGIE



*'You have so much potential, Georgina. But if you carry on like this, all you'll see in your life is the inside of a police station.'*

My old head teacher, Mr Montgomery, was eagle-eyed and fierce, but fair too. He saw through my bravado and my cheeky grin, through the detentions and the half-finished assignments. I'd laughed off his warnings at sixteen. I thought school was just a place to socialise and show off. I didn't see the point of grades when life outside those school gates was waiting for me.

Then I'd left school with barely a handful of qualifications and reality hit hard.

My dad found me a job sweeping hair at a salon. *'People always need their hair cut. It's a job for life.'*

He meant well, but even then, living with my parents in a tiny flat in a run-down part of town with no prospects, I knew I was someone special. I knew I could be someone. So one day, I begged my mum for some money, bought a charity shop suit a size too small that clung to my curves, and got the train to London. I walked into an investment bank with my head high and my smile wide, and I charmed my way into an administrative role. I started at the bottom and climbed my way up, year after year. I made a name for myself as a trustworthy personal assistant.

It was a world where no one cared about your past or grades, only what you could do for them in that moment. Failure could flip to success in a heartbeat. It was long hours, fast talking and high stakes, and I loved it. I belonged.

Until I met Nate and a whole new life opened up. After the fake Christmas he threw me, we got serious fast, and as soon as we did, Nate said one of us had to leave the bank because his job investigating his co-workers meant it was a conflict of interest to date anyone in the office. He offered to move to a different firm, but after thirteen years in the company, I was tiring of the lifestyle. The late nights partying were fine when I was single – grabbing thirty minutes of sleep in a locked toilet cubicle at lunch – but I wanted to spend time with Nate. I'd reinvented myself when I'd stepped through the doors of the investment bank. I wasn't the mouthy kid with bad grades, no money and an attitude problem. I was cool and confident. Someone who could make anything possible. And I was ready to reinvent myself again and become the perfect wife for Nate. So I left and we got married in a gorgeous church in a Suffolk village, and we bought our house in Magnolia Close. A little over a year later, Oscar was born.

Over the years, I've thought about Mr Montgomery. How badly I wanted him to see he was wrong about me. Except, as the door of the interview room opens and DS Sató steps back in, it seems he may have been right after all.

I square my shoulders and inhale deeply. *I am in control. I choose my path.* I repeat the mantra in my head and take a sip of tepid water from the bottle Sató gave me on her last visit. It sloshes uncomfortably in my empty stomach.

'What time did you sneak away from the quiz night unseen

to murder Jonny Wilson?' Sató asks, no preamble or niceties. No easing me in this time. Just the accusation, laid out between us like a ticking bomb.

My eyes flick to the folder. What's inside? What's changed? What does Sató know?

I swallow, keeping my voice steady. I'm doing this for Oscar. 'It was after the quiz. We were all cleaning up. I said I was going to take the empty bottles to the nearby recycling bins, but instead, I ran back to the close. You know the rest.'

Sató studies me. 'Let me be clear. You're telling me that you left the quiz night wearing' – she checks her notebook – 'a red sequin dress and heels. Went to Magnolia Close, gained access to Mr Wilson's house, killed him and then went back to the quiz night without being seen by any of your neighbours, who were also returning home at a similar time?'

'Yes,' I reply.

My heartbeat thuds in my ears. She doesn't believe me. Of course she doesn't. It sounds ridiculous. It sounds like a lie.

'And then you went back to the school to finish tidying up with Tasha and Beth?' she asks.

I nod. 'Yes.'

'Why?' she asks.

'Excuse me?'

'Why did you kill Mr Wilson?' Sató clarifies.

I freeze. Muscles tight. Body still. I expected this question. Rehearsed it in the time I've been sitting in this room alone, but now I have to say it, the lie feels too clunky. 'Because he was a predator. He was constantly harassing me. He made me feel uncomfortable every time I left the house, and I just snapped. I couldn't take it anymore.'

Sató tilts her head slightly like she's thinking. 'Why is it, do you think, that when I speak to the men in Magnolia Close, I receive a very different picture of Jonny? In fact, your own husband describes him as a "good friend". Someone who checks in when he knows you've got a bad day ahead of you.'

'Jonny was manipulative,' I say. 'He liked playing games.'

'What kinds of games?'

I shrug. 'It's hard to explain. It was little things, like how he liked sleeping with married women. He told Nate once that he finds them more of a challenge, like women are a sport to him. And he was a different person around men.'

'But you didn't feel able to tell any of this to your husband – how Jonny treated you?' she asks.

'No,' I reply, dropping my gaze and studying my hands. The forest-green nail polish has chipped on my thumb. My next manicure appointment is on Monday. It's only two days away, but I have no idea where I'll be.

I think about all the things I've hidden from Nate. The lies I've told – the big ones and the little ones. Keeping the veneer on our beautiful life shiny and new. He can't know the truth about my past – the real person I was before my reinvention to be his wife – but I wonder now if he sensed the lies – that methodical, observant way of his. Is that why he's pulled away in our marriage?

'I'd like you to look at a photograph now,' Sató says, reaching into the file.

My heart slams against my ribs.

My eyes blur.

I know what's coming, and I can't stop it. Can't look away.

She pulls out a glossy photo, sealed inside a clear evidence sleeve, and slides it across the table. Panic swarms, white-hot and all-consuming. My hands shake as I reach for the photo. Inside the sleeve, the edges are slightly curled, showing its age, but the image is unmistakably me. A younger, wilder version, but it's me.

'Do you recognise this photo?' Sató asks.

I nod. I can't find my voice.

'When was it taken?'

'I don't know for sure,' I rasp.

'A guess?' she pushes.

I bite my lip. 'Twelve years ago. Eleven maybe.'

It was taken only a few months before I met Nate.

I search for a mantra, something to cling to like a life raft, but there's only this panic – a storm in my mind – and the sense of being far out to sea with no way home.

I'd like to say I haven't seen that photo since it was taken, but I have. I saw it the day of the street party last summer when Jonny followed me into my kitchen and smiled at me, smug and knowing, and showed me what he had. A piece of my past that had the power to ruin everything. A photo of the two of us side by side, grinning at the camera.

When I lift my gaze back to Sató's, I see it in her eyes. She knows this is my real motive. This is why I wanted Jonny Wilson dead.

9 DAYS EARLIER

Magnolia Close WhatsApp Group

Thursday, 9 October, 8.25 a.m.

Andrea (No. 7)
*The detective has just pulled up outside Jonny's house.*

Ryan (No. 9)
*Like we know anything! Waste of time.*

Cynthia (No. 1)
*Do they think it was someone he knew?*

Bill (No. 5)
*It usually is.*

Andrea (No. 7)
*They don't think it was one of us, do they?*

Susie (No. 11)

*If you ask me, it's not us they should be talking to but all those women who visited him.*

Andrea (No. 7)
*That all stopped three or four months ago though. The only visitor he had recently was his cleaner.*

# SIXTEEN

## BETH

It's the day after the police come to Magnolia Close when Keira reappears in our lives in the same whirlwind as the night in the pub. The day is cold and bright, the kind of crisp autumn morning that Georgie finds invigorating, but I'm struggling to shake off the fog of exhaustion. I find myself squinting at the sun, wishing for clouds. From the moment I step outside my front door with Henry and we move to our usual spot to wait for the others, the sense of unease takes hold. I don't look back to my house or to Jonny's.

*It's always you waiting.*

Because I have the easiest morning routine. I don't squeeze in a workout like Georgie or have three children to get ready like Tasha. And I'm more organised than the others.

Nate joins me first, kissing me lightly on the cheek. 'Congratulations on the pregnancy, Beth. How are you?' he asks.

From the corner of my eye, I spot Georgie and Oscar, hand in hand, running over to us. Georgie starts to speak before I have the chance to reply to Nate.

'God, this is so weird,' she says quietly, nodding in the direction of Jonny's house. 'Do you think it looks different, Beth? Emptier somehow?'

'I don't know,' I reply, still not looking. I'm not sure I ever will again.

Tasha is last as usual. Marc is with her today. His eyes are puffy, his hair lying flat. Neither of them look like they've slept. Nate and Marc go in for a manly hug, hard hands hitting each other's backs, making me wonder if Alistair should've taken the day off too.

The same silver Ford from last night pulls through the gates as we make our way out of the close.

'That's the detective in charge of Jonny's investigation,' Tasha whispers when the car passes.

I force myself not to look back and wish I'd kept Henry at home today. Baked cookies together, played matching pairs and built his train set over the living room. Just the two of us, shut away from the world. A murder right next door. My pulse starts to race. My head spins. Jonny is dead! What will this do to our lovely community? We took so long to heal after the way things ended with the Gallaghers. The way they left under a cloud of suspicion. And this is so much worse. I hope Jonny's death will bring us closer together, not drive another wedge.

I don't know how much of it is the pregnancy hormones or the weight of what's happened dragging at my limbs, but everything feels off-kilter as we reach the school gates. The school playground is already filled with parents and children. A group of older boys tear past us in a chaotic game of tag as we make our way to our usual corner to wait for the bell to ring. I instinctively tighten my grip on Henry's hand, fighting the urge to pull him closer. He tugs his hand away, desperate to join his friends, and reluctantly I let him go. He'll be fine, I tell myself. But the worry clings to me, a whisper in the back of my mind that I can't ignore.

We move to our usual spot at the edge of the playground,

and that's when I see her. A flash of jet-black hair. Pearly white skin. Bright-red lips.

Keira.

*You should have trusted your instincts about her.*

She's wearing shiny black leggings with a silver design that looks like marble running across the tight fabric, and a slouchy hoodie with a deep V revealing a flash of red lace underneath. I remember she said she owned a business selling activewear. She looks just as out of place at the school gates as she did the night in the pub. I swear every parent in the playground is trying and failing not to stare.

She's holding the hand of a little girl in the school's red jumper and pleated grey skirt. She has black hair that matches her mum's. Keira's lips curve as she catches me looking, and I hear her voice in my head.

'*Let them stare.*'

'Oh my God,' Tasha mutters.

Georgie spins round. 'What?' she asks just as her gaze catches on what we're both seeing and her mouth drops open.

'She's coming over,' Tasha murmurs.

Keira reaches us in seconds, all smiles, all confidence.

'Rowan got chicken pox,' she announces by way of hello, like she's been gone two minutes not disappeared off the face of the earth for a week. 'Came down with it the morning after the pub. First day of school – can you believe it?' Her eyes flick to Nate. 'Hi, I'm Keira. We're new, aren't we, Rowan?'

The little girl nods, looking nervously around at the other children. I feel a pang of sympathy for her. She doesn't look as though she has her mum's confidence, but I'm sure she'll be fine when she's settled into the class.

'Sorry,' Georgie says, pasting on a bright smile. 'This is Nate. My husband.'

Keira's lips twitch, her head tilting ever so slightly. 'Are you now?'

There's something about the way she says it. Something suggestive that makes the smile freeze on Georgie's face. But for some reason it makes Nate laugh. 'For my sins. Which part of Ireland are you from?'

'I was born in Kilkenny, near Cork,' she replies, 'but we've lived in England since I was thirteen.'

Marc steps forward then, his hand held out. 'And I'm Marc, Tasha's husband.'

She smiles. 'Nice to meet you.'

Then the shock of her appearance must wear thin because I register what she's said. Rowan had chicken pox. Could Keira have it now? I step back, pressing a hand to my stomach. Not wanting to catch something that could harm my baby. Keira's eyes track the movement, her brows arching.

'I'm pregnant,' I say, my voice sharper than I intend.

'I know, and don't worry, I had it as a kid.'

'What do you mean, you know?'

'It was obvious,' she replies. You weren't drinking at the pub, and you kept turning a funny shade of green and running off to the bathroom. It wasn't hard to figure out. What are you, four months?'

'Three,' I correct, wrapping my coat tight around myself as my pulse starts to race. There's something about Keira that puts me on edge.

'Sure it's not twins? You're big for three months.' Keira winks then laughs at the confusion on my face. 'I was a midwife before I had Rowan and started my own business. I'm not some random woman who goes around telling women they look more pregnant than they actually are.'

A midwife. I guess that's how she saw what Georgie and Tasha have missed in the last few months. Although I can't blame them. Georgie does everything at two hundred miles an hour. Tasha is so consumed by her parents and the girls that she barely remembers to brush her hair. It doesn't matter anyway. They know now, and they're happy for me.

'Anyway,' Keira continues, stretching her arms above her head like she's just rolled out of bed, 'I'm so sorry I missed the quiz night. I totally forgot until I was getting into bed. My brain's been nothing but calamine lotion and CBeebies for the last week.' She laughs, but the moment she takes in our expressions, her smile falters. 'Is everything OK? You all look like you've seen a ghost.'

It's Nate who answers. 'One of our neighbours died this week. We found out last night. It's hit us all hard.'

Keira's eyes widen. 'Oh.'

Georgie launches in then, explaining about the police and the investigation and just how awful it is. She's speaking fast, barely drawing breath, but I notice she doesn't say Jonny's name.

'That's awful,' Keira says, her gaze moving to each of us in turn.

A shout rings out across the playground, drawing our attention. Another dad waves to Nate, and he and Marc step away to say hello. As they move, I feel the weight of Keira's gaze settle on us, her expression unreadable, but the question in her eyes sends a ripple of unease through me.

'Your neighbour who died... it was Jonny, wasn't it?' Keira says, eyebrows raised again.

Georgie nods.

'That's scary.' Then her expression shifts. 'I assume you haven't told anyone about our little chat at the pub?'

Keira holds my gaze like she's trying to read something in me.

'Why would we?' I ask as a finger of cold traces down my spine. 'It was only a joke.'

She opens her mouth to reply, but then Mrs Gardner, the

head teacher, is striding towards us, calling out to Keira and Rowan, hand waving, smile wide.

Just before Keira turns to greet her, she steps closer, eyes darting between the three of us before landing on Georgie. 'Joke or not, can you imagine if anyone found out?' she says before whirling round, shaking Mrs Gardner's hand and introducing Rowan.

They move through the crowds of parents and children, and I stare after her, my pulse thudding in my ears.

'What the hell?' Tasha whispers. 'Did that feel like a threat to anyone else?'

'What do you mean?' Georgie asks.

'The way she said, "Can you imagine if anyone found out?"'

'I don't think she meant it like that,' Georgie says, but there's something in her voice, some tiny fracture of doubt, that tells me she isn't sure.

I shake my head. All I can think about is that moment when Nate told her about Jonny's death. She didn't even flinch. It was like she already knew.

Beside me, Tasha wipes a tear from her cheek, and I wrap an arm around her.

'Sorry,' she says. 'It's just... on top of everything else...'

'I know. It'll be easier when they've caught whoever did this. Like we said last night, it had to be an angry husband or someone else Jonny upset.' I try to sound reassuring for Tasha, but the truth is, Keira's appearance now, after Jonny's death, has rattled me too. It's awful, and yet, like Georgie said last night, I'm not upset he's dead either.

When I changed everything about myself, praying it made the difference to my fertility and Alistair's low sperm count, there was still one thing I couldn't change – the stress I felt every time Jonny played his music loud or revved his engine in the middle of the night. Every time he looked at me with that mocking smirk Alistair never seemed to notice. Jonny was a creep. I felt certain the stress of living next door to him was a factor in my continued failure to fall pregnant. And even though my dreams have finally come true, the hate for him never softened.

I feel no sadness. Only relief. With his death, my secret has died too. Jonny was the only one who knew I'd visited the fertility clinic in London earlier this year. Alistair and I had agreed we'd keep trying, but only naturally. Our savings were gone, and more fertility treatment meant getting into debt. I knew he was trying to protect me too. He saw how the failure was tearing me apart.

'*Let's take a break and relax,*' he said one night, brushing away my tears of another negative pregnancy test. '*If it happens, it happens. If it doesn't, Beth, everything is still perfect.*'

Except it wasn't perfect. And even though I agreed with Alistair that night, I couldn't give up. I knew how much he longed for a second child, just as I did. The need to give that to him became all-consuming. So I did what I always do. I researched. I found a way. I hated lying to Alistair, but seeing his face when I showed him that positive pregnancy test after six years of negatives made it worth it.

And yet I can't escape the feeling that, with Keira's return, something is coming for me.

## SEVENTEEN

### TASHA

There's another officer with DS Sató waiting on our doorstep when we return from the school drop-off. I fight the urge to spin on my heels and walk away. I fight the panic squeezing me tight. I want to forget this day is happening. Forget Keira's strange comment.

*'Can you imagine if anyone found out?'*

There's something about her that scares me. It isn't just that she knows what we talked about. It's something more. But I can't explain what.

*Wish for the devil and he shall appear.*

My hands tighten on the pushchair. There's no time to dwell on Keira. No time to talk to this detective again either. I need to pick up the new prescription for my dad's sleeping pills on the way across town. I still can't believe I lost them. I should get my parents some fruit from the market stall too. They'd like that. And I still haven't called the plumber about the leak under their kitchen sink. I meant to do it yesterday, but then Matilda needed help with her reading homework, and Lanie was crying, and I just... forgot. Already, I feel the six precious hours of the school day slipping away. No matter how hard I try, no matter what I do, there is never enough time. Never enough of me.

If I could just leave right now—

Sató turns on the doorstep and our eyes meet. She nods a greeting and, no matter how much I want to escape, I force my feet forward. I find myself searching her face for any sign that she has her own growing list of things she needs to do – her own burdens – but all I see is an alertness.

Marc is a step ahead and reaches them first, pulling out his keys to open the front door, smiling a greeting. I wonder what Sató sees as she looks at us. Marc looks dreadful. Like a man who hasn't slept. His black hair is limp, his dark stubble two days old, his clothes rumpled, but it's the expression on his face as he greets the detectives that stops me dead. I've known Marc for over half my life. I know every inch of his face – every expression. And the one drawing on his features right now is guilt.

But what does my husband have to feel guilty about?

'Mr and Mrs Carter,' Sató says with a smile that borders the line between friendly and professional, 'this is my colleague DC McLachlan.' She gestures to a woman younger than Sató and wearing a white shirt with a navy V-neck jumper that's a size too big, like she's borrowed it from someone else, but her smile is kind, her eyes warm, and I find myself wishing it was just this younger detective on my doorstep. 'Do you have a few minutes to answer a couple of questions please?' Sató asks.

'Of course,' Marc says. 'Come in.'

'I'm due at my parents' shortly,' I say. 'Will this take long?' I glance from Sató to Marc, expecting him to mention that he needs to get to work, but he remains silent. He won't meet my eye. He hasn't said a word to me since last night. The first I knew of him coming on the school run was when he stepped out of the door ahead of me this morning, holding Sofia's hand.

'This won't take long,' Sató replies, and I turn to unclip Lanie from the pushchair just to break eye contact. I don't like the way the detective is watching me.

Marc leads Sató through to the living room. The girls were playing 'The Floor is Lava' before school, and the evidence of their game is everywhere – cushions scattered across the floor, the sofas pushed at odd angles from being climbed and jumped on, last night's dolls game now scattered into the corners.

I place Lanie in a ring of cushions with one of Sofia's Barbies her sister doesn't let her play with. She squeals with delight and starts a string of babbling before shoving the doll in her mouth. I must remember to wipe it clean and dry the hair before the school pick-up. Another thing added to the list. But worth it for the joy it brings my youngest daughter.

Sató declines my offer of a drink, and she and DC McLachlan perch on the edge of the sofa as Marc and I settle on the one opposite. Sató pulls her notebook from the inside pocket of her blazer. 'We now have a time of death for Mr Wilson,' she says. 'We believe he was killed by someone he knew, and we're starting our enquiries with establishing where all the residents of Magnolia Close were at the time of his murder.'

'You can't think it was one of us,' Marc says, scrubbing a hand over his face.

'It's just a formality at this stage,' Sató continues. 'But I do need to ask you both where you were between eight p.m. and eleven p.m. on Tuesday evening – two nights ago.'

A silent scream lodges in my throat. I clench my jaw, fighting to keep the fear from playing on my face. The murder window. The same murder window Keira suggested that night in the pub. *You could murder Jonny next week, during the PTA quiz night. One of you could slip out and kill Jonny. Then all three of you swear you were with each other all night.*

Then I think of Beth last night. *'We say nothing to the police. Only that we were together all of yesterday evening.'*

'I was at the Magnolia Primary School PTA quiz,' I reply, almost tripping over the words in my hurry to get them out. 'Georgie, Beth and I were running the event. All three of us were together the entire evening from six thirty until around eleven. The quiz ended around nine, but we stayed to clear up.' The words feel wooden – too practised – but there's nothing I can do about it now.

'And you, Mr Carter?' Sató asks, looking at Marc.

'Alistair and I got back to the close around nine thirty,' Marc continues. 'We had babysitters to sort out. The local teens do it. We used Florence from next door – number eleven. We didn't see anything out of the ordinary. Believe me, anything happens in Magnolia Close and we notice. We're a close-knit community.'

'So I understand,' Sató replies with a meaning to her comment that makes me nervous. She believes someone close to Jonny killed him.

She scans her notes before looking back at me. 'That's Georgie and Nate Bell from number six, and Beth and Alistair Smith from number three?'

We both nod.

Sató makes another note, and we sit in silence. I swallow, my mouth dry. I remember the tea I made myself at breakfast, sitting cold and untouched on the kitchen counter. When was the last time I drank anything? I want to get a glass of water, but I force myself to stay sitting.

'Thank you for confirming that for us,' she says, and I think they're going to leave, but then the other detective, DC McLachlan, leans forward. Eager and ready. And I have to bite back another scream and the need to escape.

'Mrs Carter—'

'Call me Tasha,' I say, the words automatic. I always thought I'd grow into being called Mrs Carter, but, at forty-two, I'm still waiting.

McLachlan nods. 'Tasha, one of your neighbours mentioned that you had an issue with Mr Wilson.' Her tone is casual like she's making conversation.

I'm back underground – buried in the earth. Can't breathe. I lick my lips and make a show of rolling my eyes, adding an amused smile, a head shake that says it was nothing. 'Really? Who told you that?'

No reply.

Marc breaks the silence. 'We had a small disagreement with Jonny in the summer,' he explains, like Jonny didn't ruin our lives.

I think of Georgie's comment last night. Now Jonny is dead, we can reapply for planning permission. I wait for the relief, but all I feel is the weight of my burdens. Georgie and Beth both hated Jonny too, but I had the most to gain from his death. And considering this is DS Sató's second visit in less than twenty-four hours, I think she knows it too.

'I guess someone could've meant that,' Marc continues.

'I've been told Mr Wilson blocked planning permission for an extension for your elderly parents, and that you were very upset about it,' McLachlan says.

There's a ringing in my ears. A deafening clang. I scoop Lanie into my lap and let Marc explain the plans for the extension and my parents and the care they need from me, still making it sound like it wasn't a big deal. I fight back the lump stuck in my throat and watch Sató's pen move across the page of her notebook before looking back at me.

'You're very close to Beth Smith and Georgie Bell. Is that right?' Sató asks, taking control of the questions once more.

I nod. 'We have children the same age.' I lick my lips again.

God, I'm so thirsty. 'Is this going to be much longer? It's just that my parents are expecting me.'

'I'm sorry to be holding you up,' Sató replies. 'We're almost done.' Sató looks to McLachlan, and something silent passes between them.

The younger detective sits forward again, hands clasped in front of her. Lanie babbles, reaching a hand out, making McLachlan smile. 'In homes like this, we'd expect to see doorbell cameras or CCTV. But I haven't noticed any in Magnolia Close.'

'It's against the bylaws,' Marc replies. 'Because the houses all face each other, a doorbell camera would capture everyone's comings and goings. It was considered an invasion of privacy. With the gates, it never felt like we needed to worry about extra security. We're a community. We take in each other's deliveries and look out for each other.'

Sató nods before closing her notebook, and finally the two detectives stand. It's an effort not to sag with relief.

'Thank you for your time this morning,' Sató says. 'I'll be back if I have any further questions, but if you remember anything unusual about Tuesday evening, or anything pertinent to the investigation, here's my card.'

She steps forward and I stand, shifting Lanie onto my hip and taking the card with my spare hand before showing the detectives out, Marc following behind. I close the door, and we wait in silence until they are down the path and on the pavement. Out of earshot.

I try to get a hold of myself, like scooping up the grains of rice from a bag that's spilled, but I can't remember what I needed to do today.

Prescriptions and plumbers and...

In my arms, Lanie tugs at my hair, trying to suck the ends. I look up to find Marc is still standing in the hall. I don't know what to say, but Marc does. He steps forward, slipping his hand into mine.

'I'm sorry, Tesoro,' he says. 'I shouldn't have gotten mad last night.'

Another wave of relief floods my body. I didn't realise how much I needed to hear him say that.

'I'm sorry too.' I squeeze his hand before I step into the kitchen and place Lanie in her high chair, handing her a breadstick.

'You have nothing to apologise for,' he says, voice hoarse. 'I was upset about Jonny, and I lashed out.' He pulls me into his arms and holds me for a long time. Lanie shouts, hands up to be lifted from the high chair and join in our embrace.

A part of me – the part thinking about everything I have to do – wants to kiss Marc's cheek and carry on with my day. I'm already running late, and there is so much to do. But our neighbour is dead, and Marc's reaction last night was so unlike him.

'What aren't you telling me?' I ask, pulling back and searching his face. 'What did you mean last night when you said I have no idea what you've done for me.'

Marc freezes. I feel the muscles in his back tense beneath my hands.

Oh God.

I want to take back the words. I want Marc to tell me everything is fine. But, instead, he's stepping out of my arms. His dark eyes are glassy and wide, and the anguish is back on his face.

Lanie shouts again, and I lift her from the high chair, kiss the top of her head, hold her close as I carry her through to the living room then place her in the playpen. She grumbles for a moment, but then I switch on the TV and she's lost to *Peppa Pig*.

Only when she's settled do I turn back to Marc. He's running a hand through his hair, and when he looks at me, a strangled noise escapes his throat.

'I'm sorry,' he says, and even though he doesn't say it, I know it's not another apology for last night but for whatever he's about to tell me. Fear slams into me. I glance at Lanie, making sure she's happy with the TV, then nod to the kitchen.

He pulls me to the table, not letting go of my hand as we sit down.

'I've made a terrible mistake,' he says, his voice breaking.

# EIGHTEEN

## TASHA

My heart pounds in my chest as Marc's hand squeezes mine. For a horrible second, I think he's going to tell me he's having an affair. He's going to tell me he's leaving. My throat starts to close, but I force myself to speak.

'What do you mean?' I ask, barely recognising my own voice.

'I wasn't in Brussels last week,' he says.

I shake my head, not understanding. 'But the client—'

The words spin in my head. Not landing. But already I see another truth – my husband was lying to me but not to his friend because Jonny knew.

'There is no client,' Marc says. 'There's no job. I... was made redundant.' The devastation contorts his features, making him look smaller somehow.

'Oh, Marc,' I breathe. 'I'm so sorry.' A shaky relief starts to weave through me. He's lost his job. It's awful for him, but he'll get another. He'll—

He squeezes my hand gratefully, and the movement causes my thoughts to catch on his words. *I've made a terrible mistake.*

My gaze fixes on him, trying to read every flicker of

emotion in the face I have loved for twenty-five years. The man I thought I knew as well as myself. 'They flew you out to Brussels just to let you go?' I ask, knowing even as my thoughts spiral that my question is dumb. He wasn't in Brussels.

There's a long pause. Then, slowly, he shakes his head. 'I was made redundant in July.'

'July?' I repeat. 'Three months ago?'

'I couldn't tell you,' Marc replies in a strangled voice. 'Not until I had something else lined up and a plan. I didn't want you to worry.'

My stomach twists. Three months of getting up early, running around with the girls, juggling Lanie and school drop-offs and playdates and dinner. Three months of rushing to after-school clubs and swimming lessons, cooking dinners, caring for my parents, driving back and forth, and back and forth. All while he pretended. All while he kissed me goodbye and came home talking about a job he didn't have.

'But you've been going to work. I've been ironing your shirts.' My voice rises, like the shirts are the important thing here and not the lies beneath them.

His hand is suddenly too hot, squeezing too tight. I yank mine away, hugging my arms to my body. Sitting back, trying to gain some distance. Three months of lies on top of lies.

'Where have you been going?' The question flies out. Suddenly, all I can think about are those shirts I ironed, and all the times Marc stepped through the door, tired and strung out, and I felt terrible for asking him to help me with the girls because I was tired too. All those times he made me feel bad. All those times he was back late when the girls were already in bed.

'I... I'm sorry,' he says, tears pooling in his eyes. 'I didn't mean for the lie to get so big, Tash. You have to believe that. I only meant to pretend for a couple of days while I got my head around the redundancy and came up with a plan. And then it just spiralled.'

'Where?' I don't recognise the ice in my voice.

He drops his head and shrugs. 'Lots of places. I went to the library a lot. And to cafés. I was still working,' he says quickly. 'I was trying to find a solution.'

'The library? Cafés. And what about when you were back late? Where then?'

'A pub in town,' he admits.

I close my eyes, unable to look at him. 'So all those nights when you knew I was struggling with getting the girls to bed, you were sitting in a pub?'

'I... I didn't want you to get suspicious. And then I really was going on business trips. I found—'

I stand suddenly. I can't be here. I can't listen to this. The chair scrapes against the tiled floor. 'I can't do this right now. I need to go to my parents'.'

Marc reaches out, grabbing my arm. 'Tasha, please. Just wait.'

'Last week, when I got back from the pub late,' I say, snatching back my arm. 'You were so angry. So worried you'd miss your flight. But you didn't even have a flight to catch, did you? You made me feel terrible.'

'I know. I'm so sorry. The lie just kept growing, and I didn't know how to unpick it all. I was just... I didn't know how to tell you, and I was just so desperate to fix it. I know I don't deserve this, but please hear me out.' He looks up at me, eyes pleading. For a moment, I think of storming out anyway, but there's a rawness in Marc's gaze that makes me sink back into my chair.

'No more lies,' I whisper.

He gives a fierce shake of his head. 'I won't lie, I swear.'

Marc sits forward, his energy changing. It's not guilt I see in his expression now; it's hope.

'There's a vineyard,' he says. 'In Devon. It's small, but

there's a house for us and a single-storey annexe for your parents. I could run the business – make wine like we always talked about, Tasha. A real family-run vineyard. There's a school in the next village with a good reputation.'

I shake my head. I can't keep up. 'What are you talking about? What vineyard? The girls have a school here.'

'It's for sale,' he pushes on, sounding excited now. 'The girls could grow up outdoors, in the fields and fresh air. We'd have space. Peace. Isn't that what we always dreamed of?'

'What you always dreamed of,' I correct, my anger pushing through. How can he be talking about a vineyard now? 'It wasn't real. It was something we'd talk about like winning the lottery. It wasn't like the extension we planned. My parents living here. That's real. That's what we should be focusing on. You getting another job and applying for planning permission again now that Jonny is—'

'I've already bought it,' Marc says, voice strangled. The guilt is back on his face, but I don't miss the spark of hope just beneath it.

'What?' I cry, confusion and anger warring inside me. 'How?'

'I've already spoken with your parents, and they're happy to move—'

'What? Marc! You spoke to them without telling me first? You've made them lie to me too. Who else knew?'

'Just them.'

'And Jonny,' I correct him, as something else clicks into place. 'He knew, didn't he?'

Marc nods, his expression paling. 'Jonny lent me some money for the deposit. He saw the potential in the vineyard. He was going to become an investor. It was such a good deal, Tasha. I know I should've spoken to you first, but I knew you'd react like this, and I couldn't wait. The deal was too good to miss.'

I don't answer. Instead, I stare past him, through the kitchen window to Magnolia Close beyond. The tidy, manicured gardens. The sense of safety, of belonging. Our community. Our home. Marc has bought a new home and a new business on the other side of the country without telling me. He's forcing us to leave this behind for something we talked about as a faraway dream. It was only ever a fantasy. Never a real plan. At least that's what I'd thought.

Tears swim in Marc's eyes. 'I'm sorry, Tasha. I'm so sorry.' The apologies keep coming. Pleading and begging until I don't hear him anymore and I stand again. He doesn't reach for me this time, and when he looks up at me, his expression is sad but lighter, like he's unburdened himself, shifting the weight onto me. I don't know how to carry it.

'It's a lot to take in,' he says. 'But please, Tasha, just think about this. Think about the life we could have.'

'I have to go to Mum and Dad's,' is all I can say.

He nods, squeezing my hand again. 'Leave Lanie with me today and I'll cook dinner tonight,' he adds.

It's not the answer. Not a way forward, but it's something.

I stand, kiss Lanie goodbye and walk out of the house without a word.


All day, Marc's lies sit heavy on my chest, shoving against the plans he's made. The lies he's told. The future he's promising. It feels like there's no room for both. But whichever way I look, everything has changed.

The one thing I know for certain is that I can't tell Georgie or Beth. They're my best friends. But so was Lily Gallagher. Lily, who once hosted the summer garden party every year. Who brought brownies to every PTA meeting. Who was one of us. Part of our friendship group. Right up until the moment she said she was moving to Brighton and everything unravelled so fast. She wasn't the kind, honest woman I thought she was. By the time the moving vans pulled up to number two, no one in Magnolia Close was speaking to her or Kevin. No one said goodbye.

If I tell Georgie and Beth what Marc has done, if they realise I'm leaving, will they push me out the same way we did to Lily? We said we'd say nothing to the police. Just tell them we were all at the quiz night together. We're each other's alibis. If I'm pushed out, will they still protect me?

It's a question I don't want to know the answer to. Whatever happens, they can't find out what Marc has done and the plans he's made for us.

# NINETEEN

## GEORGIE

'Keep going, Georgie,' I gasp to myself as I push through the final climb, legs burning as I pedal faster, the rhythmic whir of the Peloton beneath me drowning out the sound of my breath coming hard and fast. The spare room is small, but the sage-green palm-print wallpaper gives it a boutique studio vibe – perfect for the reels I post about my fitness motivation. There's just enough room for the bike, a yoga mat, a set of hand weights and a head-height phone stand. And after Nate's study, it has the best view of Magnolia Close.

I stand as I pedal, forcing my legs to keep pumping as I watch the police forensic team in white plastic overalls move in and out of Jonny's house. Every time they walk out with another box – another evidence bag – I feel myself flinch. What have they found? The question nags and pokes until I close my eyes, scrambling for a mantra to quiet them.

'You can conquer every obstacle facing you,' I tell myself before pulling in a deep breath that fills my lungs. 'You are in control of your thoughts.'

I exhale slowly, my heart pounding in my ears from the intensity of the workout. Then I open my eyes just in time to see the detective leaving Tasha's house with a colleague in tow. I expect them to head straight to the Fletchers at number eleven, knocking on each door one by one, but instead, they set off in a determined stride, heading straight for my front door.

I'm suddenly nervous and not sure why. What did Tasha tell them? I push the question aside. Tasha wouldn't be so stupid as to mention the night in the pub with Keira. We agreed to say nothing to the police.

'Last sixty seconds,' my Peloton tells me, and I sit back in the saddle and dig deep for the final minute. As the bike shifts into cool-down, there's movement from the floor above, followed by the thud of feet on stairs. I climb off the bike and reach the door in time to see Nate jogging down each step, a hand on the front door before the first knock comes. I guess I wasn't the only one watching.

I don't follow Nate to the front door but slip into the hall, padding to the kitchen while I catch my breath and compose myself.

The morning sun streaks through the bifold doors, spilling light across the marble worktops. I listen to the click of the front door and Nate's greeting, followed by the low murmur of voices moving down the hall.

'Come through,' Nate says with his usual charm. 'I was just about to make a coffee. Would either of you like one?'

The detective with the dark hair and boring suit appears in the kitchen. She hesitates, and for a moment, I think she's admiring the space, but then her gaze fixes on Nate's coffee machine and a small smile tugs at her lips. 'That would be great, if you don't mind.'

Nate flashes a boyish grin as he sets to work. 'Life's too short for bad coffee, right?' he says before gesturing to me as though only just noticing I'm in the kitchen. 'This is my wife, Georgie.'

'DS Sara Sató,' the detective in the suit says before nodding to her colleague. 'This is DC Amanda McLachlan.'

The second detective has a heart-shaped face and is dressed more like a schoolteacher than a detective.

'Nice to meet you,' I say, aiming for bright and bubbly, but my welcome is drowned out by the hum of Nate's coffee machine.

Sató takes her mug from Nate, inhaling the steam appreciatively before drinking slowly. 'That's good coffee. Thank you.'

He gestures to the stools at the island, and we settle with the detectives on one side and Nate and me on the other. I rest my hand on the countertop, hoping Nate will get the message and take it. A show of unity. A team. But he doesn't.

'Thank you for taking a few minutes out of your day to talk to me,' Sató begins, reaching into her jacket for her notebook. 'I'm the SIO – the senior investigating officer – of Jonathan Wilson's murder.'

Murder. The word clangs in my mind. Last night, the PC on our doorstep called it an investigation. Today it's murder, and even though I'm not surprised, the word still sends an inky dread circling through my veins. It's so extreme. I wanted Jonny dead. I even talked about it. But someone went through with it. Who? And how was he murdered? The questions swim alongside the dread inside me.

I sip my coffee, swallowing past the tightness in my chest. *I've got this!*

'We're happy to help in any way we can,' Nate says, his tone light and friendly. 'Do you know how he died yet?' He wants to know what's going on. I'd say he's desperate for it, in fact.

Sató lowers her mug, ignoring Nate's question. 'We're currently searching Mr Wilson's house—'

'What are you looking for?' I ask, the words bursting out before I can stop them.

Both detectives look at me. So does Nate. I keep my head high, my eyes level. 'I mean... isn't that what you do in these situations?' I add quickly. 'Go through the victim's things for clues? Phones, letters, that sort of thing?' I'm rambling now.

A beat of silence stretches between us. My heart hammers. I should have kept my mouth shut, but it's hardly my strong suit. I've always been a talker. But I need to get a hold of myself. If they'd found the photo of me, they would've said so by now. This is just routine.

Sató studies me for a second too long before she replies. 'Mr Wilson appears to have been quite a private man. No social media, no active digital presence. We're looking through his belongings for contacts – friends, family – anyone who might be able to provide insight into his life and how he died. It's one of the reasons I'm keen to talk to his neighbours. I'm told this is a close-knit community, so I want to talk to anyone who can shed some light on Jonny's personal life.

'Have you found his sister?' Nate asks, and I'm grateful the conversation has moved on from my outburst.

Sató nods before she continues talking. 'Do you know if Jonny had a girlfriend?'

Nate shakes his head. 'There was someone he was interested in. He called her fiery, but that's all I know. I got the impression she might have been married.'

Sató fires off another question, asking Nate when Jonny spoke to him. I barely hear them, my mind snagging on Jonny. I hate that he knew about my past – that wild, up-for-anything time with my boss, Reggie. I hate that he had proof.

I'm not proud of some of the things I did back then. I made bad decisions in my past and mistakes in my present. I should've just admitted to knowing Jonny the first time I saw him in Magnolia Close. Instead, I panicked. He connected me to a life Nate had no idea about – could never know about. Jonny saw it straight away. My face when I welcomed him.

'Nice to meet you,' I said, shooting him a pleading look.

He played along at first, but then we had the street party and he followed me inside.

I still remember how he leaned casually against the worktop, arms folded, smile in place, like he'd been inside my house a hundred times before.

'I've just had a very interesting chat with your husband,' he said. 'Nate, isn't it?'

I busied myself with the ice and scrambled for a reply.

'He just told me how the two of you met,' Jonny continued.

I gripped the ice bucket tighter, eyes shooting to the doorway, hoping for someone to interrupt. 'Jonny—' I started to say, unsure what would come next.

Jonny pushed a hand through his hair, his smile widening. He was so goddamn relaxed, like we were talking kitchen fittings. 'I'm guessing you haven't told him we know each other.'

'No,' I said quietly, closing the freezer. 'And I'm not going to.' I shrugged, pretended it wasn't anything but ancient history.

He saw straight through the lie, pulling something out of his back pocket. 'You won't mind if I show Nate this photo then?'

I stared at the image – the moment frozen in time. A version of me I wanted to forget. One Nate could never know about. Would never forgive.

I opened my mouth, unsure whether to beg or threaten. Both felt impossible.

All the years I'd spent building this life – the bright, beautiful world of matching pyjamas on Christmas morning and laughter and fun and the host of every party. A vision of perfection for my neighbours and my followers and myself too. Proof I was someone. And then this man – this smug, swaggering man – stood in my kitchen, holding my past between two fingers like a lit match. He had the power to burn it all down.

He must've read it on my face – the horror, the helplessness – because he laughed. 'Don't worry, Georgie,' he said. 'I'm not going to tell anyone about your past. Or that we knew each other.'

I almost believed him. Almost let myself breathe again. But of course it wasn't going to be that simple.

'I'm sure we can think of a way for you to repay me for my silence,' he added, stepping closer, running a finger down the bare skin of my arm like he owned me. Then he pushed his lips onto mine.

I lurched away, disgusted and upset. 'Don't even think about it,' I spat, my voice too loud in the hush of the hallway.

His laughter had followed me out. 'By the way,' he called, 'you can keep that photo. I've got a copy.'

And when I turned, there it was. My past, in plain sight. Taunting me.

It took everything not to scream. I waited until he left, then I destroyed it before anyone could see it.

Maybe I should've fought harder that day. Threatened him. Paid him off. Told Nate first, on my terms. Spun some half-truth before Jonny could twist it into something worse. But like the detectives sitting at the counter drinking Nate's fresh ground coffee, Nate never would've let it go until he had all the answers. I couldn't let that happen.

Besides, as soon as I pretended not to know Jonny, it felt too late to admit our connection to Nate or anyone else in Magnolia Close. The more time that passed, the more impossible it became to take the lie back.

I was trapped in it. With Nate and everyone else. Something Jonny reminded me of whenever he'd caught me on my own.

So I stayed quiet. I told Beth and Tasha just enough to explain my feelings towards Jonny, but not enough to invite questions I couldn't answer.

I avoided Jonny as best I could. Bided my time. And now, finally, my secret is safe.

# TWENTY

## GEORGIE

It's the clink of a coffee cup in a saucer and Nate clearing his throat that has me blinking away the memory of Jonny and everything that came next – squashing it down, hiding it away like it could show on my face. Because Nate might know Jonny was interested in a married woman, but he doesn't know that woman was me.

'Georgie?' Nate's prompt causes a squirming in the pit of my stomach. I'm suddenly aware of the silence in the kitchen and the three sets of assessing eyes on me.

'What was the question?' I ask.

There's a pinch to Sató's brow. 'I asked if either of you remember anything odd about the night Mr Wilson was killed? A car on the street you didn't recognise? Even something that seems insignificant could be important.'

I shake my head, force myself not to think about seeing Jonny on my way to set up for the quiz. The silence in the kitchen presses in on us. I feel like the detectives are waiting for me to say more. My fingers twitch against the counter. I fight the instinct to fill the silence with energy and talk and rambling.

It's the second detective who speaks then, pushing her dark-blonde hair behind her ears. It's wispy at the top, how mine gets in the rain. If she were anyone else, if we were anywhere else, I'd recommend the serum I use to keep my hair looking sleek. DC McLachlan looks at Nate, and I catch that familiar appraisal all women give him.

'Nate,' DC McLachlan starts with a friendly smile, 'I wanted to check a few details with you. Is that OK? I believe you told PC Henshaw last night that you left with Marc Carter and Alistair Smith at the end of the quiz.'

Nate gives a small nod as he shifts on the stool beside me.

'Neither of your neighbours mentioned you when giving their version of the evening's events. And I wondered if you wouldn't mind confirming what time you left the quiz and who was with you please.'

Nate pulls a face, an exaggerated wince like Oscar when he's been caught sneaking out of his room after bedtime. 'I might have left ten minutes before the end. Sorry, I should've been honest with the PC. I didn't think it was important at the time.' He shoots me an apologetic look I haven't seen for a long time on my husband's face. One that's all for show now, I'm certain. 'I didn't want Georgie to know I'd left early. The PTA is important to her, and I didn't want to let her down, but I was exhausted and had a full day of meetings the next day.'

I keep my expression neutral, playing along. Inside, the worry tightens. He left early, and he lied about it.

Sató scribbles something in her notebook, head still lowered. Then it's McLachlan's voice cutting through the silence.

'OK, Nate. Just so we're all clear, can you tell us your exact movements between the hours of eight p.m. and eleven p.m. last night?'

'Sure,' he says, placing his hands on the counter. The gesture is open and honest, but I'm suddenly not so sure the same can be said for his words. 'I was at the PTA quiz night until nine. That's the time it was supposed to end, but the raffle draw was dragging on. Georgie was the one drawing the raffle, and I knew she wouldn't notice if I ducked out early.'

I think back to the quiz night. The evening is a blur. I was loud and energetic, buoying everyone along, keeping the night running smoothly. Tasha was managing the kitchen. Making up the cheese boards, bringing out more wine, tidying up. Beth was carrying it back and forth when she wasn't in the toilet throwing up – the smell of the cheese triggering her morning sickness. Nate's right. I didn't notice him slip away.

'I came straight home,' Nate continues. 'So that would've been by ten past nine. I paid Rosie – Bill and Jean's daughter next door at number five – she left and I went to bed.'

'Yes. I spoke to Rosie,' Sató says. 'She confirmed you were home around fifteen to twenty minutes before her parents. She also mentioned that, as she left the house, she heard you talking on the phone. She said it sounded like you were arguing with someone.'

Nate frowns. 'I don't think so,' he replies. Then he snaps his fingers like he's just remembered. 'It was probably the TV. I put it on when I got home. It was one of those reality shows Georgie likes. They're always shouting about something. Oscar must've turned the volume up too loud. That's what she must've heard.'

'I see,' Sató says.

I sip my coffee, keeping my gaze on a swirl in the marble countertop. My husband is still all charm, and yet woven into his recount of the night Jonny was murdered, there are lies. The thought burrows beneath my skin. Nate doesn't lie. His entire career is about following the rules and stopping people who break them.

Before either of the detectives can ask another question, Sató's phone rings. A sharp trilling that makes me jump. I knock my coffee cup in the saucer, and it clatters on the worktop before I can right it.

'Excuse me,' Sató says, standing and stepping into the hall to answer.

Barely a moment passes before her head pops back into the room, phone pressed to her ear, and she's motioning for DC McLachlan to join her. I strain to listen but can't hear what they're saying.

I think of those men in white overalls carrying their boxes of evidence out of Jonny's house, and my stomach churns with that slippery, dark dread. Have they found the photo in Jonny's house? The copy he said he had.

Nate's gaze is on me. I can almost hear the questions running through his mind. 'You're quiet.' His tone is probing. 'Are you OK?'

'I'm fine,' I say, ignoring the way his eyes flick over my face. It's the investigator in him. He's looking for my tells. He opens his mouth, and I can tell he's going to push again, so I get there first, voice low and fast. 'I'm not the one lying.'

He lifts his eyebrows in question, gaze flicking briefly to the door and the detectives still talking in the hall.

'Reality TV?' I say.

Nate's jaw tightens. He doesn't say a word, but I can tell he's annoyed. It's the look he gets when he shuts down, shuts himself away, won't speak to me for the rest of the day. I drop my gaze, feeling suddenly lonely. In that moment, it's impossible to ignore the truth. Our marriage might be bright and shiny on the surface. From the outside, we look polished. But inside? Inside, it's something else. Not rotten. More like... dried up. Disintegrated. Poke too hard and that shiny surface will crumble.

I try to remember the last time I felt truly close to Nate. The last time he didn't shrink away from my touch. The last time we had sex was... Christmas? Even then, it had been a drunken fumble that I could tell he hadn't really wanted.

I don't know how we've drifted so far from the people we

were at the start. The couple everyone wanted to be. But I know one thing – I will fix this.

Before either of us can say another word, DS Sató and DC McLachlan step back into the room. 'Sorry about that,' Sató says.

'No problem.' I offer a smile. 'Can I check how long this is going to take? I'm due at work soon, and I'll need to let them know if I'm going to be late. I work a few days a week at Benton's Estate Agent's on Park Street.'

'This won't take long,' Sató replies, taking her seat once more. 'Some new information has just come to light that I'd like to ask you about, and then we'll be on our way.'

They settle back into their seats, Sató with her phone still in her hand.

'I'm going to show you a photo one of the officers has just sent me,' she continues, placing her phone on the counter between us.

The fear grabs me – fierce and unrelenting. I swallow, trying to ready myself for the one thing I've been working so hard to stop. Sató taps the screen, but the image that appears isn't of me. It's the black iron gates of Magnolia Close.

She zooms in slowly, and there – nestled in the upper curve of the scrollwork – is a tiny black circle. No bigger than a coin. Almost invisible unless you knew exactly where to look.

'It appears there is a small CCTV camera here,' she says, her voice giving nothing away. 'We believe it's motion-activated. As you can see, it's well hidden inside the ornamental crest.'

I blink, heart hammering against my ribs. A camera. Not watching who is coming into Magnolia Close but watching the houses. Watching us.

How long has it been there? What has it seen?

'Do you know anything about this?' Sató asks.

I shake my head. 'No. I'm on the residents' association and there's no way we would've allowed this. Who would do this?'

'That's something we're very keen to find out,' Sató replies as she and McLachlan move to stand. 'Whoever owns this camera will likely have captured the person who murdered Mr Wilson.'

The detectives thank us for our time, hand us their cards and we show them to the door, promising to be in contact if we think of anything else.

As soon as the front door closes, I'm whirling around to Nate.

'A hidden camera,' I breathe out. 'It has to be one of the residents, doesn't it? The camera is facing inward. Watching all of us. Why would someone do that?'

Nate doesn't reply. Doesn't look at me. Just moves towards the stairs in the direction of his study.

'Can we talk?' I call after him.

He doesn't answer. Doesn't slow. Just disappears like he hasn't heard me.

I stare after him, my mind racing in a hundred directions. I want to ask him about what he told Sató just now. The TV on loud. A reality show. It sounded plausible, and Sató seemed to buy it.

Except I don't watch reality TV. So why did he say it? Why did he lie? And who was he arguing with that night?

Then my thoughts drag back to the hidden camera. Who would secretly watch Magnolia Close? I think of Nate, checking his phone at odd times of the day and night. Always with the screen faced away from me. I think about his desk by the window and that desperate need he has to know everything that's going on.

What have you been up to, Nate? What did you see?

PRESENT DAY

# TWENTY-ONE

## BETH



A young PC brings me a cup of tea before leaving me alone once more with DS Sató. The tea looks watery and unappealing, the milky-brown liquid swirling inside the flimsy white cup. Just looking at it makes my stomach churn. I press a hand to my lower back. It's stiff from sitting in the plastic chair, but I keep myself still, spine straight, hands folded in my lap. And I wait.

*I told you it wouldn't be easy.*

The voice has taken on a nagging quality. Whiny and needling. But I never thought it would be easy. Sató asked me if I knew how many people confess to a crime before they're charged. I wonder how many people confess to a *murder* they didn't commit.

DS Sató is smart. Since Jonny's body was discovered, she's dug and poked and prodded. Asked her polite questions. I've felt her sharp, constant gaze on all of us. Sensed her closing in, to the point where it felt like I could barely draw the shallowest breath. As though every hour – every minute – we were moving closer to the point where one of us in Magnolia Close would be arrested.

Sató's gaze is on me now. She's hoping I'll fill the silence, break down like I'm certain Tasha has or talk without drawing in breath like Georgie. I do neither.

*The silence is making you look guilty.*

God, how I wish I could silence that voice. Like ironing out the creases in Henry's polo shirts. They come in packs of five with a non-iron sticker. So many of the mums don't bother ironing them, even though they really do need it, despite what the sticker says. Lazy.

The detective taps her pen against her notebook. 'Your knowledge of the murder tells me one of two things,' she begins like I asked her what she's thinking. 'Either you're telling the truth and you killed Jonny, or you know who did.'

I lift my gaze, schooling my expression into something I hope looks like guilt. 'I told you. It was me. What more do you want?'

Sató leans back in her chair. 'What I want is the truth. Which isn't what I'm getting from anyone right now.' She sits forward again, hands resting on the table. 'See, here's my problem, Beth. I've been in this job for a long time, and in my experience, people who commit murder don't usually hand themselves in. So tell me again, why did you kill Jonny?'

My fingers tighten around the edge of my cardigan. I picture Henry's face. Those cheeks that flush red in the cold and the heat. The sprinkling of freckles I pretend to count every morning when he wakes, convinced another has appeared overnight. The way he drags out, 'Mummy,' in playful exasperation when I smooth down his hair. Or the way he pretends to dive when I tackle him for the ball when we play football in the garden.

'*Foul*,' he always cries, rolling on the ground like they do on

TV until we're both laughing too hard to play anymore. There's nothing I wouldn't do for Henry.

It's why I went to Jonny's house that afternoon nine months ago in January, when the sky felt like it was darkening in the middle of the afternoon and there was frost on the ground. The coldest January on record. Alistair was in London, not back for hours. Henry was off school with a fever, his small body burning up against mine despite the Calpol I'd given him. I'd barely slept for two days, dishing out medicine. Comforting him when he cried. I was exhausted, strung out. And then there was Jonny's music. I could hear the thump, thump of it. Relentless. Non-stop, rattling through every last frayed nerve.

When Henry finally fell asleep, I slipped out and went to Jonny's front door. The music seemed quieter out here. Muffled compared to what I could hear from my own house. I tried the doorbell first. No answer. Then a hard knock. Still nothing. Finally, I banged my fist on the door. When the minutes passed and I was still on that doorstep, the anger took over. Henry needed sleep and rest. We both did. We needed quiet. We didn't need our home invaded with the incessant drumbeats from whatever awful music Jonny was listening to at maximum volume.

I flew back into my house, grabbed the spare key Jonny had given Alistair the last time he went on holiday. If he wasn't going to let me in, then I'd let myself in. A moment of madness perhaps, but one I'd been driven to by exhaustion and stress and that constant thrumming drumbeat.

The music system was in the living room. The speakers pushed right up against the back wall nearest to our house. No wonder it seemed to be only us that heard it. The number of times I'd raised it at the residents' association meetings, only to be met by the baffled looks of my neighbours. Even Cynthia and Phil at number one had said they only heard the occasional noises, and it had never bothered them. Still, we'd sent a polite letter to Jonny signed by the residents' association, asking him to be more considerate with the volume. A letter he'd ignored.

The music system was a complex monster of a thing with too many buttons I didn't understand. In the end, I yanked the plug from the wall, throwing the house into a silence that felt eerie. I swear the pulse of music still pounded in my temples.

'Jonny?' I called out, suddenly hesitant. In the silence, it seemed obvious I'd massively overstepped, letting myself into my neighbour's house to turn off his music. But it was too late to undo it now.

There was no reply. I remember wondering if he'd had an accident. Wishing even back then that he was dead. I crept forward, half expecting to find him collapsed on the floor in the kitchen. A heart attack. A stroke. It happened all the time. Why not to him? But the downstairs was empty. I stood by the staircase for a moment, wondering what to do. Walk out now or search upstairs. 'Jonny?'

*He has to be here*, the voice in my head reasoned. Who leaves their music on and goes out?

It turns out Jonny did.

Because I did go upstairs that day. Checking every room as my pulse hammered in my ears as loud as his music had. The house was neater than I'd expected. Clean but bland. Grey walls. Plain furniture. Like a show home, devoid of any real personality. And a house that was most definitely empty.

Until it wasn't.

I was coming down the stairs when the front door opened and Jonny's tall frame filled the doorway and then the hall. Dark hair and darker eyes. Attractive from a distance perhaps. Until he showed his repulsive personality.

His eyes narrowed the moment he saw me. 'What the fuck are you doing?' The question came in an exhale. Annoyance or humour or maybe both. Either way, it caused a fear to ripple through me.

Only my exhaustion and anger kept me from cowering an apology. 'I was knocking on your door for ten minutes,' I said. 'Henry is unwell, and your incessant music meant he couldn't sleep.'

Jonny smirked. 'So you broke into my house? Christ, Beth. Didn't take you for the type.'

'Turn your music off before you go out and next time I won't have to.' I moved towards the door, wanting out, wanting to be home with Henry, but Jonny was still in the hallway, and in one movement he was blocking my path.

'By all means, feel free to let yourself in any time, Beth,' he said, voice dripping with an innuendo that made my skin crawl. 'Maybe I'll use my spare key and pop over to yours next time.'

My gaze snapped to his. I was already shaking my head as I asked, 'What spare key?'

Jonny smiled. 'Didn't Alistair tell you? We did a swap. You have mine, and I have yours. For emergencies, of course. And for whenever we feel like it too, it seems.'

My blood turned to ice. His tone was still friendly, but I didn't miss the undercurrent of threat. 'Don't even think about it,' I said.

'But it's OK for you?' he asked.

'When you leave your music on, yes.' I shoved past him, my breath coming too fast as the anger consumed me. Fear too. I was in this man's house. Alone. And I shouldn't have been.

'You're ruining my life, you know.' My voice was barely a whisper. 'Maybe if I wasn't so stressed with your music and your car engine revving day and night, I'd be pregnant by now.'

Jonny's laughter followed me out the front door, but then DS Satō's voice drags me back to the small, stuffy interview room. 'Beth, why did you kill Jonny?'

I look up, blinking. My heart is still hammering from the memory of standing in Jonny's house.

*You're too scared to do what needs to be done. You've come this far, and now you're stalling.*

I swallow hard, reach into my handbag and pull out the Ziploc bag. Whatever it takes, I remind myself. 'You want proof,' I say by way of reply. 'Here it is.'

Sató's gaze moves from me to the object in my hand. Inside the clear plastic, the metal of the knife glints under the harsh lights, except for the places where the blood has dried dark red and dull.

Something in Sató's face changes. Her jaw tightens. 'I assume you're showing me the murder weapon?'

'Yes. I've told you how I killed Jonny. I'm showing you the knife I used. His blood and DNA will still be on it.'

'Will yours?' The speed of her question nearly knocks me off balance.

I grit my teeth and don't reply. We had to confess. It had to be this way.

## 8 DAYS EARLIER

Magnolia Close WhatsApp Group

Friday, 10 October, 7.05 a.m.

Ryan (No. 9)
*A hidden camera! This has to be a joke. Who was it?*
*Time to own up.*

Andrea (No. 7)
*Yes, own up please. Any form of CCTV security violates*
*the bylaws of Magnolia Close.*

Bill (No. 5)
*Forget the bylaws. This violates our bloody privacy.*
*Someone's been watching us.*

Tasha (No. 12)
*Can the police trace who installed it?*

Bill (No. 5)

*They'll try but a lot of security equipment isn't registered nowadays. Could be anyone.*

Dan (No. 9)
*Whoever killed Jonny will be on that footage.*

Susie (No. 11)
*Unless the person who installed the camera also killed Jonny.*

Beth (No. 3)
*Let's wait to see what the police say today. It won't do us any good to start accusing each other.*

Ryan (No. 9)
*There's no point pretending one of us didn't put that camera up. We should be talking about who!*

Marc (No. 12)
*Does anyone know if the camera had audio?*

# TWENTY-TWO

## GEORGIE

By Friday, Jonny's murder is all anyone can talk about. The Magnolia Close WhatsApp group is humming with tension and accusations. The gossip from the school gates isn't much better. I thought being at work today would offer a distraction, but with Jonny's murder still the top story on the local radio's hourly news bulletin, it feels like there's no escape. Especially with the police statement released this afternoon suggesting they're pursuing strong leads. What does that mean? Every time I try to think about who did this, it's like a vice squeezing my chest. A murder in our community...

Now all I want is to collect Oscar and go home. Shut ourselves away for the weekend.

My eyes land on the clock for the tenth time in as many minutes – 2.57 p.m. My daily mantra circles my thoughts, and for once it feels taunting instead of reassuring.

*I have all the time I need.*

Three more minutes. That's all. I try to focus on the computer screen and the new property listing I was supposed to finish an hour ago that's barely started. I manage a line of words before my gaze is back on the clock.

2.58 p.m.

Benton's Estate Agent's is a small, dark-green shopfront on a smaller stretch of the high street, away from the main strip of restaurants and chain shops. Family-owned and with a reputation for finding buyers and selling fast, it's always busy. I usually love my three afternoons a week. It's mostly admin and house listings, helping walk-ins, but sometimes I show the homes too. The pay is terrible, but Tim Benton is kind, and the other staff are fun. I pride myself on knowing exactly what a person is looking for the moment they step through the door. Sometimes I think I know it better than they do. A forever home. A renovation project. People think houses are about status and comfort, but they're about so much more. Our homes are part of our identity. They mean so much to us. Like Magnolia Close. At least, it used to feel that way before Jonny's murder three days ago and the discovery of the secret camera. It isn't just the WhatsApp group that feels toxic now.

In just a few short days, Magnolia Close no longer feels like the inviting haven it once was. I've seen my neighbours hurrying in and out of their homes, no longer stopping to say hello and chat about the weather and plans for the weekend. Packages left on doorsteps instead of being taken in by one of us.

Not even Andrea gave me a wave from her window earlier when I left for work, and it was me who helped her from the bathroom floor last year after she slipped getting out of the shower and twisted her ankle.

The police presence has become suffocating. Their unmarked cars come and go at all hours, headlights flicking across bedroom windows at night.

3 p.m.

'Thank you,' I say to the universe as I shut down my computer. I grab my bag and call a hurried goodbye.

Outside, the cool October air makes me wish I'd replaced

the gloves I lost that night in the pub. I walk fast, taking the road that borders the park, barely registering the crunch of leaves beneath my boots. The sky is grey, but it's not wet, and I know Oscar will jump at my feet and beg for a trip to the park. It's what we usually do on Fridays, always followed by a playdate at mine with Henry and the girls. Bags, coats and shoes piled high in my hall. The house filled with noise and laughter.

Maybe I should suggest it. Do something that feels normal. But I know we'll all want to talk about Jonny's death and Keira's appearance this week and that strange comment. The way she smiled when she said it.

There's still a dread in me I can't shake when I think about Keira. The hum of something not right. We've all tried to keep our distance in the playground, but she's hard to avoid. Hard to miss with her red lips and charcoaled eyes that seem to flash trouble. She doesn't belong here. Not in our quiet little world of PTA meetings and park trips and coffee mornings. I think she knows it too. I think she likes it.

Maybe Oscar will be happy to snuggle together and watch a film this afternoon. We could make a den of blankets and pillows on the floor.

One of my heels has rubbed into a blister in my new boots as I round the corner and the school gates come into view. The playground beyond is already filled with parents standing in clusters. I see one mum looking up, catching my eye before nudging her friend. A second later, the whole group is staring. A flush rises on my neck. I shake it off, but the sensation clings like static.

'It's not Magnolia Close anymore. It's Murder Close,' I heard one of the dads say at the drop-off this morning. A loud man with a large belly and sweat stains under his arms.

My stomach knots every time I think about the murder. The thought that it could be one of us in Magnolia Close. These people I've lived with for years. People I trust. They are more than neighbours. They are friends. Can one of us really have killed Jonny? Could someone have hated him more than I did? Had more reason to kill him than I did? I search for any hint of who could have done this, but there's nothing beyond my own hate and how I was too much of a coward to do anything about it.

'This too shall pass,' I whisper quietly to myself.

The mums are no longer looking my way as I reach the gates. I'm being paranoid. It's the police discovery of the hidden camera yesterday. The announcement of strong leads. The growing sense that Sató thinks it's one of us. It's making me paranoid. Like I've done something wrong. It hasn't helped that I feel Nate watching me more carefully at home since the detectives' visit. He thinks I was acting strangely. I think he was lying about the TV being on loud. We haven't talked about it since, but every time I turn around, I find him lingering in the doorway, studying me.

I reach the school gates and pause, forcing the thoughts away with a breath. The second I step inside the playground, my gaze snags on a familiar figure. Sharp black bob. Bright-red lips. I watch her head tilt back. That familiar laugh I remember from the pub. Another step and fear clutches at my heart as I see who she's talking to. Nate.

He's standing close to her, smiling. Relaxed. His lips are quirked up, that smile he saves for the other mums that's just a little flirty, giving them his 'look what a great dad I am' routine that isn't a lie but isn't quite the truth either.

Oscar adores Nate. And he is a great dad. When he wants to be. When he decides to shine a spotlight on our son and dazzle him with attention. But sometimes it feels like neither of us exist in Nate's orbit. In those times, I double down on being the best mum I can be, keeping Oscar's attention on me like it's a magic trick – a sleight of hand to make sure he doesn't notice what's missing.

What are they talking about?

Any second now, they'll turn and see me. I have seconds to paste a friendly smile on my face and act like this woman doesn't know we planned to murder a man who is now dead. Something I don't want Nate to find out. Nate knows Jonny wasn't my favourite person, but he doesn't know why I hated him. If he discovers I went so far as to wish him dead, he'll want to know why.

I won't let that happen.

My pulse kicks up again, and without a second glance, I spin on my heels and stride away so fast, I scuff one of my new boots on the pavement. A minute later, I'm at the top of the road leading to Magnolia Close, firing a message to Nate to tell him I've been held up and I'll meet him and Oscar at home.

I can't paste on that smile. I can't pretend everything is fine.

My hands are shaking as I tap my key fob and slip through the gates, breathing a sigh of relief to see no sign of Sató's car this afternoon. And still, there's something different about the circle of homes today. Like I've stepped into a warped reality where the world looks the same but everything in it is different.

As soon as I'm in my house, I bolt up the two flights of stairs. There are only two rooms on the top floor. Nate's study and a small bathroom with a white suite with small sand-toned tiles I chose to feel like a spa. Not that anyone but Nate uses it. The top floor has always been his domain.

Both doors are closed.

It was announced on the local news headlines today that the police believe Jonny was killed by someone he knew. Considering how much time they're spending in the close, it's clear Sató believes it was one of us.

Nate said he left the quiz early. He said it was only ten minutes before the end, but he could be lying about that too. And then there's the camera. Someone spying on us all.

I reach for the handle of Nate's study. It moves, but the door doesn't open. I try again, but it's the same. What the hell? It's been a while since I came up here, but I'm certain there was never a lock on his door. When did he have it installed? And why?

There's a loud crash downstairs – the front door slamming open – and then Oscar's familiar voice: 'I'm hungry!'

Panic jerks through me. I race down the stairs and dive into our bedroom, flipping the laundry basket lid and grabbing a towel as if that had been my destination all along. But I needn't have worried. Nate's scrolling through his phone, a frown pinching his brow as he passes me on the stairs, muttering something about a meeting before disappearing. I listen and yes, there's the click of a lock being turned. The door opens. Closes. Another click as the lock is turned again – this time from the inside.

I throw myself into spending time with Oscar, but I can't stop thinking about the door and what Nate could be hiding in that room. I can't escape the growing feeling that beneath the sheen of our perfect marriage is something not just crumbling, but dark and rotten.

5 DAYS EARLIER

Magnolia Close WhatsApp Group

Bill (No. 5)
*I heard there was a breakthrough in the investigation over the weekend.*

Ryan (No. 9)
*With the hidden camera or Jonny's murder? I've got my suspicions.*

Susie (No. 11)
*We all have!!!*

Jean (No. 5)
*If you're accusing one of us, just come out and say it!*

Ryan (No. 9)
*Fine. Andrea – you always want to know what's going on, and you're the one who is always out there trimming the bushes around the gate. Is the camera yours?*

Andrea (No. 7)
*How dare you! I'm not the one who hated Jonny because he objected to our planning permission.*

Marc (No. 12)
*That's completely uncalled for.*

# TWENTY-THREE

## TASHA

Where the hell is Sofia's reading diary? I had it in my hand last night. I really don't want to have to explain to her teacher, Mrs Pepperbridge, that I've lost another one. It's her second since the start of the new school year. I mustn't forget to reschedule Mum's hospital appointment so it's not in half-term week. We're out of bananas. And the good bread. If I'm popping into a supermarket, then I really need to get something different for dinner. I swear we had fish fingers and potato waffles nearly every night last week.

I abandon the hunt for the diary and grab a pen to make a shopping list. Even as my mind races, I wonder how I have the capacity to think about anything other than Marc buying a vine-yard without telling me. It's all I've thought about over the weekend. Through cleaning and tidying the house on Saturday and cooking his parents a lunch yesterday, pretending every-thing was normal for the sake of the girls and his parents. At least I wasn't the only one Marc lied to.

'They'll be devastated with us moving away,' Marc said on Sunday morning. 'Let's not upset them today.'

*I'm* devastated, I wanted to reply.

Three months of juggling bath times and school trips and the summer holidays and Matilda's clingy nights, and Marc's been chasing a fantasy. Lying to me. Drinking coffees in cafés and sitting in pubs, letting all those quiet hours slip away while I was doing everything. How could he have lied to me like that?

I can't decide if I'm angrier with him for the lies or the fact he's made this huge life decision for all of us. Spent our savings and decided to move us across the country, without a single conversation.

Why didn't he just tell me at the start of all this when he was first made redundant in July? I rake over the events of the summer. It's a blur. Writing and rewriting the planning application. Long days of trying to entertain the girls. The heatwave that didn't seem like it would ever end. My dad's radiotherapy. Yes, I was stressed. But I still would've listened and supported Marc.

There's a niggling voice in the back of my mind that questions if that's true. If Marc had asked me to pause the planning application, would I have done it?

I glance up as Marc walks into the kitchen. He's holding something in his hand. He lifts it wordlessly. Sofia's reading diary. I breathe a brief sigh of relief. That's one thing at least.

'It was under the sofa,' he says. His voice is cautious as though he's not sure what he's walking into. Tears and hurt or anger and accusation. I don't know myself half the time. It's been six days since Jonny's murder. Only four days since Marc confessed his lies. I need more time.

'Thanks,' I murmur, taking it from him and setting it on the counter.

He lingers. Not moving. 'How are you?'

It's not the question he's really asking. He's asking where my head is at. It's the same gentle prod he's given me every day since his confession. He's lied for three months, but I'm not allowed three minutes to process them.

I sigh and lean back against the worktop, retying my hair in its ponytail. It needs a wash. 'I know you've already bought the place, Marc, but—'

'I did it for us,' he cuts in. 'I know the vineyard was my dream, but I did it for you and the girls and for your parents. This is the solution, Tasha. This is a life of outdoors and calm. No more manic mornings and rushing around. You've seen the photos. Imagine all that space for the girls to play in. Imagine Christmases with your parents in the annexe, walking into the village for carols. This is a whole new kind of life we can have.'

I fight back the tears as I think of the property description Marc showed me on his phone last night in bed. The house and the annexe need freshening up, but they're not in bad condition. And the views... they're breathtaking. I want to want it. I really do. There's a longing in me for exactly what he's describing. But it's been built on lie after lie.

'I'm trying,' I tell him. 'But I can't get past all the lies. It isn't just that you went ahead and bought a property without telling me. It's that you deceived me for three months, Marco. You made me think you were exhausted from long hours in the office when you weren't. Then you asked Jonny of all people for a loan when it was him who blocked the planning permission for our extension here.'

Marc freezes, his expression morphing into guilt once more.

'What is it?' I ask, already dreading the answer.

He swallows hard. 'Jonny objected to our extension because I asked him to.'

The world tilts. Hurt cuts through my chest.

'You were so fixated on getting the extension,' Marc continues, speaking fast now. 'But then I was made redundant, and I wasn't sure I'd be able to get another job, or if I even wanted to keep being a project manager. I knew if we got the planning permission, we'd be locked in. Deposits paid, work starting, and I wouldn't have time to figure out another option. I didn't know how to tell you. I just needed time to think.'

'So we don't have the money for an extension, but we do have enough for you to buy an entire vineyard? How is that possible?'

His face pales. 'Because the vineyard is a business. Jonny helped me put a business plan together for the bank, and they agreed the loan. With that and Jonny's loan, I scraped it together. Selling this place will give us a cushion while we get the business up and running.'

Hurt cuts straight through my chest. He's thought it all through. Business plans and meetings and loans. I hold up my hand, and he stops talking.

'All you had to do was sit me down and explain, Marc,' I say. 'I'd have understood. You make me sound like a monster.'

His eyes shine with tears. 'I wanted to show you I was still worth something when I got made redundant. You never pursued your career, Tash, but supported me in mine. I promised you when you gave up your degree to make our relationship work that I'd always look after you. I felt like I'd failed you and the girls. I wanted to tell you, but I wanted to give you something better when I did. Because you have to see, you're not happy. And I haven't been either. I know we can be so much happier than this. I asked Jonny to delay the planning permission. That's all. But his buddy said he'd need an objection to delay things, so Jonny objected.'

I close my eyes. I can't grab hold of the emotions flying through me. All those hours I cried and raged about Jonny and what he'd done. All the blame I put at his feet for making my life harder, impossible. And it wasn't him at all. It was my husband. The man who was supposed to stand by me, support me, no matter what. I stare at Marc. I don't know what to say any more.

'Is there anything else I don't know?' I ask. 'Anything at all you haven't told me. Because now's the time, Marc. I can't take any more lies. So if there's—'

He shakes his head. 'That's everything. I swear it, Tasha.'

We stare at each other for a long moment. I wish I could believe him. But the trust of twenty-five years has been shattered, and I don't know how to rebuild it or if it's even possible.

A thud and scream from the living room wipes everything out of my head. I move fast, holding my breath, waiting for the crying that usually follows, but there's only another shout and laughter.

I poke my head into the living room. It looks like a tornado has hit it. Frustration grips me. It took me an hour to tidy it last night. Matilda and Sofia are playing another high-stakes game of 'The Floor is Lava' that involves jumping from the arm of one sofa to the other while squealing with delight and dread every time their feet touch the floor.

Lanie is sitting in the middle of the chaos, drooling happily over my phone, swiping at the screen with sticky fingers. If she stays distracted for five more minutes, maybe I can get the girls ready for school.

'Mum, I need a new lunch box,' Matilda calls out as she flies onto the sofa with such force it nearly topples back.

I gasp. 'Matilda, please don't jump onto the furniture like that. And why do you need a new lunch box?'

'I dropped mine in the playground on Wednesday and it broke, remember? You said you'd buy me a new one. Can I have a football one like Henry?'

Damn! I'd forgotten the broken lunch box.

'Yes. But only if you stop playing right now and get your shoes on please. We're going to be late to meet Oscar and Henry.' Again.

'We can't,' Sofia shouts. 'We can't touch the floor.'

'Please, girls.' The urge to cry suddenly wells up, lodging in my throat. A weight squeezes my chest, stopping me from drawing in my next breath. It's the feeling that makes me want to change something – to escape.

I was so desperate for things to change, and now everything has.

The detectives haven't visited again. I should be relieved, but I'm not. I'm scared. Is DS Sató building a case against me? Is the next time she visits going to be to arrest me? I had the biggest motive. It's what the neighbours think, ignoring the fact Beth and Georgie said I was with them all night.

I blink hard, force the tears back and take a deep breath. It would be so much easier if I wasn't so tired. My thoughts feel stretched too thin.

A loud shriek breaks my thoughts.

'That's not fair,' Sofia shouts, stomping her foot on the floor. 'You said the game was finished.'

'Tricked you,' Matilda sing-songs, causing another cry of injustice from Sofia.

My gaze catches on the clock. Eight thirty already. Beth and Georgie will be waiting. I glance at the girls. They haven't even got their shoes on, and Lanie's not strapped in the pushchair. I have half a mind to text and say we'll catch up, but they'll know something's wrong. They'll prod and ask questions I'm not ready to answer.

Then Marc is by my side, scooping Lanie into his arms.

'OK,' he says, and in that one word, the girls stop shouting and turn to him. 'Last one with their shoes on and ready and out the door is a rotten tomato.'

And just like that, we're all bundling to the door. I make a grab for the pushchair, but Marc stops me and passes me my phone. 'I've got Lanie.' He kisses me lightly on the lips, and I try not to flinch. Try to be grateful instead of still so angry.

I throw open the front door and hurry out. Drizzle clings to the air as we run, the girls rushing to greet Oscar and Henry. I wrap my cardigan tight, shivering, wishing I'd grabbed a coat but not wanting to run back.

When I glance over my shoulder, I see Marc is still standing in the doorway, watching us leave. He's tickling Lanie, making her giggle, holding her close. Something in my chest softens, and I know that no matter how furious I am for all the months he's lied, and for what he did, I know I will eventually forgive him. Because that's what families do – we survive.

We'll survive Marc's betrayal. We'll start our new life together. But I'm not leaving like the Gallaghers – cast out and shunned. I won't do that to the girls. Oscar and Henry are like brothers to them. Beth and Georgie like aunts. It would shatter their trust forever to see these people turn their backs on us. Georgie and Beth are my best friends. And right now, I need them. We have to protect each other during Jonny's murder investigation. Be each other's alibis.

But if it comes down to it – if I have to choose between my friends and my family – there's no choice at all.

I'll protect what's mine.

# TWENTY-FOUR

## TASHA

The bell rings across the playground, and the children begin lining up in their neat little rows, looping their book bags over their shoulders. I wait. Poised. Tense. Any second now, Matilda's lip will wobble, and the tears will spill onto her cheeks, and she'll rush at my legs, cling on for dear life, and it will take five minutes and the help of the teaching assistant to coax her into class. Four years at this school and it's always the same. I've tried reward charts and bribes and threats and everything I could think of, but nothing has worked. It's just another burden to add to my day.

Parents scatter, already peeling away to begin their days, but not us. We wait in our usual spot near the fence, our huddle tighter than usual, our smiles more forced. I feel more exposed without the pushchair.

The sky is a flat grey above us, and the drizzle has started again, frizzing my hair and chilling my body.

Beth nudges my side, keeping her voice low. 'Is it just me, or are people looking at us differently?'

'Not just you,' Georgie replies as she waves to someone at the gates. 'Julie – Katie's mum – gave me a look like I'd kicked her dog a minute ago. And did you see the way Lydia practically turned her back on us this morning? I mean, come on. It's like we're radioactive. I was supposed to meet Mrs Gardner this afternoon about PTA spending, but she cancelled, and that's a first. Didn't even give a reason, just said something had come up. It's weird, right? Like, why now?'

'It's because of the police update on the local news last night,' Beth whispers.

'I didn't see it,' I reply, feeling sick.

'Detective Sató said they're talking to Jonny's neighbours and building a picture of his last known movements,' Beth replies.

Georgie shakes her head. 'She basically suggested it was someone inside Magnolia Close.'

I glance around, my chest tightening. Beth is right. People are glancing our way, watching and pretending not to.

'Can you see her?' Beth asks, and I know instantly who she means.

I scan the playground. 'Rowan is here,' I say, nodding towards the year three line where Matilda is standing hand in hand with Keira's daughter. The two of them are giggling and pointing at a group of boys, heads together like they've been best friends for years. And for once, Matilda isn't looking back at me or beckoning me over. No wobbling lip. No tears.

I should be grateful she's happier – that she's found a friend – but seeing her with Rowan causes my stomach to knot. Even though I've avoided Keira since that day in the pub, I can't escape how she looks at me when we pass – like she knows all my secrets.

'Keira must have dropped Rowan and gone before the bell,' Georgie says as the children disappear inside. Matilda doesn't even look back.

We wait for the playground to empty before we begin the five-minute walk back to the close. The road outside the school is heavy with traffic – mums in SUVs. Delivery vans. The air smells faintly of petrol and wet leaves.

We pass the long stretch of detached Victorian houses, tall and grand, their paint peeling around sash windows and balconies. Most are apartments now – rented out to commuters who make the forty-minute train journey to London. Beside me, Georgie is bouncing on the balls of her feet like her energy has been turned up too high, too forced.

'Are you OK, Georgie?' I ask.

She flinches just a fraction before nodding. 'Yeah. I just want everything to go back to normal. The weekend felt like it dragged, right? And did you see the WhatsApp messages this morning?'

I shake my head. 'Lanie took my phone again this morning. I haven't had a chance to look since I got it back. What did it say?'

Beth pulls out hers and shows me the screen. 'Ryan accused Andrea of installing the secret camera,' she says, scrolling down. 'And—'

She shows me the screen, and I gasp. 'He's saying he thinks I killed Jonny.' The anxiety tightens around me in a stranglehold.

'Try not to think about it, Tasha. They just want someone to blame. It's pathetic,' Georgie says, giving my hand a gentle squeeze. 'They'll move on soon enough.'

'I hope so,' I say quietly.

We fall silent as we step through the gates and into Magnolia Close. The unmarked silver car is parked outside Jonny's house. DS Sató and DC McLachlan are back.

The drizzle has dampened the hedges and flowers. Even if it were bright sunshine and cherry blossoms, I don't think Magnolia Close will ever look the same again. The street feels changed. Haunted. It doesn't feel like the perfect home anymore. I can't shake the feeling of being watched – as if the whole close is holding its breath, waiting to see which one of us will be arrested. My gaze scans the windows. Who are the detectives talking to right now?

I want to ask Georgie and Beth what questions Sató had for them last week. But then a noise cuts through the hush. The ping of a phone. It's followed by another and another. Three sharp sounds that seem to echo off the dripping roofs and hedges. Georgie is already fumbling with her bag, but Beth is ahead of her, swiping to unlock her phone. She gasps, the sound making Georgie and me lean in. The screen is open on WhatsApp. A blank chat. No messages yet. Just a new group name. Four words.

*Strangers on a Train.*

A split second later, a message appears in the chat. Two words next to a waving-hand emoji:

*It's Keira.*

A creeping prickle moves up the nape of my neck, spreading outward, setting every nerve on edge.

'What's Strangers on a Train?' I ask, eyes darting between Georgie and Beth as I pull out my phone and see the same message.

The others look as confused as I am. I don't know what the title of the group chat means. Or what Keira wants. But deep down, in that part of me that never stops panicking, I know. Whatever this is, it's bad.

Strangers on a Train WhatsApp Group

Monday, 13 October, 9.05 a.m.

*You've been added to a new group.*

*Tasha has been added.*

*Georgie has been added.*

Keira
*Voice note.*

# TWENTY-FIVE

## BETH

We stand in my kitchen like we've done hundreds of times before. But there's no use pretending this is just another coffee after the school run. The air is too tight. The tension in the room feels like it hums around us.

I'm glad the children are at school. Henry is like me. He doesn't like people in his space. Even friends. I feel it too. Especially with Georgie, who always surveys my colours and homemade touches like she's cataloguing them.

But whatever this new WhatsApp group is, we couldn't talk about it standing in the middle of Magnolia Close. It's been painful to watch our community fall apart. DS Sató wants us to believe that one of us killed Jonny. If her aim is to drive a wedge into the community, it's working.

Which meant standing in the middle of the close wasn't an option. But we couldn't go to Tasha's house with Marc there, looking after Lanie. It's strange he's not at work again, but that's a thought for another time. And we couldn't go to Georgie's because of Nate. Even though Nate seems nice and always asks thoughtful questions, there is an edge to Georgie's husband sometimes. Like he's keeping himself apart. Like he's observing us from the outside – animals at the zoo. And right now we need privacy. So we're here, in my kitchen.

I stand beside the sink, trying to find calm in the scent of vanilla from the candles I made yesterday, now lining the worktop in the reused glass jars. Each one is perfectly uniform, the wick dead centre. I only had to throw one away that didn't measure up.

'Maybe Keira just wants to invite us for a drink,' Georgie says, trying for breezy, but it lands wrong.

'Only one way to find out,' I say, unlocking my phone and tapping the play icon on the voice-note file that's been added to the WhatsApp group.

There's a moment of muffled sound, the clink of a glass, then Georgie's unmistakable laugh crackles from my speaker. It hits me. I know what this is before the words come.

The pub.

That night.

The conversation we never should have had.

'*I'd stab him,*' Georgie's voice says from my phone. '*Right in the gut. Three times. One for each of us.*'

From across the kitchen, Georgie's hands fly to her mouth. Her eyes widen with horror as they lock on to mine. 'Oh my God,' she whispers, gaze flicking from my phone to me to Tasha. 'How did she get that?'

I force out the words I'm sure the others are thinking. 'She must've been recording us that night.' My pulse is thudding against my ribs. My phone shakes from the tremor of my hand and the recording that keeps playing from that night and our reckless, awful words.

'*I'd sneak up on him,*' Georgie says. '*Bill and Jean have a key to Jonny's house from when the Gallaghers used to live there. I've got a key to Bill and Jean's. I'd sneak into theirs, get the key, then sneak into Jonny's and bam!*'

Tasha's voice follows, slurred from the wine but unmistakable. *'I would use sleeping pills. These are my dad's prescription tablets. They'd knock Jonny out so he couldn't overpower me. And then—'*

I look up and catch Tasha's eye. Tears slide down her face. Her mouth is open, tension knotting her brow.

My voice is next, sounding alarmingly calculated. *'Stabbing is messy. Suffocation would be better. A pillow over his face while he's knocked out from the pills.'*

The recording ends. The kitchen falls silent. Fear scurries over my skin as I stare at my friends. Their eyes are wide with shock and fear. We joked about killing Jonny, but there's no humour in our voices. We sound deadly serious.

'Keira.' I say her name on a rushed breath. 'I can't believe she recorded us.'

We've been avoiding her all week, fearing she could tell someone what we talked about. Scared for how bad it looked. But this is so much worse.

Tasha lets out a strangled sound – somewhere between a sob and a gasp. 'Why would she do that?'

'She's cut the recording,' Georgie says. 'She's cut out the parts where she was pushing us to say more. Right?' Her eyes land on me. 'I know I drank a lot that night, but I'm not imagining it, am I, Beth?'

I shake my head. 'You're right. She's cut herself out of the recording. It's like she wasn't there at all.'

'Like it was just us,' Georgie repeats.

Our eyes lock, and we share in a moment of horror.

'If people hear that recording,' Tasha chokes out, putting a voice to our fears. 'If the police—' She breaks completely.

Georgie rakes a hand through her hair. 'I know,' she says. 'If this gets out, everyone – our husbands, the neighbours, the police – everyone will think this recording is us planning Jonny's murder. They'll think we went through with it.' There's a tremor to her voice I've never heard from her before. Georgie doesn't panic. Georgie doesn't lose control, and yet the cracks are showing.

*It's up to you to take control.*

That's what I'm doing.

'But we didn't kill Jonny,' I say. 'We should go to Detective Sató with this and tell her the truth.' But deep down, the doubt gnaws at me. Would Sató see it that way? Or would she hear us all talking about murdering Jonny and draw her own conclusions?

I push the thought aside. 'We've done nothing wrong, and we have alibis,' I add, as much for my benefit as Georgie and Tasha's.

Georgie's head snaps up, her gaze on me sharp. 'Do we though? The time of death was between eight and eleven. The quiz ended at nine. Everyone left soon after. The only people left were us.'

'That still gives us an alibi,' Tasha whispers. 'It's like Keira said in the pub. We just have to stick to our story. As long as we don't say anything to the police, we'll be OK.'

Georgie is already shaking her head. 'If DS Sató hears this recording, she'll assume we're all guilty,' Georgie explains. 'She'll think we planned it together and one of us snuck out and killed him, just like Keira suggested we could. If the police hear this, they'll think we're covering for each other and our alibi won't mean anything.'

A sob catches in Tasha's throat. 'Everyone in Magnolia Close already thinks it was me.'

'We all had our reasons,' Georgie whispers.

I watch my friend then. Georgie, who laughed off the school mum who called her 'too much' and mocked her behind her back. Georgie, with her mantras and her positive outlook. She isn't someone who holds a grudge. But she never forgave him for making a pass at her during the welcome street party last year. And suddenly I'm wondering if there's more to it.

*You think you're the only one hiding something?*

'We can't go to the police,' Georgie says, and suddenly she's the old Georgie again. The one making the decisions we follow without thinking. But this isn't a fundraiser or a Magnolia Close event. I can't allow Georgie to take over and drag us further into trouble.

'It isn't just about whether DS Sató will believe us,' Georgie continues. 'If Nate hears it, he'll never forgive me. He and Jonny were friends, and I'm talking about how I'll kill him.' Georgie looks like she might say more but pins her lips shut.

Tasha nods, freeing more tears that spill onto her cheeks. 'No one in the close will believe we didn't do it. We can't go to the police. We can't tell anyone.'

Tasha tugs on her ponytail. 'I just don't understand why Keira recorded us?'

Georgie shakes her head. 'That's not the question that matters, Tash. It's what she wants from us.'

'Is it possible she thinks we actually went through with it and killed Jonny?' Tasha asks. 'It's a massive coincidence he was killed the same night we talked about murdering him, isn't it? Maybe she's going to ask us for money. She wants to blackmail us.'

Tasha and Georgie continue to talk, voices low and fast, bouncing theories off each other. I stare again at the phone in my hand. It's been fifteen minutes exactly since that recording was sent. A prickle runs down my spine as another ping rings through the kitchen.

I don't breathe as all three of us unlock our phones to see the voice recording disappear from the chat. Replaced with a message:

*You can't avoid me forever. It's time to talk.*

'Where did that recording go?' Tasha asks.

I glance down at the now-empty WhatsApp group before my eyes move back to Tasha. I can see the panic coiling around her. She's seconds from unravelling. I shoot a look at Georgie. Her mouth is a flat line, her hands rubbing at the pressure point on her palm.

'Disappearing messages,' Georgie mutters. 'Or she's deleting them the moment she sees one of us has viewed them. It means we have nothing to show anyone. Nothing to prove what she's sent us.'

The kitchen feels suddenly too small, the air thick with our fear for whatever is coming next. My heart is banging against my ribcage.

*Getting upset won't be good for the baby.*

As if I don't know that. I close my eyes for a second, my hands gripping the counter, holding on to something solid.

Another ping sounds on our phones. I check the time. Exactly five minutes have passed since the last message. This time it's another voice recording.

A fresh chill rolls through me as Georgie presses play and Keira's voice fills the room. It's quiet, like it was recorded in a car or outside, but the Irish accent is clearly hers.

'Let's talk movies,' Keira says, her voice casual, like we're still in the pub. 'Ever seen *Strangers on a Train*? Alfred Hitchcock. Two strangers – each needs someone dead. They swap murders. One kills for the other, giving airtight alibis on both sides. No connection. No motive. Completely untraceable.'

There's a pause in the recording. My gaze lifts. Georgie's face has drained of colour. Tasha's eyes are wide and glassy. Blood roars in my ears. Everything is muffled, like I'm underwater. I feel the panic everywhere in my body.

'My ex is called Richard Philips,' Keira says. 'He's just like your Jonny. A piece of shit who is making my life hell. He works at Fordly Woods Business Park and runs back to town just after five p.m. every day. It'll be easy. All you have to do is hit him with your car. That quiet stretch of lane – no one around. I'll be at a Pilates class tonight. Make sure you do it then.'

The voice note cuts off.

Silence. Thick and suffocating. 'What does that mean?' Tasha asks. Her voice is childlike. Terrified. 'What is she saying?'

I can't answer. My hand instinctively moves to the soft swell of my stomach. To my baby and everything I have to lose. Everything I must protect.

Georgie presses her fingers to her temples, her voice barely a whisper. 'It means... Keira murdered Jonny.'

Then she lifts her eyes, staring at both of us with a wild terror. 'And now she wants us to kill someone for her.'

# TWENTY-SIX

## GEORGIE

Keira killed Jonny.

The thought spins in my mind. A vicious, unrelenting turn.

I've been so wrapped up in myself. In what Keira might tell Nate. In whether the police would uncover my connection to Jonny and what that would do to my already failing marriage. I've been so busy panicking over secrets and consequences that I never considered the possibility it was Keira behind Jonny's death.

We all told ourselves it was a coincidence he died the same night we'd joked about in the pub. But of course it wasn't. Keira killed him. It was stupid of me not to consider the possibility earlier. There's something dangerous about Keira. We all felt it that first night and in the days we've seen her since. And now that feeling makes sickening sense.

I unleash a breath, the exhale shuddering through me. I force myself to look at my friends. Tasha is crying, wiping her eyes on her sleeves, barely holding herself upright. But it's Beth who crumbles, throwing a hand over her mouth and rushing from the room. I hear the bathroom door click shut a second later.

And I'm just standing here. Frozen.

I stare at my phone. The group chat is still open, but the voice note is already gone. A heaviness builds in my chest that isn't just fear. It's confusion and frustration and a what-the-fuck? feeling that threatens to eat me alive.

Did she really think we were serious that night in the pub? We were just drunk and angry and venting into our wine glasses.

The police believe Jonny knew his killer, but that doesn't make sense. Keira had no connection to Jonny. So if the police are closing in, then they're chasing the wrong person. This isn't just about Jonny anymore either. It's about another man. And a murder she wants us to commit for her.

My fingers fly across my phone screen, thumbs stabbing furiously at the glass. A second later, I press send.

*You can't just decide to kill someone and expect us to do the same!*

'I'll check on Beth,' Tasha whispers, wiping her face. 'I feel like she should be here for this.'

I barely register Tasha leaving the room as I stare at the screen. At the notification that appears telling me Keira is online. Keira is typing. The reply comes a minute later.

*It's a bit late to develop morals, Georgie! It's simple. I did something for you, and now you do something for me. And if you don't, I'll send the recording I made to the detective along with some evidence I took from Jonny's house. I'll also make sure everyone at the school and in your pretty little Magnolia Close finds out.*

I gasp, pushing my phone onto the counter, like physical distance will make her words any less sharp. This is exactly what we just talked about. The knowledge that it isn't just the police we have to fear. It's everyone in our lives. This community we've built for ourselves and our children.

A second later, another message from Keira lands.

*Not sure Nate, Marc and Alistair will understand!*

Before I can think of a reply, Beth and Tasha return to the kitchen. Beth looks paler than ever against the terracotta tiles and matching walls. I glance around the kitchen, taking in its homely vibe. Dried herbs. Jars neatly stacked with pulses and rice and pasta. Everything has a home.

Everywhere I look is a reminder of Beth's determination. Even with the infertility and all those years of failure, she never gave up. She tried everything. New diets, new health kicks. I wish I could be happier for her about the pregnancy, but with Jonny's murder and now this... we're all scrambling.

'So Keira is saying we have to kill her ex tonight?' Tasha says, voice trembling. 'And if we don't—'

'She's going to make sure everyone thinks we killed Jonny,' I finish, sharper than I mean to be, but there's no time for Tasha's tears right now. 'The police and our husbands. Everyone.'

Tasha sniffs, trying to gather herself. 'She never once mentioned us wanting to kill her ex. How can she think we'd do this?'

'Tasha, we don't have a choice,' I reply. 'And she knows it. There's a recording of us talking about killing Jonny. Even if the police see past it, no one else will. Once that's out, who's going to believe we didn't do it?'

It feels like the world is collapsing in on us, brick by brick.

Beth is quiet. She's deathly pale, sipping a glass of water. Tasha stares at the floor. My own panic claws beneath the surface. I press my thumb to the bone of my wrist, grounding myself the way I always do when the world spins too fast.

*I will not let my fear control me.*

That's the mantra. That's the rule. But even as I repeat it, something inside me cracks. I don't know how to fix this. I always know how to fix things. I talk my way out of trouble, smile my way through it, reinvent myself when I need to. But this time? There's no spin. No way out. Only a choice that doesn't feel like a choice at all.

I have a flash of memory of Jonny the evening of the quiz, when he caught me on my way to the school.

'I had a little dig through my boxes the other day,' he said, stepping too close. The overwhelming scent of his aftershave and the whisky on this breath hit me like a wall. 'A trip down memory lane and all that.'

I managed to sigh like I was bored. 'What do you want, Jonny?' I asked.

He grinned. 'What I've always wanted, Georgie. You,' he said simply. 'If you want me to keep my mouth shut about your past to Nate and all of your precious friends, then you need to give me something.' He winked, making it clear what that something was.

'How is your marriage right now, Georgie? Think it can withstand Nate learning the truth?' he asked before moving back to his car, throwing his final comment casually over his shoulder. 'I've been patient for long enough. I want an answer tomorrow.'

Except there was no tomorrow. Because Jonny was murdered just hours later. And Keira has the recording of us planning it. And if Nate hears it, hears the hate in my voice, the fantasy of Jonny's death falling from my lips, he'll start digging. He'll connect the dots I've tried so hard to keep hidden. He won't stop until he knows everything. And when he does, he'll leave me. And he'll fight for full custody of Oscar. He'll use my past to claim I'm an unfit mother.

I'll lose everything.

*Power comes from action. You have the power. Take the action.*

'Georgie,' Tasha whispers, 'you're not seriously suggesting we actually do this?'

I look between my friends. I think of Beth's quiet determination and the way she makes sure everything is always perfect. And Tasha and the way she keeps going, even when she doesn't want to, even when it all feels like too much – she never gives up.

This is about survival.

I keep my voice steady as I speak. 'I'm suggesting we do whatever it takes to protect our lives.'

PRESENT DAY

# TWENTY-SEVEN

## TASHA



The yellow top is gone. Taken away in a sealed evidence bag.

How was this the only way?

If only Marc hadn't confided in Jonny. There's so much about his betrayal that stings. Borrowing money from Jonny. Asking him to block our planning permission. I've turned it over and over in my mind, trying to make sense of it. Why trust Jonny and not me? That's what I keep coming back to. Not just the three months he pretended to go to work, drinking coffees alone in cafés. Sitting in parks and bars, leaving me to feel like I was being buried under the weight of everything I had to do. But that he'd trust Jonny over me.

All he had to do was talk to me. Yes, the summer was chaotic. Yes, I was short-tempered and distracted. But I'm still his wife.

My eyes sting with fresh tears. I draw in a breath of stale air. I miss my mum. Not the frail, worried version of her that I care for everyday – the one who won't walk to the shop on the corner anymore because she's too scared she'll fall. But the mum who raised me. Who took me to London once a month to ride the red buses and wanted me to know I should never be afraid.

'In this country, Natasha, you can be anything you want to be.'

Except, however hard I tried, I didn't know what that was. As a teen, I thought I'd be a children's book editor, even write my own stories one day. But then I met Marc when I was seventeen.

When it came time for university, he chose business in Bath and I chose English at Edinburgh, and the distance felt impossible. Still, I went. Everyone on my course seemed so together, so sure of themselves. The old feelings surfaced. I wasn't like them. I didn't belong. The feelings I'd felt my whole life, except when I was with Marc. He'd made the world make sense in a way it didn't when I was on my own.

I dropped out after one term, moved home, took a job as a receptionist at a dental practice and visited Marc in Bath every other weekend. My dream changed. It became about being needed. Belonging. A wife. A mother. A family of my own. I have it all and yet, instead of contentment, I feel burdened – buried alive.

The door opens again. Sató returns. There's a pinched line between her brows, and as she takes her seat once more, the air feels heavy, hard to breathe.

It must be gone lunchtime by now. Lanie will be rubbing her eyes, trying to fight her afternoon nap. She needs to be rocked when she gets overtired, cradled against my chest with her warm cheek resting against my skin. I sing her favourite nursery rhyme, quietly, the hum of my voice soothing her. Will anyone know to do that?

I wonder if all three girls are crying for me now. The thought causes a hurt to crack open in my chest and a pulsing need to escape. Except I can't.

Sató opens her notebook and fixes that all-seeing gaze on me. 'Do you have a key to Jonny's house, Tasha?'

The conversational tone throws me. I blink back the tears. Try to focus. 'No, I don't.'

The next question comes a little faster, like a move in the games of chess I used to play with my dad. 'How did you get into Jonny's house the night you murdered him?'

'I...' My thoughts scramble. 'I knocked on his door, and he let me in,' I say, trying to make my tone sound less like I'm asking a question.

Sató's expression remains focused, but there's a new gleam to the look in her eye.

'I don't think you did,' Sató replies with that same casual tone. 'You see, the coroner has told us that Jonny ingested a high dose of prescription sleeping pills around two hours before his death. He would not have been capable of answering the door to anyone. In fact, he was likely unconscious, in bed, at the time of his death.'

Sató allows her words to settle – a smothering blanket. Hot and scratchy.

'I look at you sitting here,' she continues. 'And I see a woman who is exhausted and scared. So here's what I think, Tasha. I think you're covering for someone. And then I have to ask myself who—'

'This isn't just about Jonny,' I whisper, not liking the direction Sató is taking us, how easily my lies are crumbling.

Suddenly, I'm pulled away from the interview room, thinking of the day in Beth's kitchen after Keira's voice note. The details she gave us about her ex. What she wanted – murder.

Georgie never said she wanted to do it. But she didn't say she wouldn't either. But for once, Beth took a stand.

'We can't kill someone,' Beth said. 'We're not those people.'

'What do we do then?' Georgie asked, just as frustrated.

She's always been an act now, think later, damn the consequences kind of person.

'Nothing,' was Beth's reply. 'We call Keira's bluff. She's the murderer, not us.'

'But that recording,' Georgie said. 'We just talked about this – if it gets out, our lives are ruined.'

'Then we have to hope Keira is bluffing because we're not murderers,' Beth replied.

Georgie took some convincing, but Beth kept pushing and for once even Georgie agreed. So we did nothing.

It only made everything worse.

'Tasha?' Sató's voice makes me jump.

'This isn't just about the murder of Jonny Wilson,' I say again, forcing a strength into my voice that I hope Georgie would be proud of. 'There's a police report from the country lanes around Fordly Woods on Thursday night. It's connected to everything,' I add, allowing the tears to consume me. Giving in. Crumbling. I bury my face in my hands, knowing Sató is running out of patience.

A chair scrapes. Sató stands. 'I'll give you a few minutes to compose yourself while I find this police report you claim exists,' she says. 'Would you like some water when I return?'

I shake my head. I want to go home.

Except I don't know what home means anymore. There's so much more to this than Sató understands. We thought we could ignore Keira's demands. Move on. As if that was ever an option.

I really didn't want to kill anyone.

4 DAYS EARLIER

Magnolia Close WhatsApp Group

Tuesday, 14 October, 7.32 a.m.

Andrea (No. 7)
*Did anyone catch the local news this morning? The
police have said they're close to making an arrest in
Jonny's murder. I'll be glad when this is all over. It's
been a week since they found his body. How much longer
is it going to take?*

Ryan (No. 9)
*Like I said – it has to be one of us. Who had a key to
Jonny's place?*

Bill (No. 5)
*We had a spare key when the Gallaghers were there. We
kept hold of it for a while, but Jonny asked for it back a
few months ago. He wanted someone else to keep hold
of it.*

Beth (No. 3)
*Please, everyone, let's not start accusing each other.*

Andrea (No. 7)
*I agree. This will all be over soon, and we'll all need to
live with each other.*

Ryan (No. 9)
*Not us! We're moving as soon as this investigation has
blown over.*

*Ryan has left the group.*

Dan (No. 9)
*Sorry, everyone! Ryan has found this all really stressful.*

*Dan has left the group*

# TWENTY-EIGHT

## GEORGIE

'Do nothing.' I shake my head as I cross the school playground the next morning, Oscar's lost coat slung over my arm – found exactly where he said it wasn't, on the classroom coat hooks.

'Do nothing,' I mutter again, like I have every hour since Keira's ultimatum yesterday.

It's not like I wanted to drive to the country lanes of Fordly Woods last night and kill her ex. But ignoring her isn't going to make it go away. I did nothing when Jonny first showed me that photo at the street party. I told no one I knew him. A mistake. And this feels like another one.

I couldn't sleep last night. I lay awake wondering if Keira was doing the same. If she was waiting for her phone to ring or someone to knock on her door and tell her the news her soon-to-be ex-husband was dead.

She must know by now we haven't done it. The thought causes a jittery energy to pulse through my body. I'm scared and wired and uncertain. What will she do next? Send the recording to our husbands? Send it to the police? All I know for sure is that she won't do nothing. Keira didn't go to the trouble of murdering someone to stop now.

I sidestep a group of reception mums clustered around a pushchair, cooing over a newborn, and I'm halfway back towards the gates where Tasha and Beth are standing, when I spot her. Keira.

She's impossible to miss in cherry-red activewear. The Lycra set hugs her body, full hips, a soft stomach, breasts that look barely contained. She looks like a woman who owns her strengths and is happy to use them. And Nate – my Nate – is talking to her again.

My mouth turns dry. Is she telling him?

I stop walking and watch his eyes roam discreetly over Keira's body. And despite my fears, something clenches in my stomach. My body is strong, lean. I train seven days a week. I use the best creams, oils and scrubs. My skin is polished. My stomach is flat and defined. But my husband doesn't look at me that way anymore. Doesn't look at me at all most days.

I draw in a deep breath and try to chase the thought away with one of my mantras, but nothing comes. Nate and I used to be good at the surface stuff – the chatter, the easy smiles, the teasing and jokes. Even if there was nothing beyond the surface, at least we had that. At least we could pretend we were OK. Now he watches me when he thinks I'm not looking. I catch the look in his eyes I remember from all those years ago during the investigation into my boss, Reggie. Like he's trying to solve a puzzle. Trying to see how the pieces fit.

Nate told the police he was messaging with Jonny hours before his death. Could Jonny have shown him the photo of us?

The image is innocent enough. A group of people sat side by side in a leather booth in a bar. My boss Reggie on one side of me. Jonny on the other. All of us grinning at the camera. Jonny always was a cocky piece of shit. He was a good friend of Reggie's and would join us on some of our nights out, celebrating a good deal or a good quarter. The kinds of nights when my champagne glass never emptied and the music was good, the mood better. A night celebrating our success.

It was about a month after that damning photo was taken when Nate began his investigation into Reggie. He asked me about the nights out, and I lied and told him I wasn't invited. A white lie to cover the bigger lie. The truth Nate would never forgive about my past – I wasn't just Reggie's personal assistant; I was helping him with inside trading. I used to photocopy deal sheets I wasn't supposed to see. Forward calendar invites to his burner phone under the guise of booking travel. I overheard things – upcoming mergers, earnings reports, quiet restructures – and passed them on. It didn't feel like we were hurting anyone. It felt like I was being smart, taking my cut, being a team player. But it all came crashing down when Nate began investigating Reggie's team. I convinced him I was innocent, sharing details of Reggie and his junior, pretending I didn't understand what I was giving him.

I had no idea Jonny knew the truth about the insider trading and my part in it. I barely remembered him until he moved into Magnolia Close and showed me the photo. It isn't my smiling younger self that's the problem in that photo. It's what it means that I was there.

Nate's job is to investigate and stop any wrongdoing by the bank's employees. If he ever learns that not only did I get away with my part in the crimes we committed but that he married the woman he should've fired, should've had charged, he'll be furious. His moral compass will never allow him to forgive me. If he finds out the truth about who I was before we met, there will be no fixing us.

The wail of the newborn yanks me back to the school playground. A little girl barrels into me before darting off after a friend. I stumble and catch myself, realising I've been standing still. Staring. I glance at Tasha and Beth. They're watching me watch Keira and Nate. I see the same fears pinching their expressions, wondering what she's telling him.

When I glance back towards Nate and Keira, their body language has changed. Keira's arms are folded across her chest, her gaze fierce. Nate is no longer smiling, his expression stony. Keira leans close, and whatever she's saying, she's talking in a fast whisper.

Cold fear floods my chest. Blood thuds in my ears. I fight the urge to turn and run, and instead start towards them. Keira catches the movement, and her face breaks into a wide smile that seems forced. She's wearing bright-red lipstick again. The colour of trouble. Of danger.

'There you are,' Nate says as I approach. His voice is a little too bright as he leans forward, dropping a kiss on my cheek. It's a fight to keep the surprise from my face. When was the last time Nate kissed me in public? Or at home for that matter?

'Everything OK?' I ask, matching Keira's smile. Nate isn't the only one who can fake it.

'Absolutely,' he says. 'Keira was just telling me about a birthday party for her daughter next month.'

'Rowan,' Keira supplies, like she's reminding him. She doesn't look at me when she says it.

Nate checks his phone, hissing an expletive under his breath. 'I forgot I've got a meeting in five minutes. I'll see you at home.' He kisses me again and strides away, leaving me with Keira – a murderer. She killed the one man who could destroy my entire life, only to replace him. The woman whose ex she expected us to kill last night, and we didn't.

'What do you think you're doing?' I hiss before I can think better of it.

Keira's smirk is quizzical. 'Talking to your husband?' she replies.

'About what?' I ask.

Another smirk. 'Maybe you should ask him.' Then she

laughs. 'Relax,' she says. 'He just asked how Rowan was settling in. I said she was making friends. Planning a pirate party. Apparently, pirates are all the rage at lunch break.'

'You said something more,' I push. 'He looked upset.'

'Oh,' she says, waving a hand in the air like it's nothing. 'I said I thought I recognised him from somewhere. We were trying to work it out.' She shrugs, tucking a wisp of jet-black hair behind her ear before she continues. 'God, you mums are intense. I'm not after your husbands.'

'That's not what I'm worried about,' I reply.

'You're worried I'm going to tell him about your drunken chat about your neighbour,' she says, dropping her voice into a faux whisper like this is all a joke to her.

Anger burns through me. 'And the rest,' I say through gritted teeth, thinking of her voice note and what she asked us to do yesterday. 'Come on, Keira. This is too much now. You need to stop,' I say, fighting to keep my voice even and my expression schooled into something normal. The last thing I want is everyone staring. 'This isn't a joke. You're playing with people's lives.'

Something in her eyes hardens. It's like a mask has slipped and I'm seeing the monster underneath. When she speaks, her voice is low and menacing. 'Just so we're clear, Georgie,' she says, her Irish accent sounding stronger as my name rolls off her lips, 'I don't give a shit about your little school-mum kingdom. I don't care what you or anyone else thinks about me, and I don't need to stop doing anything I don't want to do.' She points a finger at me. 'Remember that.'

She makes to leave, stepping back, turning, but before I can stop myself, I'm reaching out, grabbing her arm, my grip tight as I step close. 'Stay away from me. Stay away from my friends. Stay away from our husbands.'

Her gaze drops to where I'm touching her, then her eyes lift to meet mine. 'Or what?' she asks, her smile fierce. 'You planning another murder, Georgie?'

Her words hit square in the chest, knocking the air from my lungs. My grip loosens, and I drop my hand, suddenly aware of how exposed we are and how many eyes might be watching.

She's asking me if I'm planning to kill her ex. Reminding me what happens now I haven't.

My heart drums a frantic beat against my ribs.

Keira checks her watch with maddening nonchalance. 'Run along now,' she says. She waggles her fingers and turns, hips swaying, weaving through the crowd like she owns it. I stare after her.

Keira's planning something. I saw it in the flash of menace behind her smile. The question isn't whether she'll strike again. It's how soon. And what we're going to do to stop it. If we'll survive it...

Strangers on a Train WhatsApp Group

Wednesday, 15 October, 10.17 a.m.

Keira
*You didn't do it. This is on you!*

Keira
*A parcel is being delivered to each of you today. If I were you, I'd get to them before your husbands. And by the way, it's their names on the envelopes.*

Magnolia Mums WhatsApp Group

Tasha
*OMG! What has she sent us? I'm at my parents'.*

Georgie

*I'm at work. Beth, can you grab the postman at the gate
and take the parcels?*

Beth
*I'm on it.*


Magnolia Mums WhatsApp Group

Beth
*I've got them.*

# TWENTY-NINE

## BETH

The three parcels sit side by side on the coffee table. Each one is addressed in the same neat, deliberate Sharpie handwriting. Each one hums with a tension that presses against me, squashing and uncomfortable. A part of me wonders if I should open them before the others arrive. But it feels wrong. I need my friends with me.

I watched them step through the gates five minutes ago, Georgie and Tasha side by side, heads bent in whispered conversation as they headed to Tasha's house, the children racing ahead of them, Henry in tow.

I didn't hesitate when Tasha suggested she and Georgie collect Henry from school for me. None of us wanted to leave the parcels unattended after I grabbed them from the postman, who was happy to hand me all three.

And when Tasha suggested they leave the children with Marc – a convenient excuse ready, no doubt a 'PTA emergency' Georgie would whip up on the spot – it seemed like the perfect solution. Except now I'm alone. Just me and these three packages.

A headache starts to throb behind my eyes. My stomach

feels coiled tight. It's the stress of the last week and the taunting threats in the Strangers on a Train WhatsApp group. The voice note asked if we'd seen the Alfred Hitchcock film. I remember it well. It was one of my mother's favourites. Guy Haines and Bruno Antony met by chance and planned a murder swap. I also remember how it all went wrong. It wasn't a blueprint for how to plan a murder swap. It was a tale of disaster.

A sound from the front door makes me jump. Three light taps. They're here!

I rush forward, pulse still hammering in my ears, and throw open the front door to Tasha and Georgie. Their heads are bent again like they're whispering, then they're pulling apart like teenagers caught out, and I swear a flicker of something I'm not supposed to see passes across Georgie's face before it's gone.

The knowing voice hisses in my thoughts. *They were talking about you.*

I refuse to think like that. These women are my best friends. We need each other now more than ever. I need them. Even if the Magnolia Close community is fracturing, our friendship will stay strong. I have to trust them.

We gather in the living room, Georgie and Tasha on the sofa, me in the armchair. Each with a parcel on our lap. It's like a nightmare version of the Christmas celebration we have each year. A secret Santa for the children and a buffet dinner with crackers to pull and party hats. Then when the children are playing or watching TV, the three of us gather to exchange our gifts.

Georgie always buys us Jo Malone candles and bath oils. Tasha buys me earrings. I prefer to make them things. Last year, it was a knitted scarf for Tasha in a beautiful soft yellow with flecks of gold. For Georgie, I made a canvas bag from material of emerald green with mockingbirds on it. I had to restart the scarf twice and the bag three times to get them perfect, but it was worth it when they both exclaimed with delight.

*How many times have you seen either of them wear or use the gifts you made?*

It's the thought that counts.

But there is nothing celebratory about this moment as we sit with the parcels on our laps. The silence drawing out, tension and fear and panic heavy in the air. When I touch the parcel, there's a tremor to my hands. The parcel addressed to Alistair is long, and there's a weight to it. Tasha's looks soft. Georgie's is small.

'On three?' Georgie asks, voice tight.

I nod.

'One,' Georgie starts. 'Two. Three.'

There's a rustle of noise as we each tear at the padded envelopes. Inside mine, I find a white dishcloth. I barely have time to consider the hard lump it's wrapped around before Tasha lets out a gasp.

She's out of her chair, scrambling away, pushing herself against the wall like she could disappear through it. Her eyes are fixed on something on the floor, and I follow her gaze to the envelope and the contents lying beside it. It's a pile of yellow silk material. Tasha's favourite top. The same one she wore the night of the quiz. Only now it's streaked with a dark rusty-red stain that can only be one thing – blood.

My insides roil. The nausea is crawling up my throat again. It's a fight to swallow it down. My gaze moves back to Tasha. She's breathing loud and fast, hugging her arms to her body, head shaking, eyes wide and wild.

'That's not my top,' she cries.

I flick a glance at Georgie. She's staring back at me, brows raised. Is she remembering the end of the quiz night, after we'd finished tidying the hall, when Tasha appeared with her jacket zipped up, complaining she'd spilled red wine on her top. Her yellow top. I look back at the stain. It definitely isn't wine.

Tasha must sense our disbelief because she tugs at her

jumper with frantic hands. 'Look—' she says, revealing the same yellow top underneath. Clean and not soaked in blood or wine.

Georgie looks from Tasha to the floor. 'That's a slightly darker yellow, isn't it?'

Tasha nods. 'And it's a round neck. Mine is a V-neck.'

'You were wearing it the night in the pub as well,' Georgie continues. 'Keira must've bought a similar one and worn it...' She trails off.

'What's in your package?' I ask Georgie, delaying the moment I have to unwrap the white cloth sitting heavy on my lap. My eyes keep dragging back to the bloody top on my floor. In my living room. My home. It's out of place. Doesn't belong. I want to snatch it up, throw it away, but I'm frozen in my chair.

As Georgie peers into her parcel, Tasha moves slowly back to the sofa, collapsing down before wrapping her arms around her legs, hugging herself tight and crying quietly.

'I've got two things,' Georgie says, pulling out the first item, holding the narrow white box up for us to see.

Tasha gasps again. 'My dad's sleeping pills,' she says. 'Keira must've taken them that night in the pub. Remember how I showed them to you?'

'There's this too,' Georgie says, and this time she holds up a silver key. 'It must be Jonny's house key. How the hell did she get hold of this?'

We fall silent again. Neither Tasha nor I can answer Georgie's question. I can't drag my eyes away from the bloody top on the floor.

'Your turn, Beth,' Georgie says.

My mouth turns dry as my eyes shift to the white dishcloth on my lap. I peel back the edges. Inside is a plastic carrier bag. It rustles as I open it and peer inside.

'What is it?' Tasha asks.

Fear scrapes its way up my throat. I'm trying so hard to stay calm for the baby, but I can't. I've wanted this pregnancy for so long – years filled with the lonely ache of wanting. I saw myself taking long walks in the mornings and spending the afternoons baking and knitting tiny cardigans, talking to my baby girl. All those years, I never thought the weeks of my pregnancy would pass with my neighbour dead and a police investigation hanging over us. What if the fear – this constant hum of worry – affects my baby's development or leaks into her personality?

*You really shouldn't call the baby a girl,* the voice whispers. *You'll only be disappointed if it turns out to be a boy.*

But I feel deep in my soul that she's a little girl. As clear as the knowledge that she is already more important to me than the air I breathe. I think of Alistair and Henry. Our perfect family. Our perfect life.

And a little baby girl who needs me.

She needed me to do everything I could to make sure she was conceived. And so I did. Keira's comment in the playground the day after we found out Jonny was dead lingers in my thoughts.

*'Sure it's not twins? You're big for three months.'*

The words creep into my ears again, cold and taunting.

Of course it's three months. Three months makes the baby Alistair's. But four months ago, Alistair was ill with stomach flu. It knocked him out for weeks. It's another small white lie I tell. Always planning the midwife appointments on the days I know Alistair has lectures and meetings he can't get out of.

A white lie that's worth the guilt that sits so hard in my chest for deceiving my kind, trusting husband. Because I was perfect. I was doing everything right. But Alistair's sperm count was still low. We were told a natural conception wasn't impossible, but it wasn't likely either. And so in March, I went to a fertility clinic to use a sperm donor. It was the only way to give Alistair the second child he wanted as badly as I did.

Even if it meant a lie.

Then, of all the thousands of people who live in the city, the thousands more that visit every day, it was my neighbour who saw me on the street after my appointment.

Jonny.

I lied about my reasons for being there, but Jonny knew. Now he's dead, and sitting on my lap in a white dishcloth is the knife used to kill him.

Strangers on a Train WhatsApp Group

Wednesday, 15 October, 4.08 p.m.

Keira
*There's more bloodstained clothing tying you to Jonny's murder. You think I sent everything? Think again.*

Keira
*Either kill my ex tomorrow – or I give the police the recording of you planning Jonny's death, and the rest of the evidence they need to charge all three of you.*

Keira
*Oh – and don't even think about destroying the 'gifts' I sent. I've hidden a few extra items in Jonny's house. Missing a glove, Georgie? A scarf, Beth? You ladies really should be more careful with your belongings on nights out!*

Keira
*The police haven't found them yet. But they will.*

# THIRTY

## BETH

'Beth?' Georgie's voice is a prod to the small of my back.

I look up. Open my mouth. Try to speak.

My hands continue to shake as I lift the dishcloth, unable to touch the object inside. 'It's a knife.'

The handle black plastic. The blade long and sharp. The metal shiny except for a smudge of dark-red blood.

'Oh God,' Tasha whispers, hugging herself tighter, trying to shrink herself down.

Even Georgie pales as I place the knife on the coffee table. I sit back, wrapping my cardigan tighter around my body, around my baby. The world feels like it's spinning too fast. I can't keep up.

I like order. I like lists. I batch cook. I colour-code the calendar on the kitchen wall. I plan. But all it's got me is here – to a knife used to murder my neighbour. A knife now sitting on my coffee table and a bloody top dropped on my rug.

Somewhere outside, a car door slams. We all jump. I think of DS Sató and the other detective coming to this door. Finding the three of us here with this evidence.

Georgie is the first to speak. Her voice is low, her eyes locked on the knife. 'This is how she did it,' she says. 'Exactly how we talked about. She let herself into Jonny's house with this key. She drugged him with your dad's sleeping pills.' Georgie points to Tasha before her gaze swings to me. 'Then she murdered him in his bed. With the knife. I bet she suffocated him too. She recorded our plan, and then she followed every step of it.'

Tasha is gasping now, her breaths short and ragged. 'Oh God, oh God, oh God. She's got that recording. She's got us actually saying it... and she... she actually did it. She's crazy.'

Georgie nods. 'But smart too. She made sure it could be pinned on us.'

'We have an alibi,' Tasha cries.

'No, we don't,' Georgie snaps. 'You spent a lot of that night in the kitchen, Tasha. How do we know you didn't run back here and kill him?'

Tasha makes a noise in the back of her throat, midway between a cry and a sob. 'Beth spent half the night in the toilets throwing up.' She gestures a hand in my direction. 'She could easily have slipped out and killed Jonny.'

A sharp pang of betrayal cuts through me. For Tasha to turn on me like this when we're best friends. It stings.

'You know my morning sickness is worse in the evenings,' I murmur. 'And I'm not the one acting weird,' I add, throwing a glance at Tasha.

'I'm not,' Tasha replies, but there's something in her expression. I've hit a nerve.

'You have been,' I push, turning to Georgie. 'Hasn't she?'

Georgie frowns before nodding. 'I'm not saying you're trying to cover up a murder, but you have been acting more stressed than usual, Tash.'

'I...' She wipes her hands over her face before looking back at us. 'It's Marc,' she says. 'He was made redundant.'

'Oh,' Georgie says. 'Why didn't you tell us?'

'Because we've had a lot going on,' she replies, motioning to the yellow top still sitting on the floor of my living room. 'And...' Tasha continues. 'It happened three months ago, and he's only just told me.'

'But he's still been going to work...' My words trail off when I see the hurt on my friend's face.

'He was lying,' she says. 'He pretended to leave for business trips and to the office, and the entire time he wasn't.' Tears stream down her face. For a moment, it looks like she might say more but stops.

'Did he say why?' I ask.

Tasha shakes her head. 'Just that he didn't want to let me down.'

Georgie reaches across the sofa, squeezing Tasha's hand. 'I'm so sorry.'

I want to ask where Marc has been going if not to work. And what Tasha is going to do. I can't imagine Alistair ever lying to me like that. We tell each other everything – every mundane detail of our days, every small worry, every little thing Henry does to make us laugh. We've built our relationship on quiet honesty. On solid dependability. If something was wrong, he'd tell me. That's the kind of marriage we have.

If we can just get through this – past Jonny's murder and these messages that keep coming and the police investigation – then I'll live with the guilt if it means we can have the life we've dreamed of. The life we deserve.

'We can't turn on each other,' Georgie says, dragging my thoughts back to the room. 'I could've killed Jonny while you two were clearing up. I took the empty bottles to the recycling bins, remember? Can either of you say for sure how long I was? But this wasn't us. It was Keira. Whatever happens, we have to stick together. Together we are stronger.'

*One of Georgie's mantras isn't going to save you from this.*

But Georgie is right. Turning on each other now won't help anything.

'We need to get rid of this stuff?' I say, staring again at the top on my rug. 'If the police knock on my door right now, it's over. They can never see this evidence.'

'We can't, Beth,' Georgie cuts in. 'Keira's message said we have to keep it. She has more evidence, remember? We didn't play her game on Monday when she told us to kill her ex and look where it's got us? She's escalated everything. We have to hide this stuff and play along for now or who knows what she'll do next.'

'I can't keep that in my house,' Tasha whispers, pointing a shaking finger at her top.

'We have to,' I reply, feeling sick again. 'Georgie is right.'

Georgie nods. 'And we have to find a way out of this. The time to do nothing is gone. And no talking to DS Sató,' she adds.

Tasha bites her lip but nods. 'I want to go to the police, but I'm scared they'll hear the recording Keira has and see all this evidence, and they'll think it was me.'

'But your DNA won't be on that top, will it?' Georgie says. 'They might not—'

'They will,' Tasha cries. 'They're my dad's sleeping pills, right? And I had the biggest motive for wanting him dead. You both didn't like him, but I'm the only one who had something to gain from his death because we can get the extension now. DS Sató already suspects me.'

A tense silence winds itself like a noose around us. 'We have two choices,' Georgie says eventually. 'We either go to the police and tell them everything, or we kill Keira's ex and hope that's the end of it.'

Tasha's next inhale is sharp.

'We're not murderers, Georgie,' is all I can say. 'We can't—'

The ping of another message cuts me off.

Georgie snatches at her phone and gasps. 'It's Keira,' she

hisses. 'She says: "*Either drive to the country lanes by Fordly Woods tomorrow at five p.m. and kill my ex, or I'll come back to Magnolia Close again. How safe do you think your precious families are? I've shown you I'm capable of murder, and I won't stop until I've got what I want. Ignore me. Go to the police, and I will destroy what you love most in the world.*"

Another ping. Then another and another.

A sob catches in Georgie's throat as she turns the screen to show us. The photo stops my heart. It's the children. Henry and Oscar and Matilda and Sofia. They're standing together in their school uniforms. Not at school, not on the road, but here – inside the gates of Magnolia Close.

'Oh God.' Tasha's hands fly to her mouth. 'That was taken just now.'

'How do you—' I start to ask.

'Matilda's lunch box. It's new. I got it for her yesterday. This photo was taken less than an hour ago.'

'Inside the close,' I add, swallowing a fear that feels like it will never ease.

Georgie swipes the screen of her phone. 'There's another photo,' she says.

I lean forward and stare at the image of a man. Mid-forties. Running kit. Short hair, grey at the temples. The kind of ordinary man you'd never look at twice in the street.

It's followed by another message. Tasha and I both reach for our phones to read.

*He'll be running along Fordly Lane at 5.05 p.m. tomorrow. Hit him with your car and make sure he's dead!*

I've barely had time to finish reading when the messages are deleted.

Tasha and Georgie look up from their phones. Tears are

streaming down Tasha's face. 'She's going... she says she'll hurt our children—'

'Unless we kill her ex tomorrow,' Georgie finishes in a trembling voice. 'While she has a watertight alibi, I assume.'

The phone slides from Tasha's fingers and hits the rug with a dull thud. 'So...' she stutters, 'if we don't do this, she'll come back and hurt our families? Kill them?'

'This was her plan all along,' Georgie says, her voice hollow now, like the strength has been sucked out of her. 'That night in the pub, we were letting off steam. It was a joke. But she egged us on, didn't she? Kept pushing us to say more. She killed Jonny just so we'd kill her ex.'

I nod. 'We can't even think about going to the police anymore,' I say. 'We can't risk her hurting our families,' I choke, unable to say Henry's name.

'I can't... ...' Tasha's voice is broken by a sob.

*That one is always unravelling.*

'What choice do we have, Tasha?' I ask, clenching my jaw, fighting a flare of frustration. We need to start thinking clearly. There's too much at stake for any of us to fall apart.

'This isn't about murder,' Georgie whispers, looking determined once more. 'It's about survival. It's about protecting our families.'

I sit still – heart thudding, nausea rolling – wondering if this one choice, this one irreversible act is about to destroy my life. Or if I did that already by lying to Alistair and trying to give him the perfect family we both deserve.

# THIRTY-ONE
## GEORGIE

Later, after leaving Beth's house with the sleeping pills and key to Jonny's house shoved in my bag, I collect Oscar from Marc, and Oscar and I spend an hour running around the living room playing dinosaurs and hunters, then TV and dinner and bath time and three stories.

When Oscar is asleep, I change into my new underwear set and cook dinner for me and Nate. It's the cute lilac lacy set I picked up last week. It pinches a little at the waist, and the underwire digs in under my breasts, but I look good. Especially since it's *all* I'm wearing as I chop the vegetables for a stir fry. After everything that's happened, the last thing I feel is sexy, but live the life you want, right?

That's the mantra I gave on my reel this evening as I got ready, hinting at a romantic evening planned with Nate. I didn't give the specifics, just the sentiment and an artful flash of the new underwear. The reel has already had over a thousand views. I don't even care that I'm cold.

This has to be something I can fix – my marriage. Because I can't fix what's happening with Keira. I can't stop what we have to do tomorrow at 5.05 p.m., when Beth, Tasha and I are going to drive to the outskirts of town and kill a man we've never met.

I can't change that.

If we go to the police, Keira will send everything to DS Sató – the recording, the evidence. And if they believe her over us, she will walk free – and she will come back to Magnolia Close and...

My chest tightens as I think of the photo of Oscar taken inside the gates of Magnolia Close. She must've been hiding behind the bushes by Jonny's house. Keira doesn't play by the rules. She killed Jonny. She stabbed him with a knife and admitted it. She's a murderer. And the thought of her coming back to Magnolia Close, coming to my house, to Nate, Oscar—

No!

There's only one way out. Tomorrow, we're going to take it and it will all be over and we can finally move on with our lives. And before then, I'm going to fix things with Nate. All we need is a little fun, a little spark to nudge us back on track.

There's a sound on the stairs, drawing me back to the kitchen and the vegetables sizzling in the wok. I send a silent prayer into the universe that it's Nate and not Oscar I hear, and when my gaze draws to the doorway, there he is – my husband.

I give my best sultry smile, waiting for him to grin back and wolf whistle as his eyes roam up and down my body. But when I look at his face, his expression is blank. He stays in the doorway, leaning against the frame, hands in his pockets.

'What are you doing?' he asks. No amusement, no coy tone.

A part of me knows in that moment there will be no spark tonight. No fixing of anything, but I give it one more go. 'What does it look like?' I motion to my almost naked body. 'I'm cooking in my underwear.'

'Why?' I try not to hear the exasperated tone of Nate's voice. The one he uses when Oscar bounces around, being loud and silly and ignoring Nate's requests to sit still.

My smile slips, but I keep my head high. I am Georgie Bell and I am magnificent. 'Why do you think?' I reply with a raised eyebrow. 'I want us to reconnect. To be good again.' And then I say the words I've been avoiding. 'Because I'm scared that maybe our marriage is... not working.'

Nate watches me for a final second before crossing the kitchen without a word. I hold my breath, hoping he'll scoop me into his arms and tell me I'm being ridiculous. Instead, he moves past me and, reaches into the fridge. Grabs a beer.

'I'm too tired for this. You're acting nuts, Georgie.'

I laugh, the sound too bright, reaching for my wine and taking a long sip for extra courage. 'No more than usual.'

'You were just talking to yourself,' he replies.

'When?' I ask.

'Just now. Something about getting in a car.'

I freeze.

Oh God. I'm so used to talking to myself when I'm alone. What else have I said without realising?

'I'm just worried about us,' I say, softening my voice. 'I wanted to fix this.'

'Well, this isn't the way,' he replies, not even bothering to look back as he turns and walks out of the kitchen. His tone just now was casual, like I was an inconvenience, but the humiliation feels like a burn.

The sting is already rising behind my eyes as I stare at the empty doorway, heart thudding. I feel ridiculous, standing here in lace underwear like some desperate housewife cliché, offering myself up to a man who won't even meet my gaze.

I turn the oven off and follow him into the hall. My skin prickles with a chill that has nothing to do with the temperature. He's already halfway up the stairs, retreating. Always retreating. Back to his study, no doubt. My fists clench at my sides. What is he doing up there that's more important than this? Than me. Than saving our marriage.

'You don't get to walk away from me,' I call after him, my voice a hissed whisper. I don't want Oscar to wake up and hear us, but I can't stop the heat of my anger and humiliation either.

He turns slowly, beer still in hand.

'Why don't you want me anymore?' I ask, hating the way my voice cracks.

Nate's expression shifts, and just for a second, he doesn't look like the charming man I married. He looks like a cornered animal. Then his body sags, and he exhales slowly.

'I've been trying to find a way to say this for a while,' he says, and already the hurt is a deep welt in my chest. 'But this isn't working. I don't think we can be fixed.'

He moves to go. Like it's that easy to throw away ten years of marriage and the life I've built for us.

'Hey,' I call after him.

He pauses but doesn't turn to face me.

'Are you having an affair?' I think of the way he acted around Keira yesterday at the school drop-off. The issues in our marriage started long before Keira arrived, but I can't shake the feeling she's connected. 'With Keira?' I push.

That makes him look back. A frown pinches his brow. 'Who?'

'You know who,' I reply, my hands clenching at my sides.

He sighs. 'No. I'm not having an affair with Keira.'

'Then what happened between us?' I force out the question. 'You used to love me, Nate. You used to want me. Now you can't wait to leave any room I'm in.'

I wait for an answer that doesn't come. Instead, he just walks away, and somehow, that silence cuts deeper than anything he could've said. I swallow the anger clawing its way up my body. I want to yell after him, tell him I'm planning to kill someone for him. For us. For this marriage he's already halfway out of. For this life I'm far from done saving.

Everything can be fixed. And I will fix us, no matter what it takes.

PRESENT DAY

# THIRTY-TWO

## GEORGIE



My eyes ache from the harsh strip lighting, the kind that I know is making my skin look washed out and grey, showing my age, which no amount of Botox or retinol serum can hide. My entire body is hurting now. The effort of sitting up straight, shoulders back, face relaxed. The 'I've got my shit together' look I cultivated that day when sixteen-year-old me reinvented myself and stepped into the glass offices of the investment bank like I belonged.

I inhale slowly, stretching my fingers in my lap.

*I choose my own path.*

The mantra loops through my mind, holding me together by a thread as thin as the one that's held my marriage together for what seems like months. Now is not the time to falter.

Opposite me, Sató sits silently. I wonder if she can see the cracks appearing – the ones I feel running down my body, threatening to tear me apart. There's a black coffee on the table in front of me. Steam billows from the takeaway cup. Beside it is a sealed packet of two custard cream biscuits. The smell of bitter coffee hangs in the air, but it's the biscuits that keep catching my eye. I can almost taste the too-sweet crumbly biscuit. The sickly cream middle. I haven't eaten a custard cream in years. I can't remember the last time I ate anything sweet that wasn't the fruit in my smoothie. I've been dieting most of my life. Denying myself, controlling my eating, protecting my figure. Now I wonder why I bothered. Why does anyone else care that my waist size hasn't changed in ten years? I should've bought that donut this morning. Should've bought five.

My stomach rumbles in the quiet. Loud enough that Satō's gaze moves from me to the biscuits and back again. She's wondering why I don't eat them. I wouldn't know what to say if she asked. I've been this version of myself for so long, I don't know who else I'd be.

I reach for the coffee instead, taking a sip. It tastes foul, but at least it's something to stave off the hunger.

Satō taps the photo on the table in front of us. 'Do you know where we found this photograph?'

I nod. 'In Jonny's house,' I reply.

Satō's eyes are sharp as they watch me. 'Was he using this photo to blackmail you?' she asks.

'Yes,' I reply. The truth feels clunky after so many lies.

'When did the blackmail start?' Satō asks.

I push away the lump building in my throat before I reply. 'He showed me the photo the week he moved into Magnolia Close last year. He told me he knew everything about my past.'

'And what did he want from you, Georgie?' Satō asks.

The anxiety I've lived with for eighteen months floods back. The constant fear. The second-guessing. How I'd watch Nate watching me, wondering if he knew. If he'd guessed. Is that why my marriage fell apart? Nate – so observant – did he notice the shift? Maybe it wasn't even a conscious thing. Just a tiny alarm in the back of his mind that something was wrong.

'At first, he didn't want anything, except to rattle me,' I reply. 'Jonny got me on my own at the street party we held to welcome him to the close, and tried to kiss me.' I shiver at the memory. 'He didn't care that my husband and child were just outside. Every time he saw me after that, there were comments and suggestions. But it wasn't until the night of the quiz that he explicitly told me he wanted to have sex with me and told me what he'd do if I refused.'

Something in Sató's expression shifts, and I realise what I've admitted. 'In all the times we've talked in the last two weeks, Georgie, you've not mentioned seeing Jonny. Are you now saying that as well as going to his house after the quiz night ended and killing him, you also saw Jonny earlier that same evening?' she asks, sitting forward a fraction.

I pause. I hadn't planned to tell her about seeing Jonny. But I'm too far down the road to backtrack now. And I'm supposed to be admitting to murder anyway. The thought leaves me feeling unsettled and queasy. I'm here because I have to do this, not because I want to.

I have to do this. I repeat the words as I fix my gaze back on Sató. 'He was driving towards the gates into Magnolia Close as I was walking to the school. I was on my own. Tasha and Beth were running late, and I wanted more time in the school hall to set up. He stopped his car and got out. He said he was bored with playing games. He told me if I didn't have sex with him, he'd show Nate the photo.'

Sató taps her index finger on the photo – pushes it towards me. 'Who are the other people in this photo?'

The edges of my vision blur for a moment. I blink it away. Gather myself.

'Obviously, that's me in the centre,' I say, staring at the younger version of myself. The tailored black dress. Sleek blonde hair. Big eyelashes, bigger smile. 'To my right is Reggie

Chamberlain, my old boss. Next to him is Phil Ashford-Wells, a junior investment manager. And on my left... is Jonny.'

Satõ's brow furrows. 'Why is it you didn't want Nate or anyone else to know you and Jonny had a past?'

I press my lips together. My eyes burn with the truth pulsing just behind them. 'It was stupid of me to lie and pretend I didn't know Jonny. The moment I lied, it became this big thing. I'm sure you've seen by now how close we are as a community. We trust each other. If my neighbours – my friends – found out I'd lied, they'd stop trusting me. It's hard to explain, but when the trust is gone, people are ignored and treated differently. I saw it happen to the Gallaghers – the family who lived at number two before Jonny. I didn't want that to happen to me, or to Oscar and Nate.'

'And Nate – why did you lie to him? What's so damning about this photo, Georgie, that Jonny could use it to blackmail you?'

I hold myself still for a moment, feeling the truth squeeze me tight in its grasp. It feels pointless to lie now. 'The photo looks innocent enough, but I met Nate when he was investigating Reggie for insider trading. Nate interviewed me and asked me about these nights out. I lied to him and told him I wasn't part of it. If he'd seen this photo of me out with Reggie, he'd have known I'd lied. He'd have realised I was helping Reggie bend the rules and make extra money. Nate's entire career has been built on trying to stop these activities. If he found out the woman he married was part of it, he'd never have forgiven me. I didn't want to destroy our family over it. I thought I could fix it.'

'Fix it by killing Jonny?' Satõ asks.

I stare at the detective, open-mouthed. Silent. I've already confessed. Told her I killed Jonny, spun a version of the truth that suited the story I needed her to believe. But now she's circling closer, prodding at the cracks I thought were hidden.

The words lodge in my throat. I can feel everything starting to slip, just like it did after Keira sent those packages, after she made it clear that pretending this wasn't happening wouldn't protect us. Just like it did the night we got into Beth's car, hearts pounding, hands shaking, and drove through the country lanes to commit a murder.

I snatch at the packet of biscuits, ripping open the plastic and shoving one into my mouth. Sugary-sweetness hits my taste buds. I don't even like custard creams and yet right now this is the best thing I've ever eaten.

A single tear tracks down my face. There it is – the thought I've been avoiding. We didn't just plan to kill someone. We got in that car – me, Tasha and Beth – and we found Keira's ex, just where she said.

I did it to protect my family. To save my marriage. I keep telling myself that's my reason. That's all that matters. But sitting in this windowless room, scared and pretending not to be, I don't know if that's even true anymore.

2 DAYS EARLIER

# THIRTY-THREE

## TASHA

Beth's grey Volvo estate smells faintly of vanilla and car air freshener. I'm sitting in the back on the driver's side, wishing I were anywhere else.

Georgie can frame it any way she likes, but it's murder.

My knees press together, hands in fists on my lap. I can't stop shaking. My throat is tight, and tears are threatening behind my eyes. It feels like I've barely stopped crying for days. Every instinct in my body is screaming at me to escape. I want to say something, but the words are lodged in my throat. And what can I say now? Beth and Georgie have decided. They won't listen to me.

They're already suspicious. Accusing me of acting strangely since Jonny's murder. I had to tell them about Marc's job. Had to give them something. But I panicked and told them too much and mentioned Marc lying to me for three months. It opens the door for too many questions. Like the one I've been asking myself for days now – where has he been going if not to work? I couldn't tell them what he's really been doing. Pretending to go on business trips when really he'd been researching a vineyard in Devon and bought it without telling me. I still can't think beyond the lies to consider our future.

From the front passenger seat, Georgie twists around, checking if I'm still holding it together. Barely. She's wearing tight black leggings and a black turtleneck. Her blonde hair is scooped into a short ponytail at the nape of her neck, the front falling out and tucked behind her ears. I wonder how long she spent getting ready. How long she agonised over what to wear to commit this murder.

I look down at myself – yesterday's jeans and an old grey sweatshirt of Marc's, Lanie's mashed potatoes from lunch smeared across my chest. I look like a mess. I feel worse. I wonder what it must be like to have time to think about clothing choices. About anything. All I ever do is pull out the first thing I find, usually grabbing whatever was on the floor from yesterday or the top of the clean washing pile.

I don't know how to respond to the look Georgie offers. I can't smile. Can't speak. So instead, I drop my gaze and stare at Henry's booster seat, wondering where the crumbs are. The rice cakes and crisps ground into the footwell and the seats like in the back of my car. And where are Henry's toys? The ones brought for the journey then forgotten and left in a heap.

I'm glad I'm not driving. It isn't just the mess of my car or the car seats in the back; it's that I don't want to do this. It can't be right. Can it? But my car was never an option with the two car seats and one booster fixed in the back. Georgie offered to drive, but her Tesla has tracking on the app, and we couldn't risk someone finding out where we'd been. So it's Beth and her older-model Volvo.

The silence presses down on us as we take the turning towards Fordly Woods and the road ahead narrows into the winding country lane. Trees line both sides of the road, growing over in a canopy of browns and oranges, the shadows adding to the darkness of the evening creeping in.

The road ahead is empty, just like Keira said it would be. No houses. No people. No other cars. Just the three of us on our way to kill a man. If we don't, it isn't the threat of sending the recording to the police anymore or the evidence she has that scares me. It's Keira coming back to Magnolia Close. I think of Matilda and Sofia and Lanie asleep in their beds at night. Their silky black hair spread across their pillows, arms tucked around their favourite teddies. I can't think about that... She wouldn't... would she?

I blink away the tears and watch the trees whip by. Then we're slowing to a crawl and Beth is swinging into a layby between two old oak trees, their roots twisting through the earth like claws. And for a moment, a weight lifts and I can almost breathe. Because I think Beth has come to her senses and changed her mind.

'Why are we stopping?' Georgie asks.

'We're early,' Beth replies.

Tension crackles in the air, and I think Beth must feel it too because her hands are gripping the steering wheel. 'Are we really doing this?' she asks.

'No,' I say quickly at the same moment Georgie gives a firm, 'Yes.'

Georgie is quick to continue. 'We know from Keira that this Richard is a bad guy,' she says. 'He's a deadbeat dad, right? I know what we're doing is terrible, but maybe he deserves this, just like Jonny did.'

My heart races, my mind running just as fast. 'How do we know what she's said is true though?' I ask. 'Look at what she's making us do. We can't trust anything she says.'

'Why would she lie?' Beth asks.

'Why wouldn't she?' is all I can reply. 'For all we know, this could be about money. Or revenge. Or maybe she's just insane. She murdered a total stranger, remember? She's set this whole thing up so we'd kill her ex while she has an alibi. And she's threatening to harm our families. Our children—' My voice breaks, and I don't bother trying to fight it.

We fall silent again. I glance at the clock – 5.02 p.m. Three minutes. Three minutes until our lives change forever.

Out of nowhere, I think of Lily Gallagher. Back when she was still our friend – still one of us. I picture her in one of her floaty maxi dresses, fabric clinging to the curve of her belly, her hips, her enormous chest. She was always baking. Always arriving with a rich, sticky traybake or gooey brownies. No gluten-free almond crunch like Beth. No dry protein bars like Georgie. Just proper icing, sugar in everything. I think because Joshua was a few years older than our kids, we all looked up to her. The reassurance of hearing 'it's just a phase' when Matilda would only eat toast without crusts and Oscar refused to potty train. She softened the brittle edges of our personalities with her jolliness. Georgie was less fixated on fitness and calories and mantras. Beth was less bitter, a little chattier too. Me? I was more relaxed around Lily. Freezer food again for dinner – who cares?

God, the number of times she hugged me tight and said, 'You're doing brilliantly, Tasha. You've got this.' I felt like I lived for those hugs some days. But that was before they announced they were moving one Christmas. By January, everything had turned sour.

It was New Year's Eve at Georgie's where it all fell apart. We'd agreed a vegetarian buffet for the party. Andrea was on one of her health kicks, and Beth had recently become a vegetarian too. But Lily turned up with duck spring rolls we all ate before realising. Andrea called her out, of course – the first to speak her mind. Lily laughed it off, said it was a miscommunication. But then she and Kevin left early without helping to clear up or say goodbye. That's when Georgie noticed the missing ornament – a little burnished gold heart from her mantel. Something Lily had admired more than once.

We all leaped on it. The theft. The betrayal. Bill wanted to call the police he was so infuriated. We decided to turn our backs on them instead. No replies to messages. No greetings. No goodbye.

But sitting in this car now, seconds from doing the unthinkable – I can't help but wonder if we were wrong. The Lily I knew wasn't a liar, and she certainly wasn't a thief. What if someone set her up? Their move out of Magnolia Close wasn't the first that left a bad feeling among the residents. Beth once told me that David and Mags, who lived in our house before us had poisoned the front lawns with weedkiller after an argument over the length of grass on the close. But I remember the elderly couple who'd showed us the house on our first viewing. They didn't look vengeful. They looked sweet. They looked nervous.

I don't know the truth behind Lily and Kevin's move or the couple in the house before us, but I know I'm scared to tell anyone Marc's plans. I thought Magnolia Close was a safe place. A community where we all looked out for each other. But now Jonny is dead and someone on the close has been secretly spying on us all.

I shiver. The car feels too still, too silent. But then Beth shifts the car into gear and moves slowly away, and I'm dragged back to this awful moment. In the last few minutes, it feels like night has closed in around us the way it does in the autumn. One minute it's day. The next it's dark. Ahead of us, the lane is cast in gloom and still empty, but then we round a bend and the road straightens out and there he is. The man from Keira's phone, wearing navy shorts and a fluorescent top, jogging with steady strides down the lane towards us. Earbuds in. Oblivious to what's coming for him.

Beth taps the accelerator, and we pick up speed.

I dig my nails into my palms. It's like being on a roller-coaster. That second when the harness locks and you can't get out. The slow tick, tick, tick as you move up the tracks, knowing the drop is coming. Wanting to get off. Unable to move.

I want to shout for Beth to stop. I want to scream that this is insane. But I can't speak. Can't move. I wish I could escape. I wish I was standing in those fields I picture when the world feels too much, but there's no way out of this.

Beth changes gear again, and the car jerks forward, faster now.

The man is running on the side of the road. Beth would barely have to move the wheel to plough straight into him.

Fifty metres.

Twenty.

Faster and faster.

Ten metres.

I scrunch my eyes shut, waiting for the thud of impact.

We can't—

# THIRTY-FOUR

## TASHA

'No,' I cry out, my voice barely above a whisper, but it's enough to force my eyes open. In a split second, the world sharpens: the blur of the trees flashing past the window, the long stretch of empty lane, the grip of Beth's knuckles white on the steering wheel... and the runner. He's so close now I can see the gleam of sweat on his forehead, the shock widening his eyes, the moment he registers the danger he's in.

Guilt floods my body, gnarly like the tree roots. It's the guilt I carry every day. For my parents and how much more they need from me than I can give. For the girls, who never get the best of me or enough of me. For Marc, who despite everything I now know, bears the brunt of my fraying edges. And for my two best friends, who don't know the whole truth, who I'm starting to question if I can trust. The burden is already too much. I can't add the murder of this man.

I can't do this.

'Stop.' My voice is louder this time, high-pitched and jolting – a hammer to glass. It shatters the tension in the car, and suddenly we're swerving. Beth yanks the wheel to one side, slamming her foot on the brake. The car skids, hitting the gravel edge, veering so close to the trees I think we're going to hit them, going to die. Then we stop with a hard jolt. My body is thrown against the seat belt then slammed back as it locks in place.

The engine stalls. The only sound is the roar of blood in my ears and the heaving breaths we're all taking. Then there's a shout from outside. I twist round and look through the rear window. The runner is walking towards us, his face a mask of shock and fury.

'Hey!' he shouts, hands waving wildly in the air. 'You almost hit me!'

Beth sits forward, fumbling to restart the engine, her hands shaking. She can't get the key to turn. The man raps on her window with his knuckles.

'Sorry,' she stammers. 'I lost concentration.'

Her words do nothing to placate him. 'You almost killed me,' he says, reaching for the door handle, but it's locked, thank God. 'I'm reporting this to the police,' he shouts. 'This is dangerous driving.'

'I'm sorry,' Beth mouths again as the man unzips a pocket on his jacket and pulls out his phone. A second later, he's pointing it at the car – at us – and talking loudly. 'My name is Paul Shortly. I was running along Fordly Lane at five p.m. when this car almost hit me. The driver was clearly speeding.' He steps back, recording the licence plate of Beth's car.

He's making a video, I realise, just as his words register. It must click in Georgie's head at the same time because suddenly she's leaning over Beth and calling to the man.

'Hey, did you say your name is Paul Shortly?' Georgie asks. Her voice is inquisitive and casual, but loud enough for him to hear outside the car. And it's only because I know her as well as I do that I hear the edge to her voice that gives away the panic she's trying to hide.

The man frowns, thrown by the change of direction. He looks from Beth to Georgie and then glances in the back to me.

It's a fight not to duck down and cover my face. 'So?' he replies, stopping his recording.

Beth's hands are still fumbling with the key, and suddenly the engine starts. The man doesn't step back.

'Hang on,' Georgie says to Beth before raising her voice to be heard. 'You're not Richard? You don't have a daughter called Rowan?'

'What are you talking about?' he asks as confusion replaces the set of anger in his face. 'I don't have kids. Who are you?'

'Are you saying you don't know a woman called Keira?' I blurt out, leaning forward in my seat, needing to be sure. My mind spins, trying to make sense of what he's saying. This is the man from the photograph Keira sent us – the right face, the right place, the right time. But he's acting like he doesn't know them.

The man steps back from the window, his frown deepening. 'What is this? Was that on purpose just now? Jesus.' He scrubs a hand over his face. 'I'm reporting this to the police.'

In the next second, Beth has thrown the car into gear and is pulling away, leaving the man standing in the road, still angry, still shocked.

We drive in silence. My heart won't slow down.

Who did we almost kill? I try to gather myself, to cling on to whatever it is inside me that makes me *me*. I cast around for my to-do list. I think about tomorrow. The house needs... I really should... The girls will want...

Nothing comes.

How many times have I wished I could turn off my thoughts, step outside myself and have a break? But I never meant like this. I can't think. Nothing makes sense.


Ten minutes later, we're parked at the back of an empty retail car park. The engine off. The silence heavy.

Beth shifts in her seat and looks from Georgie to me. Her face is ghostly pale. 'Was that man even Keira's ex? He said his name was Paul, not Richard. That was the name of Keira's ex, right? Richard Philips. And that man – Paul – said he didn't have children either.'

'Could he have been a different runner?' Georgie asks.

'No,' I reply. 'She sent us a photo, remember? It was him.'

There's a wildness in Georgie's blue eyes I've never seen before. A part of me is reassured that she seems as shaken as I am, but mostly the realisation only adds to the roaring panic inside me. Nothing rattles Georgie.

'But,' Georgie says with a frown, 'if that man wasn't her ex, who did we almost kill?'

'You mean, who did I almost kill?' Beth whispers, her voice hollow.

An icy cold trickles through my blood. I'm shivering, my whole body trembling. 'But why would Keira lie?' I ask. 'Why set us up to kill that man if he's not her ex?'

'Maybe she wanted him dead for another reason,' Georgie says. 'And used us to do it.'

'If Jonny wasn't killed so we'd kill her ex, then why did she kill him?' I ask. 'And who else does she want dead?'

'Yeah. And the other thing I can't get my head around is where she got the key for Jonny's place from?'

'I assume he let her in,' Beth says. 'Then she took a key after she'd killed him?'

'Maybe,' Georgie says, not sounding convinced. 'None of this is making sense.'

'Because she's crazy,' I cry.

'It doesn't matter,' Georgie says. She sits up a little straighter, and when her eyes meet mine, they are sharp and determined. 'What matters is what we do now.'

'What do you mean?' I ask.

'I mean,' Georgie starts, 'she probably won't know we didn't kill that man until tomorrow, right? We have tonight to act.'

Beth shoots Georgie a look, her expression apprehensive. 'Act how?'

'Keira said she hid evidence in Jonny's house that incriminates us. She took my gloves and your scarf that night in the pub, remember? And I have the key she sent me. So let's go to Jonny's house and find the things of ours she's hidden.'

'It isn't just the evidence she has and the police finding out though,' I say. 'She threatened to come back to Magnolia Close. We know she's crazy. She could kill our children.' Fear is a jagged rock in my throat.

'But we have to try, don't we?' Georgie replies. 'We have to do something.'

'The police have already searched Jonny's house,' Beth says. 'If it was obvious, they'd have found it.'

'Maybe,' Georgie says. 'Or maybe they didn't know it was important, but we will.'

Beth looks at me, and I nod my agreement. The thought of breaking into a dead man's house is crazy, but it's better than killing someone.

Beth starts the engine and pulls away, the car feeling like it's moving at a snail's crawl after the speed on the country lanes.

My mind darts to Marc. To the secrets he's been keeping. Jonny knew what he was doing during those three months Marc pretended to go to work. He knew because he was helping him.

If there's any paperwork in Jonny's house that links us to the loan he gave Marc or the vineyard he wanted to invest in with him, I need to find it before Beth and Georgie do. Until we're out of this nightmare with Keira, I can't risk them turning their backs on me.

# THIRTY-FIVE

## BETH

We leave the car at the top of the road and slip through the gates, sticking to the shadows. Magnolia Close is quiet, lit only by the glow of porch lights and the ornate streetlamps. It's nearly 7 p.m. I told Alistair I'd be home by now. The dinner will be in the oven waiting for me, and all I want is to go home. My gaze drifts to our house. There's a light on in the bathroom. He'll be finishing up bath time with Henry.

Jonny's house looms ahead. It looks darker now. Empty. Sinister. Like it's absorbed the violence that happened inside. Georgie steps ahead. She reaches the front door like she's done it a hundred times before – key in hand, no hesitation. It slides into the lock with a soft click, and then she's inside, Tasha and I following a step behind.

Jonny's house is cold. Someone must have turned the heating off. Tasha shivers beside me, her eyes distant. She hasn't said much since the country lanes.

'We can't turn the lights on, so use the torches on your phones,' Georgie says. 'But keep them angled low so it's not seen in the windows.'

There are times when Georgie's 'go get 'em' attitude to life is overbearing, but right now, I'm grateful.

'We should split up,' Georgie adds. 'Beth, you and Tasha check upstairs. I'll start down here.'

'No, I'll take the living room,' I reply, the words coming in a rush. I feel Georgie and Tasha's eyes on me, but I keep my lips pinned shut and my head down as I move through the house. I can't go upstairs again. Upstairs is where Jonny was murdered, and I'm already on edge. Every time I close my eyes, I see that runner – his face, the moment it turned from exertion to terror. The way my hands clenched the steering wheel. The seconds blur in my mind. It all happened so fast, but even before Tasha shouted, I was swerving. I wouldn't have gone through with it. I couldn't kill a stranger. An innocent man. No matter what the stakes are, I'm not that person.

The living room is minimalist. A white leather sofa. A glass coffee table. I hear the floorboards creak from the room above, where Georgie and Tasha are moving around. I focus on the drawers in front of me. One after another. Batteries and cables and a stack of old phones. Nothing incriminating. Nothing tucked away that says the three of us were involved in Jonny's murder.

I search for a couple of minutes before there's movement on the stairs. Two sets of footsteps. A moment later, Georgie is in the doorway. 'Anything?' she asks.

I shake my head. 'You?'

'No.'

'We need to hurry,' Tasha says, the panic making her breathless. 'If we're caught, there's no way to explain it.'

The last drawer is filled with manuals to the sound system and a handful of kitchen appliances. No scarf of mine or gloves of Georgie's. At the bottom, there's a stack of photographs. I pick them up, angling my torch so I can look at each one. They're the usual old holiday snaps. A younger Jonny on a beach, tanned and muscular. Jonny driving a speedboat, a bottle of beer in one hand. Jonny at a bar with friends. In every shot, there's the same smug smile. My stomach knots. I swear I can smell his aftershave – always too strong, too much. That proprietary way he always stepped into my space.

I hear his voice then. After I let myself into his house that time to turn off his speakers. The gilded threat that he'd do the same. Then we saw each other again on the street in London. *'Hello, Beth. We must stop meeting like this.'*

I feel sick. Heart racing. Mouth dry. I hate him. Even now. Even dead, I hate him. I move to the next photo and freeze.

'Oh my God,' I whisper. 'Look at this.'

Georgie is by my side in a second. She grabs the photo from my hand like it's on fire.

'Oh,' she says, like she was expecting something else. 'It's Keira.'

'And Jonny,' I add quietly.

Tasha joins us, peering over Georgie's shoulder.

'They knew each other?' she says, blinking like she's trying to make the image make sense.

I move closer, shining my torch onto the photo. It's dark and a little blurry, but that's Keira's wide grin and that's Jonny with his arm slung possessively around her. Both younger but unmistakably them.

'She knew Jonny,' Georgie mutters. 'I'm surprised the police left these photos.'

It feels like a slow, creeping, awful realisation has started to wind around us. 'This was never about her ex, was it?' I say. 'Or whoever that man was tonight. It was about Jonny. It was always about Jonny.'

'If she knew him,' Georgie says, 'she probably had her own reasons for wanting him dead. We all did.'

'So she saw an opportunity that night in the pub?'

Tasha shakes her head. 'No. It was more than that. I

remember at the time feeling like she'd overheard our conversation. It wasn't just seeing an opportunity; it was seeking us out. Manipulating us.' There's a tremor in Tasha's voice as she looks between us. 'She knew we hated Jonny, and she used that. She saw a group of women drinking too much wine, all of us angry. And she saw a way to get what she wanted – and protect herself at the same time.'

'You're right,' I whisper, my pulse racing, my head light. 'But why not just kill him and disappear?' I ask. 'Every time we find an answer, it feels like it leads to more questions. I just don't get it. Why go to the trouble of finding us, encouraging us into planning his murder? Why drag us into this whole sick game? And tonight... what if we'd actually gone through with it? What then?'

Georgie's eyes narrow. 'Then she'd have had us. Properly. Not just a recording, not just us fearing for our families. We'd have been as bad as her. Murderers. It would've bought our silence.'

Tasha's face is pale. 'I feel like we're missing something.'

Georgie and I turn to look at Tasha. 'But what?' I ask.

'She could easily have killed Jonny and walked away without involving us,' Tasha replies.

'Yeah, but she's crazy,' I hiss, feeling the panic take hold. 'This was never part of a murder-swap deal. She just wanted cover. She wanted to make us the fall guys if the police ever realised her connection to him.'

'I don't know,' Tasha starts again, biting her lower lip. 'She's crazy, but she's not stupid. And bringing us into this feels really risky for her. What do you think, Georgie?'

'I'm not sure either,' Georgie agrees. 'Something isn't adding up.'

'The important thing is—'

My next words stop dead. There's a sound. A door banging.

Footsteps from my garden. A second later, a light clicks on outside.

We drop into a crouch, hiding beside the sofa.

'It's Alistair,' I whisper, heart hammering. He can't find me here. 'He's in our garden.'

We fumble to turn our torches off as the silence stretches, each second longer than the last. I don't dare move. Don't dare breathe.

Then there's a flutter in my stomach. Not fear or nerves. Something softer. Butterfly wings brushing against my belly from within. The faintest movement but unmistakable. The baby. My baby. She's moving.

Tears spring to my eyes.

I should be home. I should be with Alistair. I should be curled up on the sofa with my hand on my bump and a cup of herbal tea in my hand, not hiding in a dead man's house.

I did this for Alistair. For us. For my baby. I can't lose it all now because of Jonny.

# THIRTY-SIX

## GEORGIE

I'm shaking as I peel off my clothes in the en-suite bathroom, allowing the warmth from the heated floor tiles to seep into the chill that's settled inside me. Tonight has been... a lot. We almost killed a man. And the worst part? I wanted Beth to do it. I thought it was our only way to fix everything, to get us out of this nightmare.

What if we'd gone through with it? At least we have something on Keira now. Our own evidence to use against her like she's been doing with us.

I draw in a long, steady inhale, releasing the air slowly. I stare at my reflection in the mirror above the sink, trying to ignore the tremor in my hands and the terror in my eyes, and ground myself in my present.

I make myself look at the slate-grey tiles, the white walls, the polished chrome. Then I close my eyes, feel that heat in my toes, and the scent of eucalyptus from a diffuser in the corner. 'I am blessed,' I whisper.

I step into the shower and let the hot water wash away the fear I felt in Jonny's house tonight. Beth holding up that photograph. I swear my heart faltered, and I couldn't stop myself from snatching it from her hands as though if I was fast enough, Beth would unsee it.

But it wasn't the photo I was looking for – the real reason I suggested going to Jonny's house – it was Keira and Jonny arm in arm in what looked like an old holiday snap. Their faces slightly blurred.

The water steams around me as I scrub at my skin with the frangipani monoi salt glow body scrub. Just one of dozens of expensive indulgences I cherish in my daily routine and share on my Insta stories. But right now, it feels like a scour on my skin. Like I can rub away the fear and panic of the night.

I shiver and turn up the temperature. Hot water needles my skin, burning like the sting of Nate's rejection last night.

'*I don't think we can be fixed,*' he said.

It isn't just the humiliation of standing in my underwear, offering myself up, trying to fix whatever has broken between us. It's the fact he doesn't want to try. Doesn't care enough to try. Not for me. And not for Oscar. That's what really hurts. Our sweet little boy who loves dinosaurs and Lego and pretending to be a pirate. How do we tell him his perfect world is being torn apart?

'You'll change your mind,' I whisper, putting my back to the water and letting the needles pummel the knot at the nape of my neck. 'I haven't done all this to let you go.'

After my shower, I pull on my tartan pyjamas – the ones I bought in matching sets last Christmas and posed with in front of the tree. Oscar wore his for a week straight, but now they're too small in the legs. Nate never wore his after that first photo.

Still, I like mine. I wouldn't usually wear them downstairs. Choosing something more fitted – sexier – in the evenings, but after Nate's rejection last night and everything we did earlier, I crave cosy and warm.

I check on Oscar, slipping silently into his room, tiptoeing over the obstacle course of books and plastic toys scattered across his floor. He's asleep, duvet half-kicked off, a little damp curl of hair stuck to his forehead. I kiss the top of his head and fight back a sob as I tuck his favourite bear a little closer. I will not destroy his world. I will do whatever it takes to protect it.

I pad downstairs and find Nate by the living-room window with a glass of wine, lights off, like the night of Jonny's death. I linger in the doorway, unsure and unsettled. We've shared our lives and our bed for over ten years, and I don't know what to say to my husband.

It's Nate who fills the silence. 'I think it's about time you told me what's going on,' he says without moving his gaze from the window.

My pulse stutters. How long has he been watching at the window? We were careful when we went to Jonny's house. Beth parked her car outside the gates and we slipped through, sticking to the shadows. But if he was watching closely, he would've seen us. Anyone could have.

I force a lightness into my voice. 'I don't know what you're talking about,' I say, turning away on trembling legs. He isn't the only one who knows how to leave a room. Suddenly, the desire to flee is stronger than the need to talk to Nate and find a way for our marriage to work. He knows something. I'm certain of it.

'Georgie,' Nate calls after me.

I pause.

'I want a divorce,' he says.

Ice floods my body. Four words. That's all it takes to unravel everything I've worked for. My heart lodges in my throat.

'I don't,' I reply, the words barely a croak. 'I want to try. I want you to try. If not for me, then for Oscar. Please, Nate. We can be good again. I know it. I'll do anything.'

I step back into the living room and curl myself up on the sofa. I wonder if he's kept the lights off not to watch the neighbours but to make this moment easier. In the dark, he doesn't have to see my hurt. Coward!

I try to reach for his hand, but he moves it away and sighs like I'm just another board meeting he doesn't want to attend.

'Do you know how exhausting your toxic positivity is, Georgie? Do you know how tiring you are to live with day in day out? The constant photos you want me to pose in. Then checking how many hits and comments. You're obsessed with posting our entire lives online and going viral. It's exhausting trying to live up to the expectations of who you think you are and who you want everyone to think we are. We're just normal people. I want to be normal.'

'I can change,' I say, too fast.

He shakes his head in the darkness. 'No, you can't. And you shouldn't have to.'

'But—'

'You live in a delusion,' he says.

I grit my teeth to the hurt cracking in my chest. 'That's not true.'

'It is,' he replies. 'You think you're this amazing, superior person, but you're just... so fucking ordinary. And there's nothing wrong with that. You're a normal mum. A housewife. Maybe if you'd accepted that...' He trails off for a second; shakes his head. 'But you think you're some kind of super mum influencer who's going to take over the world one day, and you're not.'

The words slice through me. He's blaming me. The failure of our marriage isn't because of all the times he shuts himself away and ignores us. All the ways he shows he's bored of us. It's all me. After everything I've done. Every compromise, every sacrifice, every dark, terrible thing I've done to protect us, and this is how it ends? All I've ever wanted is to be enough. And instead, I've never felt more disposable.

'You can't blame me for all of this,' I reply, forcing myself not to break. I'm keeping myself together with sticky tape, but it's holding for now.

'That's not what I'm saying.'

'It sounds like it,' I push. 'Because what about you, Nate? You checked out of this a long time ago. You're a great dad and a great husband when it suits you. But a lot of the time, you can't be bothered. And you ignore us. Do you have any idea how painful that is?'

'I don't mean to ignore you or Oscar—'

'You stopped trying to see the good in me,' I carry on while I still can. 'You go out night after night instead of spending time with us.'

A niggling, awful feeling sweeps over me. Suddenly, I'm thinking of the moment in the playground when he was talking to Keira. The anger in her eyes. The hardness in Nate's expression.

'You *are* having an affair with Keira, aren't you? Admit it.' The question is blurted and rushed. I don't even know why I say it, only that even now, with my world falling apart, I can't shake the feeling I'm missing something.

Another deep sigh sounds in the dark living room. 'I told you, I'm not,' he says.

'Then what were you two talking about the other day? And don't you dare tell me it was nothing because I know it was something, and you've just told me you want a divorce, so I believe I'm owed some honesty here.'

After a pause, he says, 'Keira recognised me.'

'What do you mean?' I ask.

'From a dating app.'

My mouth drops open. I'm not sure if I breathe as I repeat his words. 'A dating app? You're using a dating app? Why?' The moment I ask the question, I wish I could snatch it back. It's obvious why, isn't it? Nate wanted to meet other women. My ears ring. I can't tell if it's rage or grief building inside me. Both.

'For what it's worth, I'm sorry,' he says. 'I never meant for it to go so far. I set up a profile just to see who would like it, and then I started getting messages.' He clears his throat. Suddenly, I'm glad it's dark and I can't see his face.

'It felt good to talk to other women,' he continues. 'And then at some point, I just... started going on dates.'

'Dates? Like one date just to chat and then you'd come home again?' I can feel myself trying to justify this. Make it OK.

Nate makes another noise in his throat. 'Sometimes.'

'You slept with them?' I force myself to ask, even though it feels more like a statement than a question. Our own sex life has been non-existent for so long.

'Some of them,' Nate admits. 'I'm sorry, Georgie. I just wanted to spend time with women who didn't drain me the way you do.'

I shatter at that final comment. The sticky tape gives way under the weight of my grief, and the tears start to fall. 'How long for?' I ask. The answer doesn't matter, but I have to know.

I sense him shrug in the darkness. 'A few months. Six maybe.'

All those nights out. I should've known, but I didn't want to see it. The hurt cuts into my throat. Tears sting my eyes, and I have to bite down on the inside of my cheek to stop any more from falling.

*Don't you dare let him see you cry, Georgie Bell.*

What the hell happened to Nate's moral compass? The man I married saw the world in black and white. Good and evil. In loyalty. Choose a side and stick with it. The man I married wouldn't...

Then I realise how wrong I've been about everything. How stupid! All those times I felt Nate watching me. Fearing he'd figured out I'd been insider trading with Reggie all those years ago. I thought he could see my lies. But it was never about me. It was about him. He was worried about *his* lies. He's been working up the courage to tell me this. I should be relieved, but I'm not.

'Did Jonny know?' I ask because suddenly I know. The memory slams into me – Jonny that night at the gates when I was on my way to set up for the quiz night. The night he died. That flirtatious smile. The threat.

Nate takes a long swig of wine before answering. 'Yes. Jonny was my friend. I told him our marriage was over.'

'When?' I ask.

'When what?'

'When did you tell him?'

Nate shrugs again. 'The week before he died, I think.'

It suddenly makes sense. That's when Jonny changed. All these months, he's been keeping my secret, dangling the threat of telling Nate over me. If Nate told him our marriage was over, he'd have realised he was about to lose his leverage. The game he was playing would've been over. It's why he was pushing me to sleep with him and scare me while he still had the chance. Bastard!

'Is the hidden camera yours?' I ask.

Nate laughs bitterly. 'What? No. Why would you think that?'

'Come on,' I reply. 'Don't pretend you don't enjoy knowing what everyone is doing?'

He's quiet for a moment. 'Fair enough. But why would I need a camera when I've got a perfect view of the street from my study?'

'You're not there all the time,' I push.

He shrugs. 'True. But it wasn't me. And I don't really care whether you believe that or not.'

'So if you've got nothing to hide, why is there a lock on your study door?'

He looks surprised for a moment, and I can see in his face that he knows I was snooping. 'For your information, I found Oscar playing on the top floor landing one evening while you were out at one of your meetings. You know what a tornado he is. I was worried about my computer equipment, so I put a lock on the door to make sure he couldn't go in there.'

In the beat of time that passes between us, I think I might hate my husband. But love him or hate him, I do believe him. I might not know Nate as well as I thought I did, but a hidden camera really isn't his style, and the explanation of the lock on his door makes sense. Oscar does have a habit of knocking drinks over and breaking things in his battles with imaginary dinosaurs.

'What's going on, Georgie?' Nate asks. 'Why are you asking about Jonny and cameras and trying to go into my study?'

'Don't turn this on me,' I say, deflecting the question. 'We're nowhere near done talking about you.'

'We're over. What more is there to say?' he asks.

'I think I have a right to know why you were dating other women, Nate? What wasn't I giving you?'

'It's honestly just like I said – I wanted to spend time with women that didn't drain me of energy. That didn't make me feel like I was living a fake life inside a magazine shoot. But it turns out all women are crazy.'

'What are you talking about?'

'One of the dates found out I was married and called me up, screaming down the phone at me. Absolute psycho.'

'The night of the quiz?' Not a reality TV show then, like he told the police.

I grit my teeth, fighting the desire to scream. To throw something. To storm out. To collapse to the ground and cry and cry. I've lied. I've schemed. I've almost helped commit murder. All for nothing. And still a part of me is clinging to the belief that everything can be fixed.

PRESENT DAY

Strangers on a Train WhatsApp Group

Saturday, 18 October, 8.14 a.m.

Georgie
*We know you knew Jonny! We have a photograph of the two of you together. We're taking it to the police and telling them everything. This ends now.*

Keira
*You think they'll believe one photo over all the evidence against you?*

Keira
*If you really want this to end, all of you meet me in the coffee shop on Portland Street. 10 a.m.! Don't be late.*

Keira
*And bring the packages I sent you.*


Magnolia Mums WhatsApp Group

Saturday, 18 October, 8.17 a.m.

Beth
*Are we going to go?*

Tasha
*What choice do we have?*

Georgie
*I agree. I think we have to go.*

*We have something on Keira now. We can end this.*

Tasha
*Marc has already left to play golf. I've got the girls.*

Georgie
*So has Nate. I don't want to bring the kids.*

Beth
*It's fine. Alistair said he'll have them all.*

Tasha
*Even Lanie?*

Beth
*He said it'll be good practice.*

Georgie
*He's a lifesaver.*

# THIRTY-SEVEN

## GEORGIE

The coffee shop is rammed with the Saturday crowd. Families with pushchairs, runners with dogs. Harassed-looking dads with toddlers eating croissants. The noise is chatter and clinking cups, the scrape of chairs against the tiled floor. It smells of coffee beans and pastries, reminding me of when we'd come here after the rhyme time session at the library when the children were little. Me, Beth and Tasha with Henry, Matilda, and Lily and Joshua too before she left. We'd order toasted tea cakes and babyccinos and talk about milestones and nap schedules and husbands and Magnolia Close.

Now we're silent. Waiting to meet a killer. Fighting to get our lives back. All of yesterday we waited for Keira's next message – next voice note. Next threat.

There was nothing.

None of us slept last night, and when I woke up this morning to the reality of Nate asking for a divorce and then leaving to play golf like his life is just going to carry on, I knew I had to do something to fix this. I couldn't stand the waiting anymore. I didn't want the threat to Oscar hanging over me for a second longer. So I messaged Keira.

Beneath the tension circling our table is a pang of sadness. Everything is changing. The children are growing up, and Beth will have another baby soon, and she and Tasha will go to baby groups together again – and where will that leave me? On the outside, watching a life I used to have slip further away. I've tried to picture what comes next – Oscar split between two homes. Nate told me this morning over coffee that he wants to sell the house. *'We'll both be able to afford something half decent if we sell this place,'* he said with the same nonchalance as deciding what to eat for dinner.

I've tried to imagine living in a smaller house on a nothing road far from Magnolia Close. I've tried to tell myself I could rebuild. Reinvent. Thrive. But every time I close my eyes, all I see is grey. Gloom. A future that looks nothing like the bright, glittering one I worked so hard to protect.

A waitress appears at our table, notebook in hand. Her hair is wispy, and her face is tight. She looks run ragged and stressed. 'Ready to order?' she asks. It's the second time she's come to our table.

'So sorry. Just one more minute,' I say with my sweetest smile as I check the time. 'We're just waiting on someone.'

The waitress frowns, the corner of her mouth twitching like she's holding back a sigh, and then steps away without a word, retreating towards the counter. The bell above the door jingles. All three of us jump, but it's not Keira. Just another group, eyeing our table, trying to work out if we've just sat down or are just leaving.

'Where is she?' Tasha hisses, eyes darting from our faces to the menu we're all pretending to look at.

My stomach rumbles. I couldn't face my smoothie this morning or my usual positivity post on Insta.

*'You're just... so fucking ordinary.'*

Hurt slices through me every time I hear those words repeated in my thoughts.

Beth's eyes never leave the door. 'Keira doesn't strike me as someone who adheres to timekeeping.'

'She's playing with us,' I say.

Beth nods. 'She knows we'll wait,' she says. 'It's a final power play. We have the photograph now – proof she knew Jonny – and this is her way of trying to remind us that she's still in charge.'

'I want my life back,' Tasha whispers, biting her thumbnail, eyes darting between us. 'Are we really going to show the photo to DS Sató?' she asks.

'I don't know,' I reply, feeling suddenly uncertain. Adrift. I want my life back too, but what life is that? The marriage I've been pretending isn't rotten and dead. I'm an admin assistant working part-time in an estate agent's. Chair of the PTA. Host of the Magnolia Close residents' group. Chief party planner for our events. An Instagram influencer without the followers I need to be seen. It's pathetic. I'm pathetic. My life isn't big and beautiful and amazing. It's empty and ordinary, just like Nate said.

'I'm sorry,' Tasha says again, and something sharp coils inside me. I want to tell her to stop apologising, to just get on with it. Sorry isn't going to save us now. 'But is there an option,' she continues, voice small, 'where Keira agrees we all walk away from today? She's got things on us. We have something on her. No one goes to the police. We pretend none of this ever happened.'

I want to believe that. I want to believe we can walk away from this today, but as I look between my friends, see the fear tightening Beth's mouth and the guilt swimming in Tasha's eyes, I know the truth – we all know it. It's not going to be that easy. Not anymore.

Keira has threatened our families. Gone to extreme lengths to drag us into something none of us understand. There's no way this is over. Not by a long shot. But still, I'm resolute on one thing – we can't go to the police. We can't talk to DS Sató. This mess we're in is ours to fix.

The bell jingles again. Another group enters the café looking for a table. The waitress gives us a pointed look, and I shake my head. 'She's not coming,' I say to Tasha and Beth. 'We should leave.'

It's as we're gathering our coats that our phones buzz in unison. I pull out my phone, my heart suddenly racing as the words of the message blur and then sharpen. Panic surges through me, tightening around my lungs like a vice.

*I have your children. Do exactly what I say or you'll*
*never see them again.*

Beside me, Tasha gasps. Beth sways on her feet like she's going to collapse. A hand flies to her mouth. Only I remain frozen. Body. Mind. Unable to process the message. She has my son. My entire world.

'She's lying,' I say. Hope. Beg. Pray. 'She has to be.'

'Call Alistair,' Tasha whispers. Beth's hands fumble with her phone as she pushes out of the café, Tasha and I following her out onto the high street. The day is bright, and the air bites with a faint promise of winter.

We move away from the shoppers on their way to the market and stand on the corner of a narrow road, leading to a used record shop. Beth taps her phone, holding it to her ear. I want to tell her to put it on speaker, but it's too late, she's already talking.

'Hey,' she says, trying to keep her voice light. 'Everything OK with the kids?'

There's a pause. A second. Maybe two. Too long. Beth's face drains of colour. Her eyes flick wildly between us. Keira isn't lying. She has Oscar. The fear threatens to crush me.

'Do you know where they went?' she asks, that same fear in her voice.

Another pause.

'You let them go? With someone you've met once? Alistair, she's a stranger. We don't know her.'

She falls silent.

'I know, I'm sorry. It's just... we don't know this woman. Please go and get them.' There's a shorter pause, and then Beth says, 'Thank you.'

Beth ends the call, her bottom lip trembling. 'Keira came to the house. She told Alistair she'd been knocking for all of us. She told Alistair that she was there to collect the children for a pirate playdate. She told him she'd arranged it with us last week, and Alistair assumed we'd forgotten and let them go.'

'And he believed her?' Tasha asks.

Beth looks like she's going to be sick. 'He thought it was harmless. He said Henry was really excited to go, and Keira gave him her address and suggested he collect them after lunch.'

'Lanie—' Tasha starts.

'She's with Alistair,' Beth says. 'She's safe.'

'But the others aren't,' I add and even though my voice is steel, I'm cracking inside. Oscar is my whole world. If anything happens to him, I won't survive it.

Beth's gaze shoots to mine. 'He's on his way there now. He's going to drive. He'll be there in a minute. I'll message him,' she says, tapping on the screen. 'And tell him to call me when he gets there.'

Another flurry of messages from Keira land.

*Do exactly what I say.*

*Go to the police station and confess to Jonny's murder.*
*Convince the detective you're all guilty. All of you. You*

*had your chance to kill my ex and you failed. Now you'll
take the blame for this before the police link me to Jonny.*

*If you do this, I'll return your children to Alistair and
they'll come to no harm.*

'Oh God,' Tasha whispers. She crouches down, head by her
knees, tears running down her face. 'This isn't happening... Oh
God, oh God.'

'Tasha.' Beth's voice is cutting in a way I've never heard
before. Tasha straightens in an instant. 'You need to keep it
together.'

Tasha wipes her face and nods. 'I'm sorry. I just don't
understand what she's asking. She's saying we—'

Beth cuts her off. 'Alistair has just messaged. He's knocked
on Keira's door, but there's no one home. He's trying the park.'

'She's hiding them somewhere,' I hiss, fighting back the
burn of tears.

'What do we do?' Tasha cries.

I take a breath. 'Be fearless,' I whisper.

'What?' Tasha asks.

'We do what she's asking,' I say. 'What other choice is there?
She has our children. She isn't just threatening anymore. She's
actually doing this.'

'So we go to the police and we confess to murder,' Tasha
replies, still breathing hard. 'And then what? We rot in prison
for the rest of our lives?'

'Our children will be safe,' I say. 'That's what matters.'
That's all that matters. Even though we're talking about doing
the one thing we've said we'd never do – talk to the police – my
words hit with the force of a shove. What we do now doesn't
matter. Oscar is all that matters. Not Instagram. Not Magnolia
Close. Not my life. Just Oscar.

Beth is staring at her phone. She's gone completely still.

'What is it, Beth?' I ask.

'Maybe,' she says slowly, 'maybe there's a way to do exactly what Keira is telling us to do that doesn't end with us getting arrested and charged with murder.'

'Of course we'll be arrested,' Tasha cries. 'She's telling us to confess. If we confess, DS Sató is going to arrest us.'

Beth shoves her phone into her bag. 'Keira's message said we all have to confess, so that's what we do. But we go in separately. We each say we killed Jonny, but we acted alone.'

'How does that help us?' Tasha asks.

My mind is already racing ahead. *Disrupt. Evolve. Own it.* Isn't that what I thought that night in the pub when we first met Keira?

'It muddies the investigation,' Beth says, her voice gaining strength. 'DS Sató will have three different confessions. She won't know who's telling the truth. She won't be able to charge any of us.'

Beth's gaze darts between us. She must see something in our faces because she takes a breath, and when she speaks again, her words come slower. 'I used to be a solicitor, Tasha. I know what I'm talking about. The CPS – the Crown Prosecution Service – has to authorise any charges,' she explains. 'DS Sató can't just charge us with murder when she wants. She has to ask them first. If she goes to them with three separate confessions, mixed stories, mixed evidence, the CPS will never agree. They won't risk taking a case that messy.'

*Disrupt. Evolve. Own it.*

'But the children—' Tasha whispers. 'Can't we just go to the police and tell them Keira has taken them?'

Beth looks thoughtful. 'We could, but—'

'But what if they don't get to her on time,' I cut in. I'm sick of the sit-back-and-wait-and-see-and-hope-it-all-works-out approach. It's what's led us to this moment. 'She has our children, Tasha,' I cry out. 'This is not the time to worry about what happens to us. It's the time to do exactly what she's telling us to.'

Beth turns to her, gently but firmly. 'Keira is clearly desperate and crazy, but she's not stupid. She isn't going to risk keeping the children for any longer than she has to. And even she won't hurt them unless she feels it's her only option. She's blackmailing us. We have to believe that if we do what she's asking, she'll return them.'

We stare at each other. The silence is loaded before Beth talks again, laying out more details of her plan, making sure we all understand our roles. What to do. What to say and when.

'I'll go first,' I say when there's nothing more for it.

And with that, the three of us hug each other tight, and I turn and push through the crowd of shoppers. The police station is only a few streets away. I think of Oscar. No matter what else happens, Oscar is special. He is the light that brightens every room. He is what makes me amazing. Because I'm his mum. Nate is wrong. My life is big and beautiful because of Oscar. I will do anything to protect him. Even confessing to murder.

# THIRTY-EIGHT

## TASHA



The door opens and I jump, my breath coming sharp. Detective Sató steps inside the small grey room.

We've been at this for hours, but the detective is still so calm. She has a folder tucked under one arm and another bottle of water she places on the table for me. I flinch at the soft clunk it makes. My nerves are frayed, completely unspooled.

Time has lost all meaning in this awful place. Minutes have felt like hours. My stomach churns with hunger. I haven't eaten since I finished Matilda's half-eaten Weetabix this morning. Sweat has dried on my skin, leaving me feeling dirty. Stale.

I want to ask if she's been speaking to Beth and Georgie? What have they said? But we made a pact: no mention of each other. Solo confessions will only work if we stick to the plan. But Beth didn't tell me what to do if the guilt inside me feels like it's eating me alive. She didn't think about what it would be like sitting in this room hour after hour while our children were out there somewhere with that woman. A sob catches in my throat.

Please, please, please let them be safe by now. And what of Marc? Is he home from golf? Did he walk into an empty house and think I left him? I wish I could see him. To tell him I forgive him. That I understand why he lied. Why he bought the vineyard for us. That he's right – it's more than a dream. It's our future. Silent tears track two lines down my cheeks. I have nothing left in me. It has to be time to end this.

Sató settles into the chair across from me, folding her hands on the table. 'Thank you for waiting, Tasha. How are you feeling now?'

'I'm OK,' I lie. I'm not, and we both know it.

'If it's all right with you, I'd like to talk about the night of Jonny Wilson's death. The PTA quiz night,' Sató says, like we haven't spent this entire time talking about exactly that.

I nod, biting back a protest. There's something like a razor's edge to Sató's voice.

My muscles tense.

'We've continued our door-to-door enquiries from the night of Jonny's murder,' she says, sliding open the folder. 'And someone's come forward today. A woman walking her dog around eight p.m. She said she saw a woman in a yellow top matching your description running down Magnolia Road heading in the direction of Magnolia Close. Not dressed for exercise. Looking distressed.'

Cold dread twists in my gut.

'I was in the kitchen helping with food prep,' I say quickly, needing to explain. Needing her to see the truth behind what she's discovered. The detail of the night of Jonny's murder I've not told anyone. 'But there wasn't much to do so I thought I'd nip home to check on the girls.'

It's not quite true, but my real reason for leaving that night doesn't matter now.

'I'm sorry,' I say. 'I should've said straight away, but I knew it looked bad. I was only gone a few minutes. Matilda – that's my oldest – she gets upset easily. I was worried about her and wanted to check she was OK.

'I got to the gates of Magnolia Close and realised how silly I was being, so I just called Florence, our babysitter. She said the girls were asleep, and I returned to the school. No one knew I was gone.'

'Would you say you were at breaking point that night, Tasha? Your parents needed to live with you, but Jonny had blocked planning permission for your extension. You couldn't find a way out.'

'I was stressed, yes,' I admit. 'But—'

'You needed something to change. You needed that extension. And Jonny was standing in your way.'

Sató is right. She knows it. I know it. I think of how desperate I felt the night in the pub when we met Keira. There was no way forward, no escape from the relentlessness of my life. And I realise I don't feel that way anymore. That even though I'm living in a nightmare, there's hope. I'm no longer buried alive. I can breathe. And it's all down to Marc and the plans he's made for us.

Sató doesn't blink. 'Did you leave the quiz night with the intention of murdering Jonny Wilson?'

I open my mouth, but no words come. I'm supposed to be confessing to Jonny's murder. I'm supposed to convince Sató, and now I have and I can't follow through. I feel myself split in two. Cracking, like the shell of an egg squeezed too tight inside a fist.

I can't carry on.

A guttural sob heaves through my body. I'm trembling all over. Can't get the air into my lungs. I close my eyes and pray Alistair has found the children. That my girls are safe.

'I didn't kill Jonny,' I whisper.

'Excuse me?' Sató replies. 'Could you repeat that please?'

'I said…' I swallow, forcing my voice louder. 'I didn't kill Jonny. I'm not really here to confess.'

'Then why are you here, Tasha? Because you told me not two hours ago that you killed Jonny Wilson.'

'I… I lied.'

'You lied about leaving the quiz that night, and now you're lying about killing Jonny.'

'Yes. I mean, no.' I scrunch my eyes shut. I can't think straight. My chest cracks open. The sob rips through me before I can stop it. 'It wasn't me. It wasn't any of us,' I cry. 'We didn't kill Jonny. We're only here because the real murderer forced us to confess. She has our children. She said we'd never see them again if we didn't do exactly what she said.'

In the silence that follows, the only sound is my heaving breath.

Sató's eyes narrow. She still doesn't believe me. 'OK, Tasha, who forced you to come here today?'

'A woman named Keira Philips. She manipulated and blackmailed us. All of this – the murder, the confessions, it's her.'

I'm changing the plans I made with Georgie and Beth, messing everything up, but right now I can't think past needing to see my girls. Why didn't we walk into this police station earlier and tell Sató the truth? How would Keira have known what we were saying to her? These questions seem so obvious now, but I was so swept up in the messages from Keira and scared for my girls, I didn't stop to question the plan we made.

But getting to my girls – making sure they're safe – that's all that matters now.

The words spill out. I tell Sató everything. Everything since Keira's sudden appearance.

'We never thought it was real. Until she sent us the evidence. The top…' I swallow. My throat hurts. Head pounds. This is the moment. I have to make her see. 'And my dad's prescription sleeping pills. She must've taken them from my bag that night. I don't know how she got it, but she had a key to Jonny's house too.

'She wanted us to kill her ex. And when we refused, she... she... threatened our families.' I can't speak the words fast enough. They tumble out, and I'm not even sure how much sense I'm making. It all seems so unbelievable. 'We went to do it, but we couldn't go through with it. But it was never about her ex anyway. Keira knew Jonny too. We think she wanted him dead. There's a photo of the two of them together. Georgie has it. Ask her. Talk to the others. She... made us come here today to confess to Jonny's murder. She has our children. You have to help us. Please,' I whisper, praying I've said enough, praying she believes me when I was so certain earlier she wouldn't. 'Help us. Help our children.'

But when I look up, Satö's mouth is a firm line. Her eyes locked on mine.

'And I'm supposed to believe you now? After all the lies you've admitted you've told me?'

'We had no choice. She has our children.'

The room closes in. My vision blurs.

Beth said this plan would protect us. She said the police couldn't charge us if we all confessed separately. But she was wrong. This isn't the way out at all. All we've done is make everything worse. So much worse.

# THIRTY-NINE

## BETH



Time is dragging. My thoughts zigzag between Henry and Oscar and Matilda and Sofia, and everything that's happened over the past few weeks. Like a pinball rolling into the drain, my thoughts find their way back to Jonny every time, and that day in London when he found me outside the fertility clinic.

I was a mess. Tearful and broken. I went to the clinic to discuss a sperm donor. I felt awful about betraying Alistair, but what other choice did I have? I love him. He's scatty and forgetful, but so kind. So generous. There is nothing he wouldn't do for me or our family. How could I not do the same?

Alistair's sperm count was low, and my age was against us. A donor was a betrayal, yes, but one born out of love and devotion. But the costs were so high and our savings were gone from so many rounds of IVF, and the interest rates on the mortgage had gone up, and we were already counting every penny. There was no way I could afford it.

My heart broke that day as I left the clinic. I'd found a solution, but there was no way to make it happen. I was at rock bottom that day. Barely able to stand. Jonny must have seen it too because he was surprisingly kind to me, whisking me into the nearest pub, buying me a drink, and listening to me as I broke down.

'Let me help,' he said, and I lifted my head in surprise, blinking back my tears.

'You'd lend me the money for the donor?' I asked, allowing the hope to shield me from the alarm ringing in my head, telling me this was Jonny – my rude, awful neighbour. All I saw was a solution.

The door to the interview room flies open so fast, I jump, cheeks flaming, the rock of guilt lodged so tight, it feels like my lies are written across my face. The second Sató steps into the interview room, I know something has changed.

Her movements are less composed. She looks like someone who's just been given information that's knocked her off balance and hasn't figured out how to steady herself yet.

'Tell me about Keira Philips,' she says.

No preamble. Just the name, dropped like a hammer.

Tasha cracked.

Of course she did. She's always been the most fragile of the three of us. I can't blame her, but that doesn't mean I'm not terrified for all that comes next. My stomach tightens. Henry. My beautiful boy. Kind and curious. The way he always holds my hand for longer than he needs when we cross the road. How he worries when I look tired. How he hugs me so tight.

*You can't wrap them in cotton wool all their lives.*

No. But I can try.

I think of his baby sister, growing quietly inside me. I imagine her nestled in my arms, not caught up in any of this horror. And then I start talking. Piece by piece, I give Sató everything just as I'm sure Tasha did. Sató listens without interruption, her eyes unreadable, just the occasional nod as she takes it all in. But something shifts in her expression – the tiniest flicker of realisation or maybe resolve. When I finish, she straightens, reaching for her notepad.

'I think,' she says quietly, 'it's time I went to talk to Keira.'

'Take us with you,' I say, ignoring the detective's look of disbelief. 'Please,' I beg. 'She has our children. And she's only going to lie to you. If we're there, it might unnerve her and get her to open up.'

Sató hesitates. I can see her mind working through the scenarios. I hold my breath. I want to beg some more, but Sató is smart. Pushing too hard will make me seem desperate.

Eventually, she nods. 'It's not conventional, and it could land me in a hell of a lot of trouble… but whatever is going on here with the four of you, it's a mess. I've been listening to you, Georgie and Tasha lie to me all morning, and I don't want an afternoon of the same. Putting you all in the same room could be the quickest way to get to the truth. But' – she stops, fixing her eyes on me – 'you do exactly as I say, or you'll be waiting in the back of the police car.'

'Yes. Of course,' I reply, getting to my feet.

We're going to see Keira. And Henry. Is this nightmare nearly over at last?

Everything moves quickly after that. Hurried footsteps. Murmured instructions I don't catch. A radio crackling too loud but incoherent. Sató leads me down a side corridor lined with scuffed walls and the faint scent of bleach that turns my stomach and has me reaching for my bag in case I need to throw up again. She pushes through a heavy door that opens onto a small car park filled with police cars and vans and a smaller row of unmarked saloon cars. A minute later, Georgie and Tasha appear. They're led by DC McLachlan and a uniformed PC.

The younger detective isn't smiling, but there's a keenness to her steps that makes me think she was behind the two-way mirror of the interview room. I turn my gaze to Tasha. She looks broken. Her eyes are swollen and red, her hands wrapped around her arms like she's trying to hold herself together. Even Georgie's trademark poise is gone. Her shoulders are slumped, and her hair is no longer sleek and glossy but dull and tangled. We don't speak. We just stand there, taking each other in. We look like women who've lived through a year in this building. Not a few hours. And we're not done yet. Whatever's waiting for us at Keira's house – truth, lies or something even worse – feels like it's already pulling at the edges of what's left of us.

We're split between two cars. Tasha travels with Sató, whereas Georgie and I travel with DC McLachlan and the uniformed officer. No one speaks on the journey, and ten minutes later, we pull into the narrow terrace road of Dove Street. There are cars lined bumper to bumper on either side of the road. Sató has to inch her way down and squeeze into a space.

When the uniformed PC has done the same and we're all standing on the street outside Keira's house, Sató turns to us. 'Let me be crystal clear,' she says. 'The three of you have each confessed to the murder of Jonny Wilson. I still believe one or all of you were involved in his death. We are here based on information about a woman you only know as Keira Philips, and a photograph tying her to the victim. Whether you return to the police station with me after this or go home will be my decision, not yours.'

The officer steps forward then, as though to remind us of his presence. As though we'd think about running. Our children are in that house. Our whole lives are resting on what happens next.

Sató takes the lead, striding up the narrow, cracked path towards a front door the same red as the lipstick Keira wears. There's a neat front garden with pruned rose bushes and ivy climbing up a brick wall. A child's scooter leans against the wall beside the door. Sató knocks three times. The wait is endless. My heart is racing so fast, I'm struggling to draw in enough air with each breath. Over and over, I pray Henry is OK. Then the door opens and it's Keira. She's mid-conversation with someone else in the house, calling back to them, smiling as she turns to us. She's wearing black leggings and a burgundy hoodie, and there's a dishcloth in her hands as though we've caught her mid-task.

Her smile freezes as her gaze sweeps across the group, eyes widening at the detective badges Sató and McLachlan are holding up, then the three of us and the PC standing stiffly at the back. For the briefest second, her whole body tenses. The tea towel tightens in her fist. She shifts on her feet like she's considering her options. Like she's wondering if there's time to run.

'Hi?' she says, too high, too light.

'I'm Detective Sergeant Sara Sató,' the detective says. 'I'm the senior investigating officer in the investigation into the murder of Mr Jonathan Wilson. May we come in?'

A tight frown pulls at Keira's brow. Something sparks in her eyes. Fear, I think. Then she steps back. 'Of course.'

We pile into a narrow hallway painted a pale blue that leads into a white kitchen with dated countertops. It's a tight space for one, and we're all squeezed in together. On the walls, photos of Keira in younger years – cocktail dress, graduation gown, a beach somewhere hot and perfect.

Then, out the kitchen window, I see them. Henry. Rowan. Matilda. Oscar. Sofia. Laughing and chasing each other through a garden dotted with small apple trees. The world seems to stop as I take in my son. Henry's cheeks are flushed, and his jumper sleeves are pushed up. I don't even mind his hair is ruffled. He's happy, and he's safe.

'The girls,' Tasha gasps.

She lunges for the back door, but I catch her arm. 'They're fine. Let them play. Just for now.'

Tasha nods, tears spilling over. I wipe mine away quickly. My throat is tight. But I hold it together. I have to.

We follow Keira into the living room just as an older woman pokes her head in. She's shorter than Keira, but has the same nose and straight hair. Grey not black.

'Mum,' Keira says. 'This is a police detective. She wants to ask me some questions. Can you watch the kids for us?'

'Of course,' the woman says, vanishing again.

Keira gestures to the sofa. Tasha, Georgie and I sit together on a two-seater sofa. Sató and McLachlan stand, while Keira takes the armchair. I glance to the door and realise the PC has remained outside. Is he protecting the exit in case someone tries to run?

I perch on the edge, too tense to sit back. I rest my hand on the swell of my belly, my heart racing. This is it – the moment everything changes for all three of us. My two best friends. We've stuck together through this. Clung to each other even when the rest of our community has fractured. Our strength and loyalty has brought us to this moment.

'Keira,' Sató begins, still with that infuriating calm, 'can you walk me through what happened today? Specifically, how you came to be in possession of Georgie, Beth and Tasha's children?'

An amused smirk pulls at the corners of Keira's lips. 'Possession? That's a bit dramatic. It was a playdate. We arranged it after school the other day.'

'No, we didn't,' Georgie cuts in, earning a sharp look from Sató.

Keira lifts a brow. 'I picked them up, as agreed after you messaged me, Georgie, and I brought them back here. They've been playing in the garden. As you saw.'

'I didn't message you,' Georgie says.

Keira shrugs. 'Someone did then, and they said they were you.'

'She's lying.' Tasha's voice is brittle. 'Alistair came to collect them and you weren't here.'

'Maybe we were at the bottom of the garden. It's a long one.

Look, I get it – you're all stressed – but there's clearly been a misunderstanding. The children are fine. You've seen that. If you want to take them home, be my guest. There's no crisis here.'

Sató leans forward. 'This isn't just about the children, Keira. This is a murder investigation. Do you know a man named Jonathan Wilson? Known as Jonny.'

Keira shoots us a look, and I think I see suspicion in her gaze. 'I know he lived on Magnolia Close and that he was murdered. I read the news. But I've never met him, if that's what you're asking.'

'Can you tell me your whereabouts on the night of Tuesday the seventh of October between eight p.m. and eleven p.m.?'

Keira taps a finger to her top lip for a moment before replying. 'The night of the PTA quiz? I was home. My mum was out visiting a friend. Rowan had chicken pox and was too itchy to sleep, so we stayed up watching cartoons.'

'I'm sorry, but that means you don't have an alibi,' Tasha says under her breath.

'This is ridiculous,' Keira replies. 'I didn't even know the man. Why would I kill him?'

'That's not true,' Tasha cries. 'You do know him. We saw the photo of you and Jonny together.'

'What photo?' Keira looks confused as her gaze moves between the detectives.

Sató taps her phone and shows Keira a photo of the original we found in Jonny's house. Lines appear on Keira's brow. 'I've never seen this photo before. It's a fake.'

'We're having the image analysed now,' Sató replies.

Tension ripples in the air. Suddenly, the decision to confess this morning, the hours stuck in that interview room, the drive here and everything I've done before today has been leading to this.

Sató speaks with the same calm confidence she's maintained

throughout the investigation. 'Earlier today, Beth, Georgie and Tasha confessed to the murder of Jonny Wilson. They did so with full knowledge of the method, the weapon and the motive.'

The words hang in the air, and suddenly it all seems too much, too hard, too impossible. Not one confession. But three. Each of us saying we killed Jonny. Acted alone. Hearing it out loud, it sounds like madness.

I watch Keira's face, expecting anger or outrage. But all I see is surprise, like she can't believe what we did any more than I can.

Sató doesn't pause for long. She presses on, voice steady. 'They now claim they only confessed because you blackmailed them. They're claiming you took their children and told them they'd never see them again if they didn't confess to a murder they claim you committed.'

Silence.

No one speaks.

Outside, the children laugh and shout. Inside, it feels like our lives hang in the balance. Panic descends – a storm coming, heavy and fast. Tasha with her tear-stained face and Georgie devoid of her mantras. All three of us wait.

Keira's assessing gaze flicks between us. And then she does the one thing I don't see coming. She throws her head back and laughs. A loud, sharp cackle that ricochets off the walls and seems to rattle inside my skull. It's so sudden, so jarring, that I flinch.

When the laughter dies, Keira looks at each of us in turn again before quirking an eyebrow at Sató as she speaks.

'I have no idea what any of you are talking about.'

# FORTY

## GEORGIE

She's laughing.

This is funny to her.

My pulse is racing, and I feel out of my depth, washed out to sea like I did that night in the pub when we first met Keira. I wonder if I've been barely keeping my head above water since.

The living room is cramped. Too small for so many of us. It should be cosy in that way floral-print sofas and dark wood furniture can be, but all I feel is suffocated.

This isn't how it was supposed to go. All the hours spent in that police interview room, lying to the detective, confessing to murder just like Keira told us to. All that time, I imagined the moment Sató would discover the truth, and she'd rush to Keira's house and drag the woman away. Lock her up and throw away the key. Sirens and handcuffs and speed and we'd have our children back. Our lives back. This feels wrong. Just sitting here.

Keira leans back, arms crossed, gaze flicking between us with barely disguised irritation.

'Look,' she says, lips still quirking at the edges, 'we had a laugh in the pub about killing your neighbour, but I'm not stupid. I knew it was a joke.'

Tasha is the first to jump in. 'You threatened us,' she says. Her voice is shaking. She looks one word away from breaking down completely. 'Don't deny it. In the school playground, you said, "Can you imagine if anyone found out?"'

'That wasn't a threat,' Keira replies. 'I was just commenting on how weird it was.' Her gaze moves between us. Beth, then Tasha, then me, then the detective, watching everything unfold. 'You talk about killing someone and then he dies. Of course it crossed my mind you might've done it. But then I realised how stupid that was. Look at you.' She sweeps her hand towards us. 'You're all far too vanilla to commit murder.'

'This is ridiculous,' I say, straightening my shoulders. 'I confronted you in the playground last week after you were talking to Nate. I told you to leave us alone and stop messaging us. You said you don't stop doing things just because other people tell you to.'

Keira looks confused for a moment, already shaking her head slowly. 'You were threatening me, Georgie. You didn't mention any messages I was sending you. You basically accused me of trying to chat up your husband. Who, by the way, is cheating on you with any woman who swipes right for him.'

A flush of heat surges up my neck, burning across my cheeks, stretching all the way to the roots of my hair. I drop my gaze to the patterned carpet, unable to meet Beth's or Tasha's eyes.

I've spent weeks – months – telling myself I could fix this. Us. But Keira's mocking voice shatters the last of the illusion I've been clinging to. My marriage is over.

The thought hollows out my chest. I let my shoulders drop, feeling myself sag into the chair, the fight draining out of me. A flash of memory dances into my thoughts – Nate laughing across the table on our first date, that sense of something magic sparking between us. How fast did that version of us disappear? How long have I been lying to myself?

The questions spiral, wild and dizzying.

What the hell have I been doing all this time?

Keira continues then. 'I told you, I don't let anyone control me. My ex always tried to put me in a box. I'm done behaving for anyone else.'

Across the room, Sató watches. Not interrupting. Not asking questions. She's letting it play out. Letting us unravel, giving us enough rope to hang ourselves, I think.

Beth pulls out her phone. 'This is crazy,' she says, voice laced with desperation and frustration. 'You can't sit there and deny what you've done! You were messaging us then deleting the messages,' she says. 'You sent us the evidence from Jonny's murder. You told us we had to kill your ex or you'd come back to the close and hurt our families.'

Keira rolls her eyes. Not laughing but still amused. 'How was I messaging you? The only number I have is from someone claiming to be Georgie.' She shoots a look to the detective I can't decipher. 'You're wasting your time. I have no idea what they're talking about.' Then she turns to Beth. 'Whoever was messaging you, it wasn't me.'

'We heard your voice notes,' I say, remembering Keira's voice in the messages. That mocking tone. Her Irish accent.

'Again, not me,' Keira says.

Beth taps her phone screen, then reads out the digits to the phone number from the group chat.

Keira looks vindicated, those lips lifting into an almost smile. 'That's not my number, but...' She pulls her phone from the pocket of her hoodie and taps the screen. 'It's the same number I received a message from Georgie on to arrange this playdate.'

And even though I can't explain what's happening, can't see through the mess we're in to what's really going on, when I look at Keira – so relaxed, so composed – I think she's telling the truth.

Tasha looks at Beth then me. I look at DS Sató.

'You could have a second phone,' Beth says.

'Call it then.' Keira shrugs. 'See who picks up because it won't be me.'

Beth glances at the detective. She gives the faintest nod, and Beth taps the screen.

The pause is unbearable. I swear we all hold our breaths. My mind races ahead, expecting nothing. The phone switched off or unanswered. I don't know what's going on anymore, but it's not going to be as simple as an answered phone.

And then it happens – the sharp trill of a ringtone slicing through the silence.

All eyes whip to Keira. She holds up her phone, showing us the blank screen. No incoming call. No ringing.

The noise is coming from somewhere else. Someone else.

A sick feeling curdles in my stomach. I rise to my feet on unsteady legs. Everything I thought I knew – everything I was trying to protect – is slipping away, faster than I can hold on to it.

*I am calm. I am in control.*

But I'm not. Because as that phone keeps ringing, I realise I've been wrong about everything.

# FORTY-ONE

## GEORGIE

In the next second, we're all standing. DS Sató moves first, her expression tight and unreadable. In two strides, she plucks up the small leather rucksack from beside the sofa.

'Not your phone,' Beth snaps at Keira. 'Yeah, right.'

'That's not my bag,' Keira replies.

She's right. It's not. I know that bag. The worn black leather. The fraying straps from where it's been overloaded too many times with jumpers and teddies and sun cream and water bottles and snacks and nappies.

'It's mine,' Tasha says quietly, just as the realisation slams into me.

Tasha's bag. Tasha's phone. I can't wrap my head around this. All those threats came from a phone in Tasha's bag. She did this?

'Tasha?' I gasp, blink, stare at the woman I thought I knew as well as myself. A woman I thought was my friend. 'What have you done?'

Sató's voice slices through the stunned silence. She's holding the bag out for Tasha to take. 'Tasha, please open the bag and remove the phone.'

Tasha hesitates for a heartbeat too long. Her eyes are wide, but I can't tell if it's shock or resignation in her expression. She fumbles inside and pulls out the phone – the screen flashing with the incoming call from Beth's number.

A visible shudder runs through Beth. 'You killed Jonny,' she says, her voice breaking. 'You killed him, Tasha, because you wanted your stupid extension, and then you dragged us into this nightmare, faked this whole thing, to cover it up.'

My brain fights the truth, tries to shove it back, make it make sense. But it won't. Tasha – sweet Tasha, who will do anything for anyone. A people pleaser. A woman completely overwhelmed by her life – playing us all. Pretending to be Keira. Faking the threats.

*No.*

And yet even as I struggle to believe it, I remember the day at Beth's when Tasha slipped out of the room just before the messages we thought were from Keira landed. I remember her anger after the planning permission was denied. All that hate and desperation.

She said her father's prescription sleeping pills were stolen from her bag that night, but now I think about it, Keira was sat opposite Tasha the entire time. She wouldn't have had the chance to take them. And the yellow top she said wasn't hers… she must've bought a replacement afterwards to trick us into thinking it really wasn't.

I couldn't work out how Keira got into Jonny's place. How she got a key. The answer seems obvious. She didn't. Tasha must've had one. I remember a message on the Magnolia Close WhatsApp group from Bill. He said he gave Jonny his spare key back because Jonny wanted someone else to have it. Jonny and Marc were good friends. Tasha had access to a key all along.

It feels like everything is falling into place and I've been too scared, too wired, too focused on trying to protect my family to see the truth that now seems so obvious. And yet something nags in the back of my mind. Something about the messages.

Tasha is one of my best friends. My neighbour. We speak every day. Message constantly. No one knows me better than she does. I can't believe she's done this. My face is hot, but goosebumps are prickling my arms.

'You killed Jonny,' Beth whispers again. She's as shaken as I am. 'All this time, it was you? Why did you drag us into this?' The final word comes in a shuddering sob, and I reach out and take Beth's hand. We've both been betrayed.

Tasha's lips tremble. 'Please listen to me—'

'I almost killed a man because of you!' Beth cries. 'What if I'd gone through with it.' Her voice cracks, and she covers her mouth with her hands.

'You hated Jonny too!' Tasha blurts out. 'All of you did! Why is this all on me? I didn't do anything. That's not my phone.'

'It's in your bag,' Beth replies, eyes darting from DS Sató to me, like she can't believe it either.

'And it was your dad's sleeping pills, and the top you were wearing that night,' I add. And suddenly I'm not only hurt and confused – head spinning with WTF is happening – I'm also angry. Furious. Blood roars in my ears. 'You let us think Keira was the threat when all along it was you.'

'I'm sorry—' Tasha starts to say, but Beth cuts her off.

'It's too late for sorry,' she hisses.

'That's enough,' Sató says, and the command in her tone cuts us all dead. 'I think you should come back to the station with me now, Tasha.'

Tasha wipes her face with the sleeve of her jumper, her shoulders trembling with silent sobs. 'Please,' she chokes out. 'Please... I didn't do this. I can explain why I've been acting differently. Marc was—'

'You threatened our children,' Beth cuts in, and Tasha shakes her head.

'No. I didn't—' Tasha's words are lost in a sob.

'Let's talk at the station,' Sató says, still so calm.

DC McLachlan moves to stand beside Tasha.

Tasha cries out. 'Let me see my girls first. Please.'

'Not right now, Tasha. You don't want them to see you like this,' Sató replies.

Tasha looks between us, eyes wild like she's searching for something – mercy, forgiveness, a way to take it all back. 'I'm sorry, but this isn't right.'

The words fall flat. Too late to backtrack and deny what she did. Beth turns towards me, covering her face with her hands. I stay frozen, not wanting to watch, not able to look away. Then gently, firmly, Sató and DC McLachlan steer Tasha from the room and out the front door. I listen to them leave. More tears. Half sentences and spluttered apologies. And then the front door clicks shut, leaving only silence. Hot and uncomfortable.

I force myself to swallow, to stay standing. I turn towards Keira slowly.

'I'm sorry,' I manage, realising how wrong I've been about her. 'We thought—'

'Save it,' she sighs. 'Apology not accepted. I get you were manipulated here, but don't think I don't see the way you all look at me. The posh mums with your matching yoga mats and perfect little lives in Magnolia Close, so quick to judge me.'

Her words hit harder than I want to admit. She's right. We did exactly that. I thought I was so much better than her, and yet my marriage has been a lie, my friend has betrayed me. Everything I fought so hard to protect didn't even exist.

'I don't wear the right clothes. I don't say the right things,' Keira continues. 'I don't live on the right street. It probably took nothing for you to convince yourselves I was crazy and fall for whatever lies that other friend of yours cooked up. You need to take a long, hard look in the mirror. Now take your children and get the hell out of my house.'

There's a pause. A fraction of time where Beth and I stand there, open-mouthed. Reeling from everything Tasha did and the sharp honesty of Keira's words. Then we do what we always do as mothers. We rally, and we put on our brave faces and bright smiles as we call the children in from the garden. They're all pink-cheeked and breathless, giggling about a made-up game they invented.

'Where's my mum?' Matilda asks as we herd them towards the front door. I watch her feet falter and her bottom lip tremble as she peers around the hall, searching for Tasha. Sofia silently slips her hand into her sister's.

'She's busy right now, sweetheart,' I say, my voice bright and bubbling and a notch too high. I crouch down, forcing a smile onto my face. 'But guess what? I bet your daddy's at home. Shall we go see him?'

Matilda nods, but her eyes are still wary. Beside me, Beth fumbles with Henry's coat, like she's trying not to shake. We step outside, and cold air hits my face. Beth and I walk in silence, barely listening as the children tell us the fun they've had at Keira's house.

'We had ice cream for lunch,' Oscar tells us.

'And chocolate,' Henry adds.

Sofia grins. 'I had sprinkles on mine.'

I stare at them all. Happy. Safe. Never in danger. Tasha made us think we'd never see them again. She's a mother too. She loves her girls. How could she do that to us?

Only when we turn into the private road that leads to Magnolia Close do the children scamper ahead and I step closer to Beth.

'I still can't believe it was Tasha all this time,' I whisper. 'How could she manipulate us like that?'

Beth shakes her head, hands cradling her bump protectively. 'It makes me feel sick. She wasn't coping. We both saw it, but that doesn't excuse what she did. She blamed Jonny for everything. She saw him as the one thing standing in the way of a life she could actually deal with.

'She used us,' I reply. The words taste bitter in my mouth as fresh hurt cuts through me. 'She made us be her alibi without us even knowing, and when it seemed like that wasn't enough and it looked like the police investigation was closing in, she pretended to be Keira. She made us confess to a murder she committed.'

Beth is quiet for a moment before she next speaks. 'I'm trying to work out how she did it all.'

'Like what?' I ask.

'I don't know. It was just so... premeditated. Her phone was on the table the night in the pub. She must have been recording us. She was the one who brought up how much she hates Jonny first. But we heard Keira's voice on those voice notes. How did she do that?' I close my eyes for a moment. There is so much I can't wrap my head around. I don't think I'll ever fully understand what Tasha has done.

'It must have been fake,' Beth says. 'You saw what Keira was like just now. I don't like the woman, but there's no way she was lying.'

'So how did Tasha do it?' I ask.

'She must have used one of those AI voice copiers. She had a recording of Keira's voice from the night in the pub. She probably used that. Then made sure the messages disappeared so we couldn't listen too closely.'

'She always had a phone in her hands too,' I say. 'I thought it was her normal phone, but it must've been the one she was sending the messages on pretending to be Keira.'

Beth nods. 'We thought she was just looking at the messages the same as we were, but she must've been deleting them right in front of us.'

'But the man... the runner?' I ask.

Beth's body tenses. Her face pales. I don't need to ask to know she's thinking how close she came to killing that man. 'She must have made it all up,' Beth says. 'A way to keep us scared and desperate. She shouted stop, remember? She probably never meant for it to get that far. Maybe she thought we'd never go through with it. The ultimate bluff.'

We're silent as we step through the gates. The twelve grand, red-brick houses glow with the autumn sunlight streaming into the close. The hedges are neatly trimmed, the hanging baskets filled with bright flowers. It looks beautiful. Perfect even. But it's not. It doesn't feel like home anymore.

The children race ahead and begin a game of stuck in the mud in the middle of the close.

'I'm sorry about you and Nate,' Beth says, voice tentative. I can feel her watching me, searching my face for answers.

I nod but say nothing. Even now, even after all this, I'm struggling to tell her I'm leaving.

'I don't know what to do now,' I say.

Beth looks tired. 'I guess we go home. Try to carry on with our lives.'

I don't know what that looks like. I've been pretending for so long. Holding it together, painting on bright smiles and saying my mantras, and suddenly I'm tired of it all. I have Oscar. That's all that matters. I know we'll be OK.

I glance at Jonny's house. A shiver races down my spine. I think about what he knew. About how many times he threatened to expose me to Nate.

He was scum. A predator. You reap what you sow. And he deserved to get what was coming to him.

I hated Jonny.

I wanted him dead. But I didn't kill him.

I didn't do it.

# FORTY-TWO

## TASHA

The cell door shuts with a clang that feels like it rattles my bones. Panic climbs up my throat – a scream fighting to get out. I blink, taking in the space. I thought the interview room was bad, but this... this is worse.

The cell is barely bigger than a cupboard. Pale-blue walls, cold concrete floor. A raised slab of the same, topped with a plastic-covered mat that reminds me of the gym mats Sofia uses at school. There's a stainless-steel toilet in the corner and a sink, and nothing else. The fluorescent light overhead hums with an incessant pulse that adds to the pounding in my head. What the hell just happened?

Everything moved so fast. The rush to Keira's house. Seeing the girls safe. The flood of relief. For one moment, it had felt like everything might be OK again. We'd done it. We'd found them. They were laughing. Happy.

Accusing Keira. Laying it all out. Everything she'd done. And then... bam! It was me. The phone ringing in my bag. The look on their faces – Georgie's shock, Beth's horror. The betrayal I saw in their eyes. I tried to explain, to tell them they were wrong, but the words wouldn't come fast enough. I saw the wall go up between us, and I knew, in that moment, I'd already lost them. Even Sató's expression was hard, like she was convinced of my guilt too.

What happens now?

I close my eyes. Try to picture the vineyard Marc has bought – wide open skies, rows of vines catching the sun, the promise of space and calm and fresh air. All those times I closed my eyes, wishing I was someone else – it wasn't just open space and rolling hills; it was his vineyard I pictured. I just couldn't see it beneath the weight of everything I was carrying. I can't be here! My parents need me. My girls need me.

I press my palms into my knees and try to breathe. The air smells faintly of bleach and something metallic. Like blood. The thought curdles in my stomach. Was I so wrapped up in keeping our secret from Georgie and Beth that I missed something? So scared of my precious girls feeling that burn of rejection, of being pushed out of the friendship group and the Magnolia Close community like Lily—

I sit up. Jolted. Alert. My mind suddenly clear. Lily was ostracised by everyone in Magnolia Close. First the duck spring rolls, then Georgie's missing ornament. We convinced ourselves – thinking as one – all turning on her and Kevin. We were so sure she'd stolen Georgie's gold heart. So righteous. Last week, I half wondered if someone set her up – someone angry at them for leaving. Like the owners of our house before us.

And now it's me being set up. Not as a social outcast but as a murderer. Someone has set me up to take the fall for Jonny's murder. It's so extreme, but it's the only thing that makes sense. And yet it would mean someone knew what Marc was planning. The only person he told in Magnolia Close was Jonny. Could he have told someone in the close? Or did the person with the secret camera pick up a conversation between them?

My heart thuds against my ribs. Cold sweeps through me. All this time, we've been speculating about what that camera caught the night of Jonny's murder. But what if the person with the camera is responsible for more than just spying?

Yes, I left the PTA quiz that night. I was meant to be helping in the kitchen, but the noise, the heat, the crowd – it was too much. My head was pounding, and all I could think about was Jonny. I hated him. But I needed him too. I needed him to call his friend at the planning office and remove his objection. That's why I left the quiz. That's why I went to his house. Georgie was playing quiz master, and I could hear Beth in the toilet throwing up. So I went. I ran. I knocked on his door. I heard movement from inside, but he didn't answer. I knocked again. Louder. Firmer. But he still didn't answer. All I'd wanted was to talk to him. To beg him to help us. I shiver, realizing the movement I heard in Jonny's house must have been the real murderer.

A dog walker saw me that night. I no longer have an alibi.

My head spins.

What else do the police have on me? A motive. Opportunity. My dad's missing sleeping pills. The phone used to send those messages in my bag. A bloody top that looks exactly like mine. I saw it in Beth and Georgie's eyes. They think I'm guilty. Sató too. I don't know how to make it right.

Yes, I hated Jonny. Yes, I wanted him dead. Yes, I went to his house that night.

But I didn't kill him.

I didn't do it.

SIX MONTHS LATER

EPILOGUE

BETH

The soft whir of my sewing machine fills the house, rhythmic and steady. It's the only sound, apart from the quiet tap of my foot on the pedal. I'm making a new bed set for Henry, cut from fabric printed with astronauts kicking footballs in space. I smile as I work, imagining his face when he sees it. He'll cherish it, like he does everything I make for him.

The window is open. A warm breeze drifts in, carrying the scent of freshly cut grass and the hum of lawnmowers from the neighbours' gardens. It's the kind of spring day made for parks and ice cream, the kind of blue sky and sunshine that makes it easy to believe nothing bad ever happened on Magnolia Close.

I glance at the clock. Nearly noon. Alistair will be home soon with Henry – and our baby girl, tucked in the pushchair, blinking up at the world, ready for her next feed. Just the thought of her makes my breasts ache. It's only the second time I've been apart from her, but Alistair insisted I take a morning for myself.

We named her Alanna. It means 'precious child'. After everything it took to have her – the years of trying and failing, the heartbreak and emptiness – it was the only name that made sense. She is perfect. Red hair, bright, curious eyes that study me when she feeds. Everyone says she looks just like Alistair. I smile when they say it and always agree. Sometimes, I almost believe it too.

*He'll see the truth one day*, the voice inside whispers.

No, he won't.

There have been so many times when my heart has raced and I've barely breathed as I feared the truth would come out. Whenever we met with the midwives, I feared they'd mention my due date and Alistair would put it together. But he never did. It's the benefit of having a forgetful, trusting husband.

It's amazing, really, the lies we choose to believe. Like Jonny that day in London. I chose not to see the trouble I was bringing on myself.

'Let me help,' he said, after buying me a gin and tonic and listening to me cry over how the fertility clinic and my plan for a sperm donor was too expensive.

I lifted my head in surprise; blinked back my tears. 'You'd lend me the money for a sperm donor?' I asked.

He smiled a flirtatious grin. 'I want to help you get pregnant, yes. But why waste money on a stranger's sperm? Why not use someone you know?'

I laughed at first. I thought he was joking.

'I'm serious,' he said. 'Use me. I'm tall, successful, smart—'

'Cocky and obnoxious,' I cut in, and it was his turn to laugh.

He leaned closer, lowering his voice. 'Free and available. We can try as many times as you need, and it will cost you nothing.'

'Why would you do that?' I asked, taking another long gulp of my drink. I told myself I would never do that. Not with Jonny. Not to Alistair. A sperm donor was one thing, but an affair was a whole other kind of betrayal.

'Because you're beautiful,' he said. 'Why wouldn't I want to sleep with you?'

I said no at first. I wouldn't do that to Alistair. But then I went home, empty and broken, and I started to see that Jonny's proposal was the only way Alistair and I would ever get the perfect family we deserved. And even though I could barely look at myself in the mirror, I told myself I was doing it because I loved my husband and would do anything to give him the second child he wanted as much as I did.

And so for three days every month, when I was ovulating, Jonny and I slept together. It wasn't unpleasant. Jonny was passionate and exploring, different from Alistair's slow tenderness. But I refused to enjoy it. I told myself it was a means to an end. And when that second pink line appeared on the pregnancy test three months later, I ended the affair.

I got what I wanted.

But Jonny wanted more.

A noise outside pulls me back. I glance out the window and see a removal van pulling into number twelve. A new family, finally filling the last empty house on Magnolia Close.

Tasha, Marc and the girls left first. Going before their house had even sold. Georgie and Nate went next. Nate moved to a high-rise apartment in London, and Georgie and Oscar to a little house near Dove Street.

We still see each other at school pick-ups. Georgie tried to stay in contact after she moved out of Magnolia Close. I gave her excuse after excuse, and eventually, she got the message. I let the friendship slip away. It was better that way. But she seems happy. She finally got her wish to go viral and become the influencer she dreamed of being. Not as someone who has it all but through posts about the stark honesty of life as a single mum on a budget. Relatable and passionate. A different version of the Georgie I knew, but then she never really knew me either.

Jonny's house sold next. A nice family moved in next door – a couple who run a florist. Their children are older – a boy and a girl around ten and twelve. They always say hi to Henry and throw his football back for him when it goes over the fence.

Dan and Ryan sold next. It's sad they couldn't heal the rift. And even though Marc and Tasha were the first to leave Magnolia Close, their sale has only just gone through. The final new family are joining our community. At last, it feels like a fresh start for all of us.

Downstairs, the front door bangs open. I hear Henry and Alistair calling up, followed by Alanna's hungry wail.

'Mummy! Quick! Alanna needs your milk!' Henry shouts.

'Coming!' I call back, already smiling.

I head downstairs. Henry stands proudly by the sofa, taller now, his neat red hair and freckles glowing in the sunlight. He sets a glass of water on the coffee table like Alistair has told him to do any time I'm breastfeeding, before he kneels beside his train set.

Alistair lifts Alanna from her pushchair and hands her to me. She nuzzles into my chest, latching on with a small tug. I breathe in the sweet, milky scent of her, feeling a contentment I always believed I would find.

Alistair drops a kiss on my head. 'I said hello to the new family at number twelve,' he says. 'They've got a baby too.'

'Oh really?' I glance towards the window, feeling hopeful.

He smiles. 'I invited them for coffee tomorrow morning.'

'Perfect,' I reply. And it is. I can already tell we'll be good friends.

Magnolia Close isn't just a street. It's a community. We look out for each other. We stick together.

I can't see number twelve too well from here – not like Georgie's old view of the entire close – but that's fine. A few more months, a little more healing and I'll set up a new camera. Discreetly of course. Somewhere hidden.

It isn't about spying. It's about caring. Protecting what we have.

The first camera wasn't about prying either. It was about Jonny. I needed to make sure no one was around to see me slipping between our houses, letting myself into his house with our key those times I was sleeping with him.

Everything would've worked out if Jonny hadn't changed his mind about our plan.

'You know,' he said, a few weeks after I ended our affair, 'I think I've changed my mind. When else am I going to get a chance to be a dad? Alistair is a sap. He'll forgive you. You can still have your happy family, Beth, but I want to be part of this baby's life.'

I knew he didn't really mean it. It was just another game to him. He didn't care about being a father. All he cared about was being in our lives forever. I suspected it was always his plan. This way he could constantly mess with us. Lord my betrayal over Alistair.

'Either you tell Alistair or I will,' he said the day I met Georgie and Tasha in the pub for the PTA meeting. The day I realised I would need a new plan to protect my perfect family.

Maybe Jonny was right about Alistair forgiving me. But it would've destroyed the sweet, honest trust we share. It would've hurt my husband and my family too deeply. And I didn't do all this for anything less than perfect.

There was only one solution – Jonny had to go.

When Keira joked about killing him that night, something clicked into place. I saw my opportunity. I bent forward, pretending to laugh as I tapped my phone to record. If I was clever, if I played it just right, I could build an alibi, kill Jonny and protect my future.

So on the night of the quiz, while the others thought I was battling morning sickness, I set my phone to play a recording I'd made of me in the bathroom retching, and I slipped out. I'd already laced the biscuits I'd made with the sleeping pills I'd stolen from Tasha's bag at the pub. I'd given them to Jonny as a peace offering just before I left for the school to help set up for the quiz, promising him I'd tell Alistair that weekend. One of the things I learned about Jonny in my time in his bed was what a sweet tooth he has, always wanting chocolate or treats. I knew he wouldn't be able to resist my biscuits. I was right. By the time I arrived and let myself in with the spare key, he was unconscious in bed.

The killing was... mechanical. Stab wounds, like Georgie said. Smearing blood on a yellow top I'd bought to look like Tasha's. Then suffocation like I described. Enough to muddy the method, enough to echo what we'd talked about.

Even then, I'd hoped I wouldn't need any of the evidence I collected. I'd hoped Jonny's death would be considered an unsolved murder. But DS Sató wasn't the bumbling detective I'd expected. She was diligent and determined. The news broke that she was close to an arrest. The police knew it was someone close to him. And even though I didn't think it was me she suspected, the panic set in. I had to take control.

Starting with the WhatsApp group pretending to be Keira. I didn't know how to set up disappearing messages that I could pre-load via a website. I didn't know about using an AI voice to replicate Keira's. But I did what I always do. I worked the problem. Found the solution.

Like planting the photo of Keira and Jonny and pretending to find it the night we searched his house. Keira was right. It was a fake. I scrolled through their oldest Facebook posts and found two photos I could use. The image was grainy. A terrible job if anyone cared to look hard enough. But just like how I trusted Jonny, just as Alistair trusted me – we see what we want to see.

I messaged Keira, pretending to be Georgie, and arranged the playdate. The calls to Alistair were fake that morning we confessed. He didn't go to Keira's house to find them. As far as Alistair was concerned, he was babysitting Lanie while the other children were safely playing at Keira's house.

I created a misdirection with my friends, built on fear and loyalty and lies. I needed them to pull it off. That's not to say it was easy. I was scared and stressed the entire time. Terrified of Georgie or Tasha looking too closely or second-guessing.

The runner was a nobody. A random man who commented in a local Facebook group that he runs home from work along Fordly Lane each night. I was always going to swerve. But I had to make it seem real so that when the scheduled message arrived telling us Keira had our children, Tasha and Georgie wouldn't question it. Another way to muddy the investigation, to keep the fear pounding through us so we wouldn't stop to think. If Keira could blackmail us into killing her ex, what would she do to our children...?

I meant what I said outside the café. I was certain if we all confessed to Jonny's murder, none of us could be charged. The CPS would never approve a case for prosecution with multiple confessions. And even if they did, a jury would struggle to convict if more than one person said they were the killer.

That's why I convinced the others to confess. Of course I knew Tasha would crack and tell Sató everything. And with the claim of four missing children, I knew the police would take it seriously. I had no idea how the final showdown would play out, but even I couldn't have planned for it to work out so perfectly.

Poor Tasha.

She was released from police custody later that same day. But she's since been charged with Jonny's murder. She's out on police bail, awaiting a trial date. Tasha, Marc and the girls moved out of Magnolia Close the day after we confessed. I heard they lived with her parents for a few weeks, then all moved to the vineyard in Devon. A happy ending all round.

Almost.

I'm sure waiting for the court date and the trial hangs over her.

Perhaps she didn't deserve this. But then... she didn't

deserve my friendship either. Not when she was already planning to leave our community. As it happened, I knew about Tasha leaving before she did. That was the other thing I learned about Jonny. Not only did he have a sweet tooth, but he liked to gossip after sex. When I was scrambling to collect my clothes and escape, he liked to talk. He told me about Marc's redundancy and his secret plan to buy the vineyard in Devon and move away from Magnolia Close. I knew Tasha would be upset, but I knew she'd accept it eventually. She's always been a follower.

Georgie leaving Magnolia Close was different. She'd have stayed if she could. That's why I slipped the phone I'd used to pretend to be Keira into Tasha's bag when I'd hugged her on that final day together, before we'd gone to the police station to confess.

Just like David and Mags – the couple who lived at number twelve before Tasha and Marc moved in. They wanted to invite people to join them for holidays at their new house in Spain. Everyone was so excited. But I knew if we kept in touch with people who moved away, it would dilute and fracture the community we had. It's why I snuck out in the early hours of the morning and poured weedkiller on people's lawns. Then gently reminded my neighbours of the dispute we'd had with David about the length of lawns in the close. He denied it, of course. But his lawn was the only one not damaged.

Lily and Kevin Gallagher wanted to stay in touch with everyone too. There was talk of them returning for the summer street party every year.

I glance at the small gold heart ornament that sits on the coffee table. It's been hidden in a drawer for so long, but there's no way Georgie or Tasha will pop over again and see what I stole from Georgie's house on that New Year's after the Gallaghers announced they were leaving. The second I heard the news, I knew I'd need to make sure it was a clean break. If they wanted to leave, they couldn't stay friends. So I stole the ornament. I knew it was Lily's favourite. She'd commented on it enough times that I knew she'd be blamed when I casually asked Georgie where it was after Lily left that night.

I caused the rift, allowing a clean break for all of us. I do feel for Tasha though. It wasn't like I wanted her to have a murder charge hanging over her. I'm not so vindictive that I'd want someone to spend their life in prison just for leaving Magnolia Close. But DS Sató was relentless. The local news kept talking of breakthroughs and arrests being imminent. I needed a fall person, and Tasha was the most likely candidate. Not just because she decided she wanted out. But because, as she said all along, she had the biggest motive for wanting Jonny dead. Or she thought she did anyway.

I was wrong about the CPS not bringing charges when multiple people confess. DS Sató must have presented a strong case against Tasha. The phone in her bag. The motive. Her own father's sleeping pills used to drug Jonny.

The case could all still fall apart before it gets to court. I hope it will. I hope Jonny's death gets lost in the pile of unsolved cases and Tasha can get on with her life, and so can our little community.

That's the problem with people when they say they're going to leave Magnolia Close. They forget our community is special. We rely on each other. You don't just get to walk away from that.

And now with the new residents at number twelve, our community is complete again. It's perfect in fact. The perfect home. The perfect family.

I did what I had to do to get here. Even murder.

*I did it.*

# A LETTER FROM LAUREN

Dear reader,

Thank you so much for picking up *Perfect Wives*! I'm genuinely thrilled to be sharing another twisty thriller with you. Whether you devoured it in one sitting or savoured it slowly, I'm so grateful you came along for the ride.

If you'd like to stay in the loop about upcoming releases, you can sign up for my newsletter here:

*www.bookouture.com/lauren-north*

I promise your email will never be shared, and you can unsubscribe any time.

The idea for *Perfect Wives* has been simmering in the back of my mind for years. It all began with a question: *Why would someone confess to a murder they didn't commit?* Then I pushed it further – *what if three people all confessed to the same murder?* Each of them insists they acted alone. Each is lying. But why?

That mystery sat with me for a while... until another spark lit up. What if I gave it a *Strangers on a Train* twist? A murder swap, but modernised and rooted in the kind of English market town where everyone waves politely but harbours secrets behind closed doors? What if the story revolved around three women whose lives look picture-perfect on the outside? Of course, it wouldn't be one of my thrillers without some husbands behaving suspiciously, school-gate gossip and a few red herrings along the way.

I suspect many of us will see glimpses of ourselves in Georgie, Tasha or Beth. I know I did. I felt Tasha's overwhelm in my bones and Georgie's need to fix everything (even the things she can't).

I love hearing from readers. Your messages, reviews, tags and shares make this journey even more rewarding. You'll often find me lurking around Instagram, Facebook and TikTok, so don't be a stranger!

And if you enjoyed *Perfect Wives*, I'd be so grateful if you'd leave a review on Amazon or Goodreads, or simply tell a friend. Word of mouth is a powerful thing.

With love and gratitude,

Lauren x

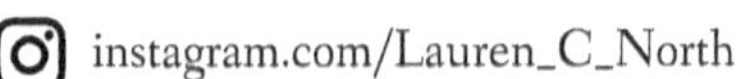 instagram.com/Lauren_C_North

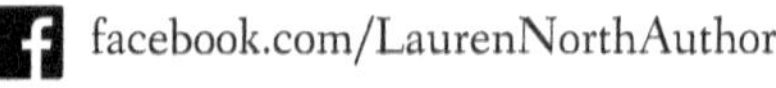 facebook.com/LaurenNorthAuthor

tiktok.com/@lauren_c_north

## ACKNOWLEDGEMENTS

To the early readers, bloggers and bookstagrammers – your passion and tireless championing of authors never ceases to amaze me. I'm endlessly thankful for every post, message and word-of-mouth recommendation. A heartfelt shout-out to @Booksta_Jon, @littlemissbooklover87 and @WhatCallyReads for the incredible support on Instagram this year. It means everything!

To my brilliant editor, Lucy Frederick. Thank you for challenging me, for your sharp instincts and for helping shape *Perfect Wives* into the book it is today. I'm so grateful that we've had the opportunity to work on so many books. I think this is book eight together! Getting an email from you always brightens my day.

Writing may be solitary, but publishing certainly isn't, and I'm so grateful to the entire team at Bookouture. This book carries all of your fingerprints. Special mention to Donna Hillyer, Laura Kincaid and Mandy Kullar. Please take a moment to read the credits page because every name there helped bring these pages to life.

To my agent, Amanda Preston – you are a master juggler, confidante, strategist, occasional therapist and brilliant pep-talk giver. Thank you for never wavering in your belief of me or my books. You have the best energy, and it's a joy to work with you. I'd also like to thank Daisy Messent and the phenomenal LBA team for being in my corner.

And, as ever, to Zoe Lea, Nikki Smith and Laura Pearson.

Thank you for the pep talks, the plot untangling and the honest reads, not to mention the numerous voice notes that always make me laugh and smile. I sometimes wonder how we get any work done.

Lastly, to my family – Tommy, Lottie and Andy. Thank you for your support on this wild, wonderful journey.

**Marketing**
Alex Crow
Melanie Price
Occy Carr
Cíara Rosney
Martyna Młynarska

**Operations and distribution**
Marina Valles
Stephanie Straub
Joe Morris

**Production**
Hannah Snetsinger
Mandy Kullar
Nadia Michael
Charlotte Hegley

**Publicity**
Kim Nash
Noelle Holten
Jess Readett
Sarah Hardy

**Rights and contracts**
Peta Nightingale
Richard King
Saidah Graham

Dear Reader,

We'd love your attention for one more page to tell you about the crisis in children's reading, and what we can all do.

Studies have shown that reading for fun is the **single biggest predictor of a child's future life chances** – more than family circumstance, parents' educational background or income. It improves academic results, mental health, wealth, communication skills, ambition and happiness.

The number of children reading for fun is in rapid decline. Young people have a lot of competition for their time, and a worryingly high number do not have a single book at home.

Hachette works extensively with schools, libraries and literacy charities, but here are some ways we can all raise more readers:

- Reading to children for just 10 minutes a day makes a difference
- Don't give up if children aren't regular readers – there will be books for them!

- Visit bookshops and libraries to get recommendations
- Encourage them to listen to audiobooks
- Support school libraries
- Give books as gifts

There's a lot more information about how to encourage children to read on our websites: **www.RaisingReaders.co.uk** and **www.JoinRaisingReaders.com**.

Thank you for reading.